He Didn't Have a Heart, He Had an Adding Machine.

"All you understand is money. You have no appreciation of grace and beauty."

Disdainful amusement flickered across his face as he tilted his head and stared at her. "On the contrary, I've always been attracted by grace and beauty. That's why I think of things in monetary terms. In this materialistic world most beautiful things cost money, and I enjoy having the power to buy whatever catches my interest, anything I want to have." He smiled, and his gaze moved intimately over her body as he walked slowly toward her.

JOANNA SCOTT

lived for many years on the East Coast, but now this teacher-turned-writer is quite happy with her home state of California. She is married and has one son.

Dear Reader:

During the last year, many of you have written to Silhouette telling us what you like best about Silhouette Romances and, more recently, about Silhouette Special Editions. You've also told us what else you'd like to read from Silhouette. With your comments and suggestions in mind, we've developed SILHOUETTE DESIRE.

SILHOUETTE DESIREs will be on sale this June, and each month we'll bring you four new DESIREs written by some of your favorite authors—Stephanie James, Diana Palmer, Rita Clay, Suzanne Simms and many more.

SILHOUETTE DESIREs may not be for everyone, but they are for those readers who want a more sensual, provocative romance. The heroines are slightly older—women who are actively involved in their careers and the world around them. If you want to experience all the excitement, passion and joy of falling in love, then SILHOUETTE DESIRE is for you.

I'd appreciate any thoughts you'd like to share with us on new SILHOUETTE DESIRE, and I invite you to write to us at the address below:

Karen Solem
Editor-in-Chief
Silhouette Books
P.O. Box 769
New York, N.Y. 10019

JOANNA SCOTT
A Flight of
Swallows

Silhouette Special Edition
Published by Silhouette Books New York
America's Publisher of Contemporary Romance

Other Silhouette Books by Joanna Scott

Dusky Rose
The Marriage Bargain
Manhattan Masquerade

SILHOUETTE BOOKS, a Simon & Schuster Division of
GULF & WESTERN CORPORATION
1230 Avenue of the Americas, New York, N.Y. 10020

ISBN: 0-671-53526-9

First Silhouette Books printing June, 1982

10 9 8 7 6 5 4 3 2 1

Map by Tony Ferrara

A Flight of
Swallows

Chapter One

A flight of swallows passed below the sun, casting a dark shadow over the mission. The now somber sky was definitely in keeping with Karin's dismal spirits. On her seat by the old stone fountain she flipped her long, softly waved auburn hair behind her ears, cupped her hand above her gold-flecked amber eyes and watched the small brown birds fly into the distance. Only the white pigeons she was feeding would remain. They were like the farmers who stayed here year round. Karin remembered the lean suntanned men from her youth. All during her childhood she had been like the swallows, spending the summer in San Juan Capistrano and the colder months in another, more elegant home, a castlelike structure in Bel-Air, an expensive suburb of Los Angeles, far to the north of this small seaside community.

Now the swallows were leaving—flying back to Buenos Aires, where it would be summer. It was time for her to leave, too—if only she had some place to go. But now, at the age of twenty-three, her life of luxury had vanished and she was practically destitute. The Tudor mansion in Bel-Air had already been sold to repay her father's exorbitant debts and she had just learned that the hilltop estate on the outskirts of San Juan Capistrano was so heavily mortgaged that her small salary would never stretch far enough to meet the monthly expenses.

A large land-development company, American International, had been interested in buying the property for years, but her father had always refused. No greedy builder was going to turn Casa del Mar into an unattractive maze of boxlike houses, he had declared firmly.

Karin couldn't argue with his sentiments, and she shook her head in silent disgust as she thought of her beautiful home being ripped apart by some calculating builder who would see it as only another money-making proposition. Frowning, she visualized the red, white and blue American International sign dominating her property—proclaiming ownership just as it did over so much of the surrounding area.

Her sensually full mouth tautened into a grimace of disgust and she couldn't suppress a hiss of hatred as she thought about American International. Although the company was one of the largest land developers in Orange County, in all of southern California, in fact, it was said to be controlled by one man—Lucas McKay. Lucas McKay: the name was salt in the wound of her despair. Just thinking about him made her hands curl into tight, angry fists. And how could she help thinking of him? How could anyone? His name leaped from the pages of countless newspapers and magazines. If he wasn't in the business section consummating some new land grab, he was in the society column cavorting with some glamorous actress. She supposed she should be grateful that she'd only had to read about him and had never been confronted by a photograph. She snickered to herself. If she *had* seen one, she would probably have used it for a dartboard.

Well, she didn't care about his social life. As far as she was concerned, he could play Don Juan with every woman in San Juan as long as he didn't bother her. Briefly considering the women his name was linked with, she decided that she didn't have to worry. He'd never be interested in her—but her home was another matter. He'd devour Casa del Mar in one greedy gulp, just another tasty tidbit to feed his insatiable appetite for land.

Closing her eyes and letting her long, dark lashes feather the dismal circles of defeat that were beginning to form below them, she tried to dispel the image of McKay's bulldozers crunching through the towering palm trees and chewing up the stately adobe mansion. The thought was as abhorrent to her as it would be to her father. He would be dead set against the idea. She tightened her lips in firm determination. No matter how she felt, she would have to convince him to change his mind. It was absolutely impossible for them to keep up the payments, and if they didn't sell quickly the bank would foreclose, leaving them homeless as well as penniless.

Casa del Mar was the last vestige of her father's aristocratic way of life, and she hated having to tell him that they had to move, especially when he was still recovering from a serious heart attack. But there was no way that it could be avoided, not that she knew of.

The problem seemed monumental and she felt herself almost physically shrinking under the weight of it. She was only five-foot-two and her fine bone structure made her appear frail, especially when combined with her slender, willowy build. But the disenchanting experiences of the last few years had proven that appearance to be entirely deceptive. She was a survivor, and no matter what actions she had to take she would make sure that her father survived along with her.

Another flock of swallows left the red-tiled roof, and Karin stood up. The Sacred Garden, just below the Campanario, was the place where she always came to think out her problems. The old bells had been brought to the mission in 1775. They had hung in the tower of the original Great Stone Church until that building was destroyed by an earthquake in 1812. Now they graced this newer Campanario, situated between the museum, filled with old Spanish and Indian artifacts, and the arched ruins of the ancient church. On the other side of the Campanario was the statue of Father Junípero Serra. The mission at San Juan Capistrano, the jewel of all missions, was the seventh in a series of missions erected by the founder of California missions.

She loved this garden just as she loved everything about the mission, a beautiful structure which reminded people of their heritage, a heritage which could never be replaced once it had been destroyed. That was why she hated Lucas McKay so intensely. He had no respect for the past; he saw everything in terms of dollars and cents, and she was sure that in his avarice he would flatten even this mission if he were given half a chance.

Shivering at the thought, she reached into the small plastic bag and tossed the last of the stale bread to the pigeons. Much as she had enjoyed the restful serenity of the garden, she had not found a solution to her dilemma. How could she hold on to Casa del Mar at least until her father was well enough to withstand hearing the truth about their financial situation? Working wasn't the answer; her job at the antique shop didn't pay enough to make a dent in their bills. As she stood up and brushed the crumbs off the skirt of her celery-green shirtwaist dress, a gentle breeze drifted in from the ocean, pasting the fine linen fabric against her high full breasts and slender hips, revealing an enticingly curvaceous feminine figure, but Karin was completely oblivious to the seductive change in her appearance. Crumpling the empty plastic bag into a pocket, she sighed at the futility of her situation and began walking away.

"You left your sweater."

She turned and saw a tall, dark-haired man holding her white cashmere cardigan. He must have entered the garden through the museum. She had been so absorbed in her problems that she hadn't even noticed him. As she looked at him now, his presence seemed so over-powering that she found it hard to believe that anyone could help being aware of him once they had seen him. He was in his early thirties and casually dressed. Well-cut blue jeans clung to long, lean masculine legs, and an open-necked white knit shirt outlined the muscular power of his chest. Yet despite his unassuming attire, there was something in his bearing that created a powerful aura of aristocratic authority. He seemed so virile, so sure of himself, that for a moment she was mesmerized, unable to stop staring at him.

He held out her sweater but made no attempt to close the distance between them, so she began walking toward him. His obsidian eyes narrowed thoughtfully as she approached.

"Thank you. It got so warm, I forgot I had it with me." She reached for the cardigan.

Instead of releasing it, he covered her hands with his and let his thumb trace a sensuous path between her fingers. She felt as if a flame was licking at her skin. His eyes lingered on her face, meticulously assessing her classically regular features. "Don't I know you?"

"I don't think so." In fact, she was positive. Meeting him was a memorable experience, and even now her flesh burned from the heat of his touch. Pulling her hand free, she took the sweater and began walking toward the old stone arch.

He followed her. "Wait. I really mean it. I'm sure I've seen you before."

She turned and looked directly at him. He returned her gaze and Karin felt a strangely sensuous excitement flutter deep within her. He wasn't the type of man a woman could easily forget, and for a moment she was tempted to accept his seductive invitation. She hesitated, and he smiled, parting his lips with the easy arrogance of someone who was experienced at this sort of thing. An ocean breeze rustled through the trees and she suddenly felt that responding to him would be as sensible as sampling the serpent's apple.

"Please leave me alone. I'm sure we've never met." She spoke in the concise, clipped tone of voice her father always used when he dismissed a person who was beginning to bore him. In truth, she was anything but bored. The problem was that she found the man's blatant virility dangerously attractive, but an innate sense of self-preservation made her want to escape.

"Perhaps we've never met, but I'm sure I've seen you before, and if we haven't been properly introduced, that's something I'd like to rectify immediately."

"Don't bother; I don't know you and I don't want to know you. I wish you'd leave me alone." She moved forward, keeping a wide distance between them as she tried to slip past him.

He grabbed her arm. "You seem more familiar to me by the minute—behaving like a childish spoiled brat. What you need is a good shaking to teach you how to speak in a civil manner."

Karin looked around her. The garden was completely deserted. Where were all the tourists just when you needed them? "If you lay a hand on me, I'll scream. Whatever fantasy you have about us knowing each other is just that, and nothing more. Now, will you please stop all this and let me leave?" She tried to shake her arm free.

He released her and moved back, a glimmer of recognition or remembrance seeming to flicker across his face. "My apologies, an unfortunate mistake." His lips were taut and bitter as he turned and walked away as if he had lost all interest in her.

The man's cavalier attitude affected Karin as strongly as had the appalling speculation about Lucas McKay purchasing her beloved mission. Shivering, she slipped the sweater over her shoulders and thought back to what had just occurred. Controlled rage had momentarily sparked deep within his eyes; her words had obviously angered him, and she was certain that he wasn't in the habit of disregarding any offense, no matter how minor. Yet, had he really imagined that she would be foolish enough to fall for a line as trite as "Haven't we met somewhere before?" Still, she couldn't rid herself of the lingering aura of ownership the man seemed to have cast over her.

She looked over her shoulder as she walked to her car. She could see him standing beside the mission arch watching her. He claimed to know her, but even if he didn't, he was certainly gathering information about her very quickly. She drove away as quickly as she could. She wanted to escape his relentless scrutiny as rapidly as possible.

She recalled the incident while she was driving home. Something about him definitely appealed to her, and she found herself half-wishing that she hadn't cut him off so brusquely—but only half. Another, less emotional, more rational part of her mind insisted that her actions had been entirely correct and absolutely necessary.

Tightening her hands on the wheel, she visualized the dark, hawklike features that had been etched into her mind with a searing permanency. What was it about him that both attracted and frightened her? Even in her musings she couldn't deny a surging magnetism that reached out, pulling her toward him—which was precisely why she couldn't afford to become involved with him. She knew he wouldn't stop until he held her completely within his power. Everything about him told her so, even his threat to shake her into obedience. He was a strong man, the kind she had always avoided, yet strength was what she needed now, and her body was responding to his powerful aura with a will of its own. The thought frightened her.

In any case, she hadn't the time to brood over him. Her real-life problems were much too serious to be solved by escaping into daydreams. Much as she would have liked to avoid it, she had to get home and tell her father that they could no longer afford the payments on Casa del Mar; it would have to be sold. She sighed and wished her world was once again so trouble-free that all she had to worry about was fending off the attentions of some stranger attempting a casual pickup.

Her father was sitting on the veranda when she walked up the steps, a tall frosty glass in his hand. She didn't have to wonder what it contained. Gin and tonic had always been Paul Andrews' usual late-afternoon indulgence, and he made the most of the single drink the doctor still allowed him.

"Ah, Karin, did you have a good day? You're just in time for cocktails. What can I get you?"

"I'm not thirsty." She sat in the white wrought-iron chair next to his. "I have something to discuss with you, Dad." She hesitated, trying to find exactly the right words. It was so hard to shatter the dreams of someone you loved, but she had no choice. It had to be done. If only she could be sure that his heart was strong enough to stand the shock.

"Nothing too serious, I hope." He smiled in his boyishly engaging manner, and Karin wondered if he would ever grow up.

She thought back to Dr. Cal Stevens' words, the words he had spoken to her father, as well as those for her ears alone—warnings about the severe mental depression which had been plaguing her father long before he had been incapacitated by his heart attack.

Something had snapped in him when her mother had

died. He lost interest in the architectural practice which had brought him such wealth, and he accepted no new design commissions, for which he had been so famous. To make matters worse, he had lost the Midas touch that had formerly made all his investments turn to gold. When he had suffered the serious heart attack, Dr. Stevens had advised him to retire, sell his home in Bel-Air and relax in the sea breezes of San Juan Capistrano. The physician had then taken Karin aside and told her that any aggravation would be extremely harmful to her father's precarious health.

She had tried to avoid mentioning the sale of Casa del Mar for as long as she possibly could, but she wasn't able to delay it any longer. She chose her words carefully. "Dad, you know this house is much bigger than what we really need."

"Nonsense. I like the extra space. A man needs breathing room. Can't understand how anyone can live in those tacky little houses they build today."

"Well, it's hard for me to maintain such a large house. Jenny wants to retire and move in with her sister, and I can't handle all this by myself." Besides, we can't afford this anymore, her silent thoughts added. She closed her eyes as she tried to find an easy way to make her father understand.

"Hire someone else. We've always had a large household staff."

Karin laughed wryly to herself as she bit her tongue to keep from speaking. Sure, I'll hire an army. Money is no object—none at all—especially since we don't have a cent and our debts could keep the red-ink business going for years. Controlling an impulse to blurt out the truth, she forced herself to remember her father's health and spoke in a softly modulated voice. "That's just it, Dad. I would be able to manage everything myself if only we had a smaller house. I'm seriously considering selling this place. There are some beautiful new condominiums that would be just perfect for us." She crossed her fingers behind her back, hoping against hope that he would agree.

"Don't be ridiculous. Where would I put my billiard table?" He lifted his glass. "Stop fretting and get some extra help. I know it's hard to find these days, but you'll have no trouble if you offer a decent salary."

The situation was impossible. Her father had no concept of how bad their financial situation actually was, and any attempt on her part to bring him more in touch with reality would certainly upset him, possibly damaging his already fragile health. She sat silently. Random thoughts knocked against each other in her mind as she desperately tried to find the right words. Something had to get through to him. Things couldn't go on this way—*she* couldn't go on this way. Feigning an optimism she couldn't feel, she decided to try a new tactic. "Perhaps we could lease this house and move into the guest cottage."

Her father put his glass on the small round table beside his chair. He took a deep breath and studied her face quietly before speaking. "Is there something I should know? I realize you haven't had much experience with money. Perhaps it's just too much for you." He tapped his fingers against the table. "I've rested long enough; I think I ought to review our financial situation. Put all the bank statements and bills in my study and I'll look at them in the morning."

It was futile. She ran her fingers through her hair as she realized that her father was in no condition to withstand the strain of learning the truth. "No, Dad, there's no need for that. Remember, Dr. Stevens said no strenuous mental or physical activity. I'm still in charge of things around here." She picked up her handbag and stood. "I'll check with Jenny and see how

dinner is coming along. Don't worry about a thing."
She walked into the house.

Jenny was standing by the kitchen sink, peeling some potatoes. She turned and smiled when she saw Karin, then wiped her hands on her apron. "Sit down; you look tired. Did you have a busy day at the shop?"

"Not very. Mostly browsers. They've really come to see the swallows. While they're here, they walk through town, stop at some restaurants and look through the stores, but they're not very anxious to buy anything."

"That realtor friend of yours came by again today. Your father told him that he wasn't interested in selling, but I took his card." She handed a small white rectangle to Karin.

"Thanks," Karin said, glancing at the name. She realized that Jenny knew exactly how serious their situation was, that Karin had to stretch every dollar to meet the household bills. Only her father was blissfully unaware of the financial problems they were facing, and she was too afraid to take the risk of telling him the truth.

At dinner her father casually mentioned that he thought he was feeling strong enough to resume some of his less strenuous activities at the country club. Karin felt her stomach contract tensely. One of the first expenditures she had eliminated had been his costly country club dues, an extravagance they could no longer afford. How on earth was she going to manage this? Their desperate situation seemed to have no solution—none that could both protect her father's fragile health and provide for them financially. She put down her fork and asked to be excused.

"I've got a headache," she said. "I think I'll get to bed early."

She walked up the wide, curving stairway, head bowed and feet dragging. A large wrought-iron chandelier illuminated the hallway, reflecting the opulence of an affluent past while mocking the reality of the difficult present. Her own room had been so exquisitely planned that it looked like a magazine layout, and Karin remembered wryly that the entire house had been featured in an article several years ago. Now, although the sheer white curtains and plush pink carpeting had lost the crisp sparkle they had had when they were new, they still provided a pleasant background for the mellow patina of the antique white and gold furniture.

She looked around and tried to remember how happy she had been here when she was a child. But the thoughts wouldn't come and now the room offered her no sense of security, no comfort. She felt totally alone and she desperately needed someone she could talk to, someone who would share her problems.

For no apparent reason she thought of the man she had met at the mission. His muscular body had vibrated with strength and she had no doubt that he could solve any problem, even hers. Briefly she regretted the harsh way she had dismissed him. Then she shook her head to free it from his image. What on earth was wrong with her?

The dilemma was hers—hers and her father's. If only her father's heart were stronger, then maybe she could tell him the truth, discuss the situation with him. She sighed and began getting undressed. All her wishful thinking couldn't change things. Her father was too sick to deal with their problems; somehow she would have to find the solution by herself.

After showering and changing into pajamas, she brushed her hair at the small French-provincial vanity table. When she had finished, she replaced the brush and glanced down at the dressing table. Her gaze fell on the realtor's card Jenny had given her. She stared at it for a long time before she made up her mind. She would call him in the morning; maybe he could suggest a way to pursue the only option she had.

Jim Simpson's office was located in the Mission Shopping Plaza, a few doors down from the antique shop where Karin worked, and she could easily see him over her lunch hour. His father had attended college with hers, which made things simpler for Karin. She felt more comfortable discussing the problem with someone who wasn't a complete stranger.

Sitting in his small private office, she explained her situation to the sandy-haired realtor. Keeping her voice calm and casual, she tried to conceal the desperation that was behind her decision. "I'm perfectly willing to sell the house. We have no need for anything so huge." She avoided mentioning their financial distress and was grateful that Jim was tactful enough not to ask. "It's just that my father is sick and can't be convinced to leave right now."

"Then it's pointless to list the property; anyone who buys it is going to want to move in."

"I'm aware of that, but I wasn't thinking in terms of a private sale. You know that American International has been building on every available inch of land between here and San Diego. They've been making offers on our property at regular intervals, but up until now I've never had to consider them." She pressed her hands together and lowered her voice. "Unfortunately, things have changed and I can no longer afford the luxury of my convictions." Taking a deep breath, she forced herself to utter the words. "I'd be willing to sell the property at a price well below current market value, but only with the conditions that my father never learn about the sale and that he be permitted to stay in the house for the rest of his life. After that, they'd be free to do as they please."

Simpson whistled softly and shook his head. "I don't

know if they'd agree to those terms. I've never run across anything like this before."

"Well, that's the situation. I'll appreciate anything you can do." She stood up, affecting a calm indifference she didn't feel. "My lunch hour is nearly over; I've got to get back to work."

Simpson walked her to the door. "I'll get on this right away. And as soon as I find out anything, I'll be in touch with you."

Karin silently prayed that he would find a solution quickly, and hurried back to the antique shop so Stephanie, her co-worker, could go to lunch. Mrs. Edison, the owner, was an elderly widow who had gone to live with her daughter in Laguna Beach. She could no longer keep up with the daily demands of the shop, but she was so attached to each piece of merchandise that she couldn't bear to sell the store to just anyone, so she had hired the two women to keep things under control until she found a suitable buyer. Karin would have loved to buy the shop herself, but there was no way she could get the money she needed. Perhaps, if the sale of Casa del Mar netted enough extra cash for a small down payment, Mrs. Edison would be willing to let her pay the rest of the price in installments.

When her stomach began growling, she realized that she hadn't eaten since breakfast. I may have discovered the perfect diet, she thought as she ran her hands over her slender hips. Fortunately weight had never been one of her problems, and she walked to the back of the shop to snack on some coffee and cookies.

That would have to do for lunch. Right now, she had to get back to work because one thing was certain, someone would be buying the shop and it was Karin's job to see that the stock was kept in impeccable condition so that Mrs. Edison could get the best possible price. She scanned the store, her eyes drifting over an intricately carved walnut card table, then shifting to the dusty Baccarat crystal chandelier which hung above it. The prisms weren't really dirty, just dingy enough not to show each clearly cut facet to its best advantage.

She maneuvered a small ladder between the card table and an adjacent bombé chest. There wasn't enough room to open the ladder fully, but Karin wasn't concerned. She had done this many times before and nothing had ever happened. She placed the bottle of ammonia at the top of the ladder, poured some onto a soft white cloth and gently began stroking each prism.

She had forgotten to replace the cover on the ammonia and the fumes combined with the near-emptiness of her stomach to make her feel light-headed and dizzy. The room began to spin, and when she reached out and tried to grab something solid, the ladder tilted, casting her toward the floor. Cold fear knotted within her as she hopelessly called out for help.

Two strong hands circled her waist, pulling her clear of the ladder and holding her securely against the firm strength of a sturdy masculine chest. Her head was still spinning and she curved her arms tightly around the man's neck, trying to reassure herself of his support. Her eyes were closed, still smarting from the ammonia, and her head rested against his chest as he walked to a Victorian settee and sat down, settling her beside him.

She felt his breath moist against her cheek while his hands moved slowly up her arms, massaging them, warming them, bringing her body back to life. Slowly she let her eyes flutter open and she looked up at her rescuer. "You!" Her eyes widened as she recognized the dark-haired man who had found her sweater yesterday.

"So we meet again." He still held her tightly as he smiled down at her. "Are you feeling better?" His gaze traveled slowly over her face, flaming against her skin, and the heady sensation she felt hadn't come from her fall.

"Yes, thank you." She tried to move away, but his arms tightened, imprisoning her. "You'd better let me go."

"Why?" He was still smiling as he bent and kissed her, his lips pressing gently against hers at first, then dominating them with their harsh expertise.

She felt his lean body hardening against the softness of hers, and the same fiery thrill she had felt at the mission surged through her veins once again. The realization frightened her. She twisted her head, pulling herself free. Her body trembled and she gasped breathlessly. "Can't you take no for an answer? I told you yesterday that I wanted you to leave me alone. Why did you follow me here?"

She stood up, and he followed her, as if refusing to let her go.

"I'm sorry, I should never have tried to help you. I'm sure you would rather have fallen to the floor than have had me touch you." He turned and left the shop before she had a chance to answer him.

Karin leaned against the settee, breathing hard and waiting for her heart to slow to its normal pace.

What did he want? She rubbed her fingers across her lips, trying to erase his imprint. She felt threatened, like a swallow being stalked by a hawk.

She pursed her lips, trying to control her anger. Yet that same half of her heart that had reached out to him in the Sacred Garden was reminding her of the seductive gentleness in his touch, which had sent her unwilling heart racing toward fulfillment.

The bell above the door tinkled, and Karin tensed, fearing that he had returned. She sighed in relief when she saw Stephanie.

"What happened in here?" Stephanie asked as she

walked into the shop. "The most gorgeous man nearly knocked me over out there. What did you do to get him so angry?"

"Nothing. We'd had a previous misunderstanding and he was just surprised to see me here."

"Judging from his attitude and your red face, I'd say that it was more than just a misunderstanding. Exactly how well do you know him?"

"Hardly at all." Karin turned away in annoyance. "I don't even know his name."

"You've got to be kidding. If I had been here, I would have gotten his name, address and telephone number."

"Well, you weren't here, and I didn't find him at all attractive."

"Then you must be crazy. Next time he comes in here, just keep him calm until I can get to him."

Keep *him* calm? Karin thought. What about me? How do I keep myself calm? It was easy enough to lie to Stephanie, but she wasn't foolish enough to deny the truth to herself. Her expression must have given something of her thoughts away, because Stephanie still didn't seem satisfied.

"Well," she asked, "do you want to talk about it?"

Karin shook her head and the need for any further explanations was brought to an abrupt halt when a customer walked into the shop.

Business was slow and Karin let Stephanie leave the shop an hour earlier than usual. She was about to lock up and go home herself when Jim Simpson walked through the door.

"Glad I caught you. With all the need for secrecy, I thought it would be easier to discuss things with you away from home."

Karin showed him to the small office at the back of the shop. "It's good you did. The less my father knows about this, the better I'll feel."

"I have some excellent news. American International is definitely interested in your property. They've agreed to let you remain, and they won't make any changes while you're there. However, they insist upon access to the property at their convenience."

"That's impossible. How will I explain that to my father?"

Jim shrugged. "I don't know. But I'll tell you this, you'll never get another offer half as good."

"I need time to think about it. What type of access do they have in mind? Are their architects going to be coming and going, surveying the land and placing stakes right under my father's eyes?"

"I don't know the details, but the president of the company has agreed to meet with you and discuss terms. Would you like me to schedule an appointment?"

"Yes, that sounds good. I can't possibly decide until I know exactly what they have in mind."

"I don't want to force you into anything, but I don't think you'll find another offer as close to what you're looking for as this one is. So, if I were you, I'd make every effort to meet their terms." He started toward the door. "I'll call and set up the appointment. Is there any special time that would be convenient for you?"

"Lunch hour or after work, but I don't suppose the president of American International is going to adjust his schedule to suit my needs. Much as I hate to do it, I'll have to ask Mrs. Edison for some time off."

Jim smiled. "I'm glad to hear you talking that way. If you're as anxious to sell as you seem to be, then they've got the upper hand, although we're not going to let them know that." He waved and left the store.

Karin locked the door and looked up. No swallows flew above the mission. They had gone, just as they did every October 23, St. John's Day. They would not return until March 19, St. Joseph's Day. The little mud nests that *las golondrinas* had built in the crevices of the old church would be waiting for them on their return. Karin envied them; they knew that the mission would always be their home, whereas her place of residence was to be determined by the president of a huge, heartless conglomerate. She only hoped that she could work things out without involving her father.

The streets were quiet as she drove through town toward the ocean. The tourists seemed to follow the swallows' schedule, staying while the summery warmth heated the ocean breezes and leaving for more favorable climates when the cold winter fog drifted over the town.

From the highway she could see the glistening elegance of Casa del Mar, the house of the sea. Built on a towering bluff overlooking the ocean, with a narrow row of steps cut into the stone and leading to a secluded private beach, it dominated the landscape. Arrogant and majestic, it spoke of wealth and permanence. It was a home demanding limitless money, money they no longer had.

Her father, as usual, was seated on the veranda. "Karin, I've been waiting for you. I really think you're spending too much time at that hospital gift shop. Even charity should have its limitations, you know." He sipped his drink. "You're looking rather pale. I think we could both do with a bit of a vacation. South America is warm this time of year. How would you like to go to Rio? I'll talk to a travel agent."

Karin took a deep breath and swallowed. She was beginning to feel schizophrenic. She was living in two worlds, the real one, and the secure fantasyland she had created for her father. In previous years, when she had been a debutante and a member of the Junior League, she had done volunteer work in the hospital thrift shop. That sales experience, combined with a knowledge of fine furnishings built up over years of living with them, had helped her get the job in the antique shop. But she had never told her father that she was now working for a salary. As far as he was concerned, she was still volunteering her time to help the local hospital.

She didn't like lying to him, but she had to. "I enjoy my work, Dad; it gives me something to do. You know I like to keep busy."

"Yes, but enough is enough. I'm beginning to feel better and I think it's time we had some fun. I know it hasn't been easy caring for me. You don't go out much, and it's just not right. What's happened to all those young people who were always hanging around here?"

Karin was silent. She knew what had happened, even if he didn't. It took money to keep up with the social set her father was discussing. So she kept making excuses until they had finally stopped calling. Actually it didn't matter anymore. Her mother's death, her father's devastating illness and the subsequent financial problems had changed her from the carefree teenager she had been just a few short years ago. A few short years, but it seemed like a lifetime. There was no way she could ever return to the frivolous way of life her father was so reluctant to abandon.

"Yes, that's what I'm going to do. Rio. We'll go there and maybe you'll meet some eligible bachelor. It's time you were married. I'm not getting any younger, you know. A man my age needs grandchildren." He smiled contentedly.

Karin laughed. "I don't want to go to South America, Dad. I think you're just jealous of the swallows. Dr. Stevens still wants you to rest, so we're not going anywhere for a few more months." She patted his shoulder and walked into the house.

Jenny looked up when she entered the kitchen. "You look tired, Karin. You need some rest. I think you should talk to your dad. He ought to know the truth."

Karin shook her head. "Not yet. I have to wait a little longer. You remember what Dr. Stevens said."

"I remember, but Dr. Stevens doesn't know the whole situation. I don't think he wants you to worry yourself sick."

"I spoke to the realtor. We may be able to work something out."

Jenny's response was delayed by the ringing of the telephone. Karin answered it and recognized Jim Simpson's voice immediately.

"Can you talk? I don't like calling you at home, but I won't be in the office tomorrow, so I had to reach you right away. I spoke with the president's secretary and set up an appointment for tomorrow at six."

"That's great. I won't even have to ask for time off."

"I know. I mentioned that you were working and they agreed to schedule the appointment at your convenience. The office is in Newport Beach." He named an address. "Would you like me to come with you?"

"That's not necessary. I won't sign any papers until I check with you."

Karin hung up the phone with a feeling of finality; there was no going back now.

Chapter Two

*J*im Simpson's phone call wound Karin's already tensely coiled nerves even tighter. Her voice and her actions seemed to belong to another person as she controlled her taut emotions during dinner with her father and while helping customers in the shop the next day. So much depended on the outcome of this evening's meeting that she could think of nothing else. She was grateful when five o'clock came and she could lock the doors of the shop.

Traffic was light on the freeway and she arrived at American International's headquarters by five-thirty. The one-story granite building with smoked-glass windows sat on several acres of carefully maintained bluegrass. The facade of the pristine structure was interrupted at regular intervals by crawling junipers and tall fluffy cypress trees; the overall appearance was one of utilitarian simplicity.

Karin frowned as she slipped her car into a parking spot. The building reminded her of the homes American International constructed: neat and simple, with no unnecessary features. She hated to think that Casa del Mar, with its lush tropical gardens and grandeur, would eventually be replaced by rows of boxlike structures. But there wasn't anything she could do about it. Her main concern was her father's health, so if American International would agree to her terms, she would sell them the property.

The heels of her bone-colored sandals clicked against the Carrara marble floors in the entryway. An attractive woman with short black hair smiled at her from the reception desk. "May I help you?"

"I have an appointment with Lucas McKay."

"Your name please?"

"Karin Andrews."

The receptionist pressed a button and spoke into the intercom. Then she smiled up at Karin. "If you'll have a seat, Mr. McKay's secretary will be out in a moment."

Karin had barely settled herself in the chair when a tall, gray-haired woman in a navy-blue business suit opened one of the double glass doors to the left of the receptionist and walked into the lobby.

"Miss Andrews?" Her half-smile was sober and businesslike. "I'm Mrs. Dunn, Mr. McKay's secretary. Mr. McKay will see you now. Please follow me."

Polished marble floors gave way to thick gray carpeting, just as cold but definitely less noisy, as if the occupant of this office was too important to be disturbed by the sound of footsteps. The atmosphere was so quietly dignified that Karin was practically tiptoeing as Mrs. Dunn tapped on the dark oak door at the far end of the room they had just entered. A muffled voice answered her knock.

Mrs. Dunn opened the door and leaned against it while Karin walked into the room. "Mr. McKay, Miss Andrews is here to see you." She stepped back and closed the door.

Karin stared at the man who came toward her, holding out his hand.

"You!" She closed her eyes, praying that she was wrong, hoping that her eyes were deceiving her.

He smiled wryly. "It appears you have a one-word vocabulary. It's nice seeing you again, Miss Andrews." He stood with his hand outstretched, his hooded eyes mocking her. "Surely you can honor me with a handshake?"

Karin felt as if she were the victim of some bizarre scheme designed to drive her crazy. For the last three days this man had materialized everywhere she went, at the mission, in the antique shop and now here. Her arrogant stranger was Lucas McKay, the president of American International, the man whose decision would affect her whole life.

Forcing herself to smile, she held out her hand. He caught it between his, holding it gently, while his dark eyes met hers. A sensuous warmth flowed through Karin's body as they stood touching and she felt a chilling loss when he released her.

"Won't you sit down?" he asked, motioning to a small alcove with a gray suede sofa, a glass-topped coffee table and two white leather chairs. "Would you like some coffee?"

"No, thank you," Karin said. Arsenic would be much more suitable, she thought. Despondently she sank into one of the chairs. She felt like crying; why couldn't she have been just a little more cordial in her previous encounters with Lucas McKay? Okay, so he had tried to pick her up—tried to kiss her. Big deal. Couldn't she have laughed it off? She looked up at the man standing beside her and instantly realized that there was no way she could ever laugh off anything about Mr. Lucas McKay.

"Well, then, let's get down to business. You seem as anxious to get things settled as I am." His eyes moved slowly over her face, almost as if he were trying to dominate her with the intensity of his gaze, and Karin sensed that no matter how relaxed he might appear to be, he knew exactly what he wanted and would let nothing stop him from achieving his goal. All her optimism vanished as she realized how foolish she had been even to think that she could bargain with someone like him. Then she remembered what Jim had said about not letting McKay know how anxious she was, and stroking her fingers nonchalantly over the arm of the chair, she attempted a posture of casual confidence. She was determined that Lucas McKay would never know about the feathers tickling the sides of her stomach.

Without breaking his piercing scrutiny, he sat on the sofa and crossed his legs. The dark blue wool of his well-tailored suit covered, but couldn't conceal, the powerful muscles of his lean masculine frame. "I've been interested in your property for a long time. Jim Simpson said there were some unusual conditions to the sale, so I thought it would be best if we talked about them privately without an army of lawyers around. They have a way of complicating things that I sometimes find unnecessary." He smiled, a comfortable, complacent smile that told her he was firmly in control and would easily have maintained that control no matter who else had been in the room.

His arrogant self-assurance wasn't lost on Karin, and that, coupled with the inexplicable excitement she always felt in his presence, made her want to run away, but she couldn't; the sale of Casa del Mar was the most important thing in her life right now. She forced herself to speak calmly. "I don't know how much Mr. Simpson has told you, but I'm very interested in selling Casa del Mar. It's really too big for us. The problem is my father. He's quite ill, and I believe he'd be very upset to learn about the sale. I'd be willing to let the property go for a price well below the fair market value if you'd agree to let him live there for the remainder of his life." She prayed that her voice wouldn't betray the sense of urgency quivering through every nerve in her body.

Lucas McKay nodded and rubbed his thumb against his chin. He seemed caught up in his own thoughts. "It's an unusual request, but I might go along with it.

As you probably know, Casa del Mar is one of the finest pieces of property on the California coast, and I really want it—so much so that I'd consider your terms. I've never really minded waiting for something I'm determined to own." He smiled confidently and Karin felt herself silently cringing at the possessive authority in his voice. "The only thing that bothers me is what Jim said about our company not having access to the land. I can't agree to that."

Karin took a deep breath, refusing to let him intimidate her. "I'm sorry, but if I were to let your workers troop all over the place, my father would suspect something. What explanation could I give him?" She shook her head. "If I'm going to do that, I might as well list the house and ask for as much money as I can get."

"I wasn't planning on sending a crew of construction workers out to the site. Just one person—sort of a caretaker to see that the place was being kept up properly. I don't mind buying the property and holding it for future use, but I can't see not having the right to inspect something I own. Those are my terms. I never back down, so the decision is yours." He stared at her coldly, sure of himself, daring her to disagree with him.

Karin thought for a moment; she wanted to get this matter settled and leave as quickly as possible. Despite her reluctance to let Lucas know how desperate she was to sell, she couldn't continue to act indifferent for much longer. She would have to agree to his terms. "There is a small guest cottage. I could tell my father I'm letting a friend use it. Do you think you could choose someone with tact and understanding?" She privately doubted that he knew the meaning of the words.

Lucas McKay smiled. "I'll do my best." His triumphant grin told her that he had gotten exactly what he wanted, and his manner once again became easily relaxed.

Karin picked up her purse and stood. "I really

appreciate this. I'll tell Jim to draw up the contracts and settle on a price. He's obviously more aware of current real-estate values than I am."

He stood to face her and Karin's gaze traveled upward. His tanned skin and dark hair contrasted sharply with his white silk shirt. His obsidian eyes seemed to burn her flesh. Suddenly an annoying flicker of remembrance prodded Karin's brain, and without realizing it, she frowned.

"Is something wrong?"

"No, it's just that you remind me of someone I used to know."

"It seems to me that remark got me into trouble when we met at the mission." His raised eyebrows mocked her.

"I owe you an apology. I thought you were—" She stopped without finishing the sentence.

"Trying to pick you up?" His mouth quirked with amusement.

"Yes." She laughed. "I'm sorry."

"Perhaps I was; nevertheless, your apology is accepted." He tilted his head and smiled. "We really should try to remember where we know each other from. Obviously it's just a matter of time. Are you busy for dinner?"

"No, but they'll be expecting me at home. I told them I'd be slightly delayed."

"Well, then, they're probably not going to wait for you, which means you'd be eating alone. Join me for dinner and we can try to jog our reluctant memories."

His voice was strangely soft, but she detected the hint of a cynical smile playing at the corners of his mouth. His somber business attire gave him an imposing aura of both masculine and financial power, and she felt that in some way he was amusing himself at her expense. She remembered the way he had touched her, kissed her—remembered everything she had ever

33

heard, had ever believed, about Lucas McKay, beliefs that meeting him and talking with him had only reinforced. His attitude, even if it was only something she was imagining, made her very uncomfortable, and once again she was anxious to escape his presence.

"It's good of you to ask, but I really should get home."

"Should you really?" His eyes crinkled at the edges as a smile spread over his face.

"My father will be worried," she lied. Her father would probably be sleeping. But she herself was worried, worried about the way her stomach plummeted every time Lucas looked at her.

"Some other time, then?" He didn't press the point and accepted her explanation with an unconcern that suggested it was only a matter of time until she did exactly as he wanted.

"Yes, of course." Turning, she walked through the door he held open for her and caught her breath as she inhaled the disturbingly masculine aroma of his spicy cologne. As she crossed the gray carpeting and entered the marble-tiled lobby, she knew he was still watching her; she could feel his fiery gaze burning into her retreating figure. The sharp staccato tapping of her heels echoed through the empty corridor as she increased her pace and almost raced from the building.

His image kept clouding her thoughts as she drove back to Casa del Mar and she made a conscious effort to dislodge it by thinking about other things. Miraculously she had found the ideal solution to her problem. She was sure she could find a plausible explanation for the caretaker who would live in the guest house. Her father would never have to know of their financial difficulties, and since Jim Simpson would handle all the details of the sale, she would never have to see Lucas McKay again. And that was very important to her right now. She despised him, despised the arrogant disdain that she had now experienced firsthand. Yet, being with him made her feel strangely vulnerable and she was frightened by the power he seemed to have over her emotions.

When she reached home, Jenny told her that her father had been tired and had gone to his room immediately after dinner, as Karin had suspected he would. Jenny had set aside some cold steak and a green salad for Karin. While she ate, Karin told Jenny about the arrangement she had made with Lucas McKay.

"McKay . . ." Jenny repeated the name and absent-mindedly tapped the index finger of her right hand against her cheek. "There was a family named McKay who had a farm not far from here. The land is covered with houses now, but when we first moved here, I used to buy our fresh produce from a stand they had at the side of the road. I wonder if they could be related?"

Karin reflected for a moment. Lucas did remind her of someone, and he had thought he remembered her. "Yes, of course; I know the family you mean. They had a son, but he was about my age. We used to go to the beach together." She had a hazy recollection of an amiable teenager with tousled blond hair. "Lucas McKay is much older, in his thirties, at least." Once again his dark image flashed into her mind and she dismissed the possibility that he had ever been in any way associated with a fruit-and-vegetable stand. "And there's nothing fresh-from-the-farm about him. He's a businessman through and through. The only thing he can envision sprouting from the earth is a small stucco house."

"Well, you never can tell. Why don't you ask him the next time you see him?"

"I won't be seeing him again. I'm going to leave everything to Jim Simpson from now on." She recalled Lucas McKay's air of cold arrogance. "And if I were to see him again, I'd be too embarrassed to even suggest that he might be related to the McKays we knew. McKay is a fairly common name . . . like Andrews. Can you imagine how ridiculous it would be if people expected me to be related to every Andrews they knew?"

The two women glanced over the kitchen to see that everything had been put in its proper place, then Karin said good night and went upstairs. She knew Jenny would stay in the kitchen for a while longer, reading the local newspaper and enjoying a cup of tea. In all the years she had been working for the Andrews family, Karin had never seen her really relax until everyone else had gone to bed.

There was no light streaming from beneath her father's door, so she assumed he had fallen asleep. Now that she had settled the matter of the house, she should have felt calmer about things, but she was more nervous than she had ever been. And their financial condition had nothing to do with the situation; now it was her confused emotional status that was causing all the problems. She knew she was attracted to Lucas; something in him seemed to satisfy a previously unsuspected need in her. Was it his aura of vibrant strength that she found so appealing? Hadn't she yearned for someone to share her problems? Yet Lucas wasn't sharing her problems; he might be solving one, but even as he did, he was presenting her with a new, more hazardous dilemma.

Lucas McKay, the builder, was someone she could hate. He represented the kind of businessman she despised, totally caught up in his company's financial growth, with no regard for the intrinsic values of environmental beauty. But the Lucas McKay she had met in the Sacred Garden and kissed in the antique shop was another matter altogether. Perhaps if she had never seen him again she might have been able to forget him, but after tonight she wouldn't even bother deluding herself with that possibility. Lucas McKay, the man, aroused sensations in her that had nothing to do with hate, and she didn't even want to give a name to what she knew she was feeling.

The next morning, she left for work earlier than usual so she would have time to see Jim Simpson before going to the antique shop.

"I'm glad you stopped by. Lucas McKay called after you left last night. He's anxious to get the property."

"And I'm anxious to sell."

"I know that, and apparently he does, too. It's good to be cooperative, but it's never wise to let a buyer know that you're desperate. He's agreed not to do any new construction on the property and to let you continue living there, but the price he's offered is considerably below the fair market value."

Karin shrugged. "The money doesn't matter; my father's health is at stake. I need a quick, quiet sale—one concluded without his knowledge. Lucas McKay seems agreeable. The most important thing is that he's willing to let us live there with just one person from his company on the premises to see that things are being properly maintained."

"I can reject the offer and hold out for a better price. I'm sure he'd come through. He really wants the property."

"Absolutely not. I want the sale finalized. Soon."

"Well, then, it should be consummated very quickly. American International is privately owned by the McKays, and the company always pays cash for its acquisitions. They like to own everything outright, no mortgages or high interest payments."

Karin nodded silently. How she wished that her father had adhered to that philosophy. Until he had gotten sick, she had never realized how much money they owed. Their extravagant life-style had been supported on a day-to-day basis, and once her father had stopped earning enough to make the enormous payments, an unbelievable amount of unpaid bills began accumulating. Now, by selling the estate, she would eliminate one of her costliest expenses and have enough extra money to pay off all of the outstanding bills.

"That's just fine," Karin said. "You settle all the legal points with American International and I'll sign any necessary papers."

"That makes everything much easier. We won't need your father's signature, since you have his power of attorney. I'll try to get things moving as quickly as possible." He shook his head. "I have to admit, this is going to be the strangest sale I've ever made."

She checked her watch. "I've got to get to work. You know where to reach me." They both rose and Jim walked her to the door.

Karin was surprised to find that Stephanie had already opened the shop because she usually arrived much later than Karin. To her added surprise, Stephanie was wearing a smock and dusting the furniture. Her eyes reflected the excitement when she saw Karin.

"Mrs. Edison's daughter called me at home. They've had an offer on the shop. She doesn't feel that her mother can continue being so selective, and she's decided to sell. They want everything cleaned up for the new owner."

Karin looked around the shop. "We always keep things clean and in order."

"I know that. I think she wanted things extra shiny."

"Did she say anything about the buyer?" Karin asked.

"Not much, but she gave me the impression that they had received a very good price and we would be keeping our jobs."

"I'm glad to hear that," Karin said in relief. The last

thing she needed now was to lose her job just when the financial situation at home was finally straightening itself out. "Does the new owner intend to work here?"

"I don't know. I didn't think to ask. I was too surprised to say much of anything after Mrs. Edison's daughter told me about the sale."

Karin slipped into her smock and began helping Stephanie. She hoped that the new owner would appreciate all these beautiful antiques as much as she did. How could anyone not admire the craftsmanship that was collected within these walls? It just wasn't possible, she thought as she put on a pair of soft white gloves and reached for a container of silver polish. She was polishing a Sheffield silver tea set when the bell above the door tinkled. Putting down the small creamer, she wiped her hands and walked to the front of the shop. His back was to her as he stroked the colorful enamel of a cloisonné lamp, but she didn't have to see his face to know who he was.

"Mr. McKay!"

He turned around and smiled. "I suppose that's better than 'You!' but I'd much prefer Lucas." His probing eyes held a hint of a smile as they gazed into hers.

Karin turned her head, breaking the eye contact he had so easily established. His large frame was so vibrantly alive that it seemed out of place in the small antique shop, crowded with curlicued furniture and dainty porcelain figurines. When their eyes had met, Karin had felt a sudden urge to reach out and touch him, to somehow feel the roughly carved features of his face beneath her fingertips. The startling impulse frightened her and she tried to regain her composure.

"Is there anything in particular you'd like to see? Somehow I didn't think your taste ran to antiques."

"On the contrary, I like quality items no matter what their age." His deep voice was strangely soft, flowing with a dynamic magnetism that pulled Karin toward him.

Once more their eyes met and Karin felt her heartbeat speed up and grow louder until it seemed to vibrate through the quiet room. A warm veil of red enveloped her skin and a childish sense of nervous embarrassment added to her discomfort. "What can I show you? Or would you like to browse for a while?"

"You're not asking me to leave?" His rugged features softened with amusement.

"I'm sorry about that." Her blush renewed itself. "I don't know what else I can do to make amends."

His smile broadened, and deep lines of laughter appeared in his face. "I'll try to think of something." His voice was seductive.

Karin lowered her eyes and tried to turn away, but he stopped her, catching her shoulders between his fingers. "I've just seen Jim Simpson and signed some papers to set the machinery in motion. I was hoping you'd be able to show me the estate."

"When?"

"Now."

"I'll be working until noon. I have my lunch hour then."

Lucas checked his thin gold wristwatch. "I'd rather not wait that long. I have some spare time right now and I'd like to see the property before we finalize the sale."

Karin hesitated for a moment. "Let me check with Stephanie." Of all days for Lucas to want to see the house, she thought. She hated to ask Stephanie to cover for her, but the sale of the house was even more important than her job. She could probably find another job, although she might not like it as well, but she doubted if she'd ever find a buyer as accommodating as Lucas.

Stephanie assured Karin that she would have no

trouble watching the shop while she drove Lucas to Casa del Mar.

"I'll try to be back as soon as possible," Karin said. "If the new owner stops by, tell him I took an early lunch."

"Don't rush," Stephanie said, her gaze moving meaningfully over Lucas' muscular body. "And I thought you said you weren't interested."

Karin was so embarrassed she could have shaken her co-worker, but instead she just said, "Thanks," and headed for the door so they could leave.

Karin motioned Lucas to her red Mustang. "I think it will be easier if I drive. I know the route."

Lucas shrugged. "Whatever you prefer, although I'm sure I'd have no trouble finding the place." His attitude indicated that he'd have no trouble doing anything, and Karin's fingers curled nervously around her car keys.

As she drove, Karin pointed out various landmarks, the old adobe houses which had belonged to the early Californios and the new tract homes which were being built on what used to be vegetable farms and fruit orchards. She stopped midsentence when she realized that American International was building the houses and Lucas would be thoroughly familiar with them.

He laughed. "I told you I'd have no trouble finding my way around. I know this area."

"Once you buy our land, you'll own most of the property around here." Her casual statement masked the hostility of her thoughts.

"A man can never own enough land. Without land a man has no roots, no heritage."

"You sound like a feudal lord."

"Exactly." Turning toward her, he smiled complacently. "Now I want to own the manor house."

This was the Lucas McKay Karin hated. The words spilled from her mouth, tumbling over each other in their eagerness to escape. She couldn't stop herself.

"So you can tear it down and replace it with a new housing development!" Her angry voice was tinged with sarcasm.

"Perhaps, but you understand that when I'm finished, I sell the houses to other people and then I no longer possess all the property you accuse me of owning."

"Somehow I think you'll never sell it all."

"That's true. I retain the land that my shopping centers are built on, and occasionally I just sell the houses while leasing the land to the homeowner. Of course, my company always keeps the oil and mineral rights."

"Hmm," Karin said, taking her eyes off the road for a moment and glancing at him. "I'll have to talk to Jim about including those provisions in our sales contract."

"Don't bother. I'd never agree to it. I've consented to your unusual request to let you remain on the property after I've purchased it, but once I own something, I own it all. I don't share my possessions with anyone." His tone of voice left her no room to argue with his statement.

Once again Karin felt strangely intimidated by the intensity of his words, as if his remark held a personal meaning for her, but she said nothing as she turned the car onto the private road that led to Casa del Mar. No longer did she feel a strong attraction for Lucas McKay; his view of the world was totally abhorrent to her and she wished she could tell him to take his filthy money and get off her property. But that was just wishful thinking, and wishful thinking, like the house itself, was a luxury she couldn't afford.

The car moved between the rows of Mexican fan palm trees which lined both sides of the winding road leading up to the house. Their arching crowns filtered the strong rays of the late-morning sun like an arboreal canopy.

"These trees look like they're a hundred years old," Lucas said.

"They are. They were planted when the house was started. The original owner was a Spanish grandee who built a small adobe cottage. When he began to prosper, he built the large mansion and planted the palm trees and gardens, then he started gambling heavily and lost everything. For a while he remained in the small cottage, then he disappeared. No one knows where he went. The house had several owners before my father bought it."

She smiled ruefully. "Now we're losing it, just like the Spanish grandee. Well, the old cottage is still behind that grove of yuccas. I suppose if the grandee could live there, my father and I should be able to. Unfortunately he doesn't have the stamina of the grandee, so I have to ask your permission to stay on in the large house."

"I've already agreed to let you remain. There's no need to discuss it anymore."

"I know. It's just that, since you've told me you don't like sharing your possessions with anyone, I feel I have to explain why I have to insist on staying here even after the house is sold."

"Forget it. I'm only agreeing to your terms because I want the property. Besides, the price I'm offering has taken into account the fact that I won't be able to do much with the place for several years."

"I hope you're right."

"What?"

"My father has a serious heart condition. I hope you're right when you say that he'll be staying in this house for several years. The doctors aren't that optimistic."

"Doctors aren't infallible."

"That's what I keep telling myself." She circled the huge front lawn that her father used as a putting green and was shocked when she saw him standing at its edge, lightly swinging his golf club along the top of the freshly mown grass. Pressing her lips tightly together, she stopped the car. "He's not supposed to lift anything heavier than a fork. He must be feeling better, so I guess he's decided to improve his strokes. He mentioned something about going to the country club. Well, I'll put an end to that right now." She opened her door and began getting out, completely forgetting about Lucas.

His hand circled her wrist, drawing her back. "Wait. Boredom can hurt his recovery more than a few easy swings with a golf club."

Karin hesitated for a moment. "He did say he was feeling better. But I hate to see him take any chances."

"All of life is a chance. You'll kill him if you try to wrap him in cotton. Come on. We'll go see him together."

Her father looked up and began walking toward them, his golf club tapping lightly against his leg. "What are you doing home this early? No customers at the thrift shop?"

Karin looked quickly at Lucas, hoping he wouldn't correct her father. Lucas returned her glance, but except for a brief questioning flicker in his eye, his face remained expressionless and he said nothing.

"No. The shop is still open; someone's covering for me." She thought quickly. They hadn't discussed how she would introduce Lucas to her father. She certainly couldn't say that he was the head of American International. Her father detested the company that was cutting the land up into postage-stamp parcels, as he called them.

"I'm afraid I'm to blame," Lucas said. "I'm an architect and builder. I was visiting the mission and the guide mentioned that your home was one of the finest examples of early Spanish architecture in California.

44

He said that your daughter worked in town and I persuaded her to take me here."

Karin was speechless. His explanation was so casual and matter-of-fact that she almost believed it herself. Her father definitely accepted it.

Taking the hand that Lucas offered, he shook it vigorously. "Well, I'm glad you came. It's a pleasure to meet someone who appreciates the beauty of an older structure; they just don't build homes the way they used to. Come up to the house. I could use a cool drink."

Karin went into the kitchen to prepare some iced tea and Lucas joined her father on the veranda. Jenny was surprised to see Karin home at such an early hour.

"I'm showing the house to the buyer," Karin said. "Father doesn't know."

"I thought you weren't going to have to show it to him."

"He wanted to see it, and Dad thinks he's just interested in the architectural features." She put the tea on a tray and walked outside.

Lucas stood as she approached. He took the tray from her and placed it on the small wrought-iron table between the chairs.

"I've invited Mr. McKay to lunch," her father said.

Great, just great. She couldn't wait to get rid of Lucas and her father was cozying up to him. "I have to get back to the shop, Dad." She might have to show Lucas the place, but she certainly didn't have to feed him.

Her father shrugged off her protest. "Nonsense. I told you that you were carrying this volunteer work too far. I'm glad someone else is filling in for you."

Karin glared at Lucas, hoping he would make some excuse so they could leave, but he just tilted his head and smiled complacently. When he reached for his iced tea, she had to control an almost overpowering urge to spill the amber liquid into his lap.

They had lunch on the small patio overlooking the pool. At first Karin was nervous, afraid that Lucas might slip and say something to let her father know that he had purchased the house, but after she saw how carefully he answered her father's questions, she began to relax. Lucas seemed as determined as she was to keep her father from learning of his true identity. She relaxed and listened to the conversation.

"I studied architecture at the University of Southern California, where I also received a degree in business administration." Lucas was more interested in talking to her father than in eating. He looked up at the red-tiled roof and graciously curving balconies. "This house is so purely indicative of early California styling that I'm sure I could find useful ideas here to incorporate into my own designs."

"Well, you're free to look around as much as you like. There's nothing I'd like better than seeing some new structures with more appeal than those cracker boxes that are springing up all around us."

"I appreciate your offer," Lucas said. "If you're really serious, I'll see what I can do about renting a place in the area so I can come here as often as necessary."

"No problem," Paul Andrews said. He looked at Karin. "We have a small guest cottage right here on the grounds. Karin can show it to you after lunch. If you like it, you're welcome to use it for as long as you want."

"I'm sure it would be fine," Lucas said. "Of course, I'd insist on paying rent."

"Nonsense." Her father dismissed the suggestion with a wave of his hand. "I'm offering it to you as a friend. Gentlemen don't deal in such commercial arrangements."

Chapter Three

$\mathcal{H}$ ow could you?" Karin asked Lucas when her father had gone to take his nap and they were walking down to the guest cottage.

"How could I what?"

"Trick my father into letting you stay here."

"I told you I would expect to have someone here. It was a condition of the purchase. I thought I handled the situation rather well. Your father doesn't suspect a thing and I'll be free to inspect the property."

"I didn't think it would be you."

"Why not? Can you think of anyone more dedicated to protecting my interests?"

"No, of course not. But what happens when he learns about your connection with American International?"

"I'll just have to convince him that I'm not quite as bad as he thinks. That's what you're afraid of, isn't it?" He cupped her elbow and smiled down at her confidently.

"Well, yes . . . that, and having him find out about the sale of Casa del Mar."

He turned her to him, his index finger tilting her chin upward and forcing her to look into his eyes. "I gave you my word on that. Don't you believe me?" Watching her intently, he waited for an answer.

She pulled away, unwilling to remain in such close

contact with him. "Of course I do. It's just that . . . well . . . accidents do happen." She continued walking.

His deep voice followed her. "Not where I'm concerned. I plan everything carefully; nothing I do is accidental."

The assurance in his voice sent shivers racing up Karin's spine. She couldn't bear for him to know the effect his touch had on her emotions, and she walked swiftly ahead of him until she reached the guest cottage. Then she stopped, reached for the key above the doorframe and opened the door. "It's quite small and not very elegant. Hardly what you're used to."

"Hardly," Lucas agreed wryly. He walked past her, through the square living room with its plain muslin-covered sofa and into the small bedroom at the back of the house. "This will be just fine. After all, it's not as if I were going to be living here forever." He ran his index finger across the hand-painted tiles covering the countertops in the small kitchen that jutted off the living room. Karin watched and remembered how that very same finger had touched her face only minutes before. She blushed helplessly and turned away.

"Jenny and I will clean it up for you. It's been years since anyone has stayed here."

He looked at the pottery dishes in the dark oak cabinets.

"There's not much in the way of kitchen utensils," Karin said. "Most of the guests ate with us. Whatever's here was only in case they wanted a late-night snack."

"It sounds like you had a lot of company."

"My parents enjoyed entertaining. We spent most of the summer here; they were known for their parties." She turned away and, glancing out the window above the small sink, recalled the laughter and music which had filled the house in her youth.

She had been too young to attend most of the parties and had either watched from the top of the stairway or been permitted to stay up just long enough to be introduced to some especially important guests who would coo fatuously over their hosts' charming child. Karin had often wondered how many of the compliments were honestly offered and how many were just a means of playing up to her parents.

Her birthday was in August, and those were the happiest parties in her memory. All her friends from the country club were invited and her parents always provided suitable entertainment. There were magicians and clowns when she was young and dancing to a live band as she got older. These days her birthday celebration consisted of a small cake shared with her father and Jenny.

Fingers danced feather-lightly across the nape of her neck. "You're far away."

"Just remembering. When I was younger, we spent only the summer at Casa del Mar, but somehow I've always considered it more of a home than any other place I've lived." She turned and smiled at him. "I don't mean to bore you with my personal reveries. Will you be spending much time here?"

"We're starting a new tract in Dana Point, so it would be easier if I stayed here. Would you mind that very much?"

I'd hate it, she thought silently. I don't like the thought of you being so close. You frighten me, in more ways than one. "No, of course not," she said. "Why should I?"

"You don't seem to want me around."

"What I want has nothing to do with it. I agreed to let someone watch the property while we still lived here. I just never thought that you'd take the job yourself." She shrugged and began walking toward the door. "Now, if you don't mind, I really must be getting back to work." She locked the cottage, replaced the key and headed for her car.

Gripping her arm, he stopped her before she had taken three steps. "What if I told you that what you wanted was very important to me? Would that change how you felt?"

"How could I be important to you? You hardly know me."

"Don't you believe in love at first sight?"

"Love?"

Lucas nodded.

"Mr. McKay, I don't think you know the meaning of the word."

Lucas' eyes narrowed and she glimpsed a flash of anger. "Why? Is it restricted to a select group of people? One that doesn't include me?"

"You might say that," Karin said and, freeing herself, continued walking toward the car. What was the purpose of this conversation? Lucas would never understand what she meant. A man who viewed life as materialistically as he did couldn't love anything or anyone.

Lucas followed her to the car and got in after her. "I keep forgetting that some people set themselves above the rest of us—then someone like you comes along to remind me." His mouth curved cynically.

Karin started up the car. Lucas' cold glare was giving her goose bumps. "Could we please talk about something else?" Anything else, she thought. Lucas and love were two things she didn't want to think about together.

"I see; I'm not worth much, but I'm okay for idle chitchat." He leaned back and looked at her. "Why does your father think you're doing volunteer work? Surely he can't object to your working in an antique shop."

Karin grimaced. Lucas was too intelligent not to realize exactly why she was selling Casa del Mar. It was pointless to pretend that she was still wealthy when Lucas was sharp enough to suspect the truth. "You heard what he said about commercialism. He's too set in his ways to understand that his daughter has to earn a living. He still thinks of me as a frivolous debutante."

"And how do you think of yourself?" They were on the freeway now, his arm resting leisurely across the back of her seat. Then his fingers dropped, casually stealing beneath the heavy curtain of her auburn hair. Her stomach muscles grew taut as she tried to disregard the delicate strokes that combed through the wispy hair clinging to the nape of her neck.

"I haven't had much time to think about myself. I've been too busy doing what had to be done."

"It seems to me that all your problems could be solved by marrying a wealthy man."

"You sound like my father. He hasn't the vaguest idea of how serious our financial problems are, and because of his health, I can't tell him. Now he's determined to take me on an extravagant South American vacation so I can meet some eligible young jetsetter and get married."

She had become accustomed to the touch of his fingers and was finding the light circular movements strangely relaxing. Although her eyes studied the road, all her other senses focused on the gently soothing motions of his hand. Lucas might not know about love, but he certainly knew about everything else.

"And you find that repulsive?"

"Going to South America?"

"No." He laughed, and his hand returned to the back of the seat. "Getting married."

Karin shrugged. "I don't find it repulsive at all. I think every woman wants to marry and have children. I just can't see getting married as a way out of our economic difficulties. People should get married only if they love each other."

"Ah, back to love. We can't seem to avoid the subject." His words mocked her, but she said nothing. "Why do you think your father would want you to marry someone you didn't love?"

She shook her head. She didn't want to pursue this conversation, but what choice did she have? After all, she was the one who had introduced the topic. "It's not that he doesn't believe in love. I know he loved my mother." She hesitated. "It's just that he has certain standards by which he judges people. I don't always agree with him," she finished dryly. Just as I'll never agree with you, she silently added.

She parked the car in front of the antique shop and got out. "I'll leave a spare guesthouse key with Jim. Jenny and I will have everything cleaned up by the end of the week." Waving her hand, she turned and walked into the shop. She sensed his eyes following her, and she leaned against the door, grateful for the thick oak barrier between them.

"Sorry I'm late," she said to Stephanie as the other girl walked toward the front of the shop. "Did the new owner stop by?" She was eager to talk about something which would take her mind off Lucas.

"No, but I got hungry while I was waiting for you, so I called the coffee shop and asked Harry to bring me a sandwich." She smiled wryly and ran her hands over her hips. "I can't stand missing a meal. I guess that's why I'll never lose weight. Anyway, Harry delivered the sandwich and you'll never believe what he told me." Her voice was breathlessly tantalizing.

Karin put her purse in the armoire at the back of the store and smiled. Stephanie had a definite flair for the dramatic. "Well, what? Is it something to do with the sale of the shop?"

"You bet it is. Someone wants to buy all the stores in

the plaza. They've made a fantastic offer on Harry's place, and he's considering it."

"Why would anyone want to buy all the stores?"

"I don't know. Harry seems to think that they want to tear them all down and build a huge shopping center."

"Oh, no! A shopping center doesn't belong here!" Karin felt as if her world was being destroyed—first Casa del Mar and now the quiet plaza.

"I think people have been complaining about the parking problem. Tourists visiting the mission park in front of the plaza and customers can't find a spot."

"But most of our customers *are* tourists. I can't believe anyone would desecrate the mission's ambience by putting up a modern shopping center. Did Harry happen to mention who was buying the stores?"

"American International." Stephanie grimaced. "Harry said they're buying everything in sight." She shook her head. "They already own most of the land around here; you'd think they'd have enough."

Silently Karin remembered Lucas' words. "A man can never own too much land." Now he would own the antique shop as well as Casa del Mar. She had the uneasy feeling that he was drawing a circle around her. Buying everything that ever really mattered to her, trying to control her life. But that was foolish. He was merely pursuing his insatiable desire for land. It was coincidental that two of the pieces of property he was buying meant something to her. Nevertheless, she was once again reminded of Lucas' destructive avarice and she hated herself for having enjoyed his gentle caresses. Gentle indeed! The man had about as much heart as an anvil. What was wrong with her? Why hadn't she pulled his hand off her neck and thrown it back in his face? Well, she was sure of one thing: she would never let it happen again.

"I don't suppose there's much point in worrying

about the stock," Karin said. "It will all be sold if they're tearing down the stores. I guess we won't be keeping our jobs, after all."

"I guess not," Stephanie said. She thought for a moment, then her face brightened. "Say, now that I've told you my big news, don't you think you ought to tell me what's with you and that gorgeous man?"

"There's nothing to tell. It's all business—which reminds me, I was out longer than I expected and it looks like another slow day. Why don't you leave? I'm sure I can manage by myself."

"Thanks," Stephanie said. "I suppose I should start looking for another job." She shook her head despondently and left the store.

The afternoon was unusually quiet. A few people walked through the shop, but they were just browsing. Karin hadn't sold anything in two days. Business always slowed down after the swallows left; then it picked up again in the spring. But this year there would be no spring for the shop. Lucas McKay would have cleared the contents and locked the doors long before then. The thought depressed her. It was just one more part of her life that she seemed to be losing—losing to the avaricious grasp of Lucas McKay. Her face was as glum as Stephanie's when she picked up a soft white cotton cloth and began rubbing some creamy wax into the small cherrywood music cabinet.

In a short while she was totally involved in polishing the furniture. It seemed as if she had to give it every opportunity to look its best before Lucas cleared it out and brought in the wrecking ball. She looked around the cozy shop, hating the thought that it would soon be replaced by a cold, modern structure. But there was nothing she could do to prevent it any more than she could prevent Lucas from tearing down Casa del Mar and destroying all the memories hidden within its walls.

A glance at the grandfather clock told her that it was

after six, yet somehow she felt obligated to remain on a little longer. After all, she had taken some time off that afternoon. It was only fair that she stay late and get the stock in good condition. Perhaps Mrs. Edison could demand a better price for the pieces if everything looked even shinier than usual. She telephoned to tell Jenny that she'd be late.

As she ran her hand over the marquetry top of a French ladies desk, she realized that she was putting off facing her father. She didn't want to answer any questions he might have about Lucas. She was having enough trouble trying to answer her own questions. Lucas McKay . . . what did he want from her? More important—what did she want from him?

She looked up in surprise when the bell above the door tinkled and Jim Simpson walked in.

"Glad I caught you. I was afraid you might have left."

"I was just finishing up."

"Can you spare a few minutes?"

"Of course." Karin led the way toward the back of the room. Jim followed her into the office.

"I told you that American International moved fast, but this is unbelievable. They've given me a cash deposit to be put in escrow, so as soon as you sign these papers I can open escrow and finalize the deal." He handed her several sheets of paper and watched silently while she studied them.

"Any questions?" he asked when she looked up. "It's the usual sales contract. I've just added the special clause about you being allowed to remain on the property and American International being permitted to have a representative on the premises."

"Everything seems fine. I'll sign these and then American International can worry about paying the taxes." She smiled as she wrote her name at the bottom of each sheet.

"I doubt if they'll have any trouble making the payments, but it's becoming really difficult for private individuals to maintain these large houses. Fortunately, the land they sit on is extremely valuable and developers are always anxious to pick up a choice piece of property." He began gathering up the papers and putting them back into his portfolio. "Do you have time for dinner . . . to celebrate closing the deal?"

Karin thought for a moment. It would certainly be easier for Jenny if she could clean up the kitchen without waiting for her to have a late dinner. Besides, if she got home later, her father might be asleep and she could avoid any explanations about Lucas. Anyway, she felt like getting out. It seemed like ages since she had had dinner with an attractive man. She smiled at Jim. "I'd be delighted. Just give me a few minutes to freshen up and call home."

They went to a well-known Mexican restaurant housed in a building which had been a stagecoach stop and boardinghouse when it was built in 1778. It had also been used as a hospital, and the wine cellar had even served as a jail. Aside from the mission, it was the oldest structure in San Juan Capistrano.

Jim asked for a California Chablis and they ordered. Strolling mariachis entertained them during dinner, and by the time they had finished their cappuccino Karin felt totally relaxed.

"I'm glad I was able to help you." Jim's hand reached across the table. "And now that we've finished our business, I hope we can get to know each other better. I'm sure your father would approve."

Karin lifted her hand and toyed with her coffeecup. She smiled at Jim; she knew her father *would* approve. Jim belonged to the right social class, and that was the only thing that mattered to Paul Andrews. But what about her? What mattered to her? Lucas' dark image flashed into her mind and she pushed it away. "I'd like that very much." She checked her watch. "We'd better be going. Tomorrow is a work day for both of us."

Jim called for the check and watched her quietly. "I hope I haven't upset you."

"No, of course not," she said truthfully. His remark hadn't upset her at all. She felt very comfortable with Jim, completely at ease. His presence generated none of the tension that Lucas' did. Lucas McKay. Even when he wasn't with her she couldn't get him out of her mind. Well, she would force herself to stop thinking about him. He was definitely not the type of man she could afford to become personally involved with. Theirs was merely a business relationship, after all—just that and nothing more. Besides, if she hated doing business with the man, how could she even think about doing anything else?

After dinner Jim walked her to her car. He took her hands in his as she was about to get in. "Remember what I said about our being friends. I really meant it." He smiled and released her hands as she slipped behind the wheel.

October drifted quietly into November. She went out with Jim once or twice, but he never managed to push Lucas from her mind. Yet while Lucas was constantly in her thoughts, he was strangely absent from the rest of her life. Even the guesthouse remained forlorn and empty. He had probably decided that she wasn't worth the effort. Unfortunately, all her resolutions to the contrary, Karin wasn't sure that was what she really wanted at all.

Nothing at the shop changed, either. She had received a bank check with the closing papers on the sale of the house, but Lucas so far seemed content to let both places take care of themselves. Although Karin hadn't reviewed the bank statements after the sale of the house, she knew there was more than enough to take the vacation her father kept talking about. Maybe it would do him good to get away to a warmer climate. Then she remembered that this was the only money they had, and since she had no way of knowing what unexpected expenses might occur in the future, she decided that it would be wise to save as much of it as she possibly could, at least until she had the chance to do a complete analysis of their finances.

Early one Saturday morning she went back down to the guest cottage. Jenny was busy enough between caring for the main house and seeing to her father's needs. Lucas was bound to show up eventually, but until he did, she got a perverse satisfaction from spending time in the cottage and keeping it clean.

Putting down her cleaning supplies, she walked through the rooms and opened all the windows. She ran a finger over the small marble-topped table beside the brass bed and it came away dusty.

She moved the small brush attachment of the vacuum cleaner across the tops of the furniture and watched as the machine sucked up the dust, leaving everything clean, if not shiny. The polishing would come next, after the dust had been cleared away. The machine emitted a constant whir as she bent down and concentrated on scooping up some dustballs that were caught between the desk and the wall. A hand touched her shoulder and she jumped back.

"Sorry, I didn't mean to frighten you. I knocked, but you didn't answer."

Karin pointed to the vacuum. "I didn't hear you."

Lucas shifted his foot and shut off the machine. Silence flooded the cottage and Karin wiped her hands nervously on her jeans. Lucas was watching her, making her feel awkward and embarrassed. Everything about his appearance made him seem immaculately attractive. His open-necked white knit shirt stretched across his broad chest while carefully pressed light gray trousers clung to his lean masculine hips and long straight legs. She brushed back a wisp of hair that had escaped from the kerchief she had tied around her head.

He placed his index finger against her cheek and began rubbing lightly. "You've got a smudge." His eyes held hers while his fingers kept edging across her face. His hand dropped to her chin and cupped it, tilting it toward him. Then he slowly bent his head, pressing his lips to hers.

His hand left her chin and moved behind her back, sliding down her spine and arching her body against the hard strength of his. Slowly, purposefully, he deepened the kiss, his sensitive lips demanding a response from hers. She closed her eyes and let herself relax against the lean power of his body.

A fiery warmth swept through her, consuming her senses and stealing her breath. She gasped against his mouth; he drew back and raised his head.

"I could apologize, but I won't," he said. "I've been wanting to do that for weeks." He held her in his arms, his eyes gazing steadily down at her face.

She looked at him, bewildered, still flushed from the passion of his embrace. "I don't know what to say."

"You *could* say you felt the same way about me."

"I don't even know you."

"You liked it when I kissed you."

"Yes." She couldn't deny the warmth of her response.

"Then I suggest we get to know each other better." His hands began caressing her back very slowly, very sensuously. She felt his fingers moving up, curving around the nape of her neck, playing with her kerchief, then flipping it off, releasing her auburn hair in a long shimmering cascade. His fingers combed through the silken tresses, biting into her scalp and pressing her lips harshly against his. Then his touch gentled as she felt his tongue tracing the outline of her lips, curving around them enticingly, reaching the center and urging them to open to his passionate probing.

Her lips parted and she sought out his masculine essence with an erotic yearning that seemed centered beneath the pit of her stomach. She found herself standing on tiptoe, trying to fit her body closer to his, trying to fill the vibrating void that had become an aching need deep within her. He caught her closely up against him and she felt his hardening response to her search for satisfaction.

His hand slipped beneath the strap of her halter top, tenderly caressing the curve of her shoulder before sliding down to flatten against her breast. For a moment there was no further movement, almost as if he were waiting for her to adjust to the intimacy of his touch, then his fingers began kneading the supple flesh and encircled the rosy aureole, expertly guiding it toward the taut response he was seeking.

His mouth left hers and circled her peaking breast as his hands went beneath her knees and carried her to the bed. She turned her head away from him, gasping breathlessly as a powerful surge of desire plunged her body into a state of mindless oblivion. As he set her on the bed, something snapped in Karin's mind and she realized where she was, what she was doing.

Things were happening too fast. She pressed her palms against Lucas' chest and rolled away. He made no attempt to stop her; he merely stood and looked at her with calm amusement in his eyes. Two weeks ago she had vowed to stay away from him, telling herself he was a man with no principles, a danger she couldn't afford. Now he was insisting that they become better acquainted, much better acquainted. She glanced at his dark face, then her gaze swept down his body, noting the self-assured way he draped himself against the wall while quietly watching her as if assessing and relishing the effect he had had on her. There was a dangerous aura about him which frightened her, yet drew her closer to him.

She needed time, time to think, time to sort out the frightening new impulses that were assaulting her. She rose from the bed and picked up a dustcloth and the can of furniture polish. She couldn't handle what had happened, so she would just avoid it, pretend it had never occurred. If only she could still the throbbing that filled every portion of her body. She tried to speak calmly, hoping Lucas would understand what she was trying to do. "I'll get the cleaning finished today. When are you moving in?"

"I thought I'd drop off some things today; they're in the car. We're breaking ground on Monday and I want to be close by. I hope that won't create a problem." His tone was as matter-of-fact as hers had been.

"No, of course not. As I said, I'm going to have everything in order by the end of the day."

"It's very nice out, too nice to work. I thought we might go for a ride and have some lunch."

"I'd love to, but I want to get things finished. Some other time, perhaps." She didn't want to have lunch or anything else with him. She couldn't afford to. She hated him, didn't she? But what about her body? What about what had happened only moments ago? Without looking up, she poured some polish on the cloth and began running it over the furniture. Why didn't he leave? She needed time alone, time to think. She leaned against a table and tried to steady herself.

He came to her and placed his hand over hers, stopping her circular strokes across the honey-toned wood. "It seems to me that I asked you to dinner the night we were discussing the sale of this property. You refused me then and agreed to dine with me at some other time. Don't put me off again. We've gone too far for that."

She knew he was referring to what had just happened, but she felt she couldn't discuss it now. She just couldn't. "I'm not putting you off. It's just that I want to get this place in order so you can move in."

"And I told you that's not necessary. You've done enough already." He pulled the cloth from her hand and led her to the door. "Now, go change while I talk to your father. I have a question to ask him about the arches between the rooms."

Before Karin could vocalize her protests, she found herself on her way up to her room. Once there, she reconsidered her decision. She had to be crazy to go out with him after what had happened at the cottage. Yet what choice did she have, after he had reminded her of the promise she had made at his office? Why was she getting so upset anyway? It was just lunch, wasn't it? What could happen over a sandwich? She dismissed her apprehensive thoughts and turned on the shower.

When she came downstairs twenty minutes later, Lucas and her father were bent over a small sketch pad and her father was making some penciled notations.

They looked up when she walked into the study. She had changed into a sleeveless white silk dress with a V neck and knife-pleated skirt. A finely woven gold chain encircled her neck and high-heeled sandals accented the slender length of her legs.

"You look very nice," her father said.

"Lucas has invited me to lunch. Would you care to join us?"

Her father shook his head. "Afraid not. I'll have something here, then lie down for a while. I'm feeling a lot better, but I still need my afternoon nap." He smiled. "You two go ahead and enjoy yourselves."

"I wonder if you'd mind if I took this paper with me?" Lucas asked, fingering the pad her father had been writing on.

"No, of course not. Let me know how it works out."

Lucas tore the page out of the pad, folded it and tucked it into a pocket.

"Where would you like to go?" he asked as he helped Karin into his car.

"I don't know. The weather is so warm it's hard to believe it's November. Actually it's a day for the beach."

"Would you like that? The beach, I mean?"

"It's a good idea, but we're not dressed for swimming."

"Well, maybe we could just beachcomb." He smiled at her and entered the freeway, heading south.

"I understand you've bought the antique shop." She couldn't keep the apprehension from her voice.

"Yes. You knew it was up for sale, didn't you?" His eyes left the road for a moment as he glanced at her, challenging the disapproval that was so apparent on her face.

"Yes, but I was hoping it would be sold to someone who wanted to keep it operating. You're going to close it."

"I'll have to, for what I have in mind."

"You've been buying up the surrounding stores and I've heard you intend to build a shopping mall of some sort."

"The area could use it."

"Perhaps, but you'd lose the charm of the town. It's a special place."

"Because of the mission?"

"The mission, the swallows, everything. You have to know Capistrano to really understand."

"Be a native, you mean?"

"Or have lived in the area for a long period of time, like I have."

"Spending the summer here? Leaving when it gets

cool . . . like the swallows. You think that gives you a real feel for the land?" His voice was edged with sarcasm.

"Not just the land. It's more like a love for the history and flavor of the area. I don't like to see any of it destroyed."

"And you think I'm doing that."

"I don't think a shopping center belongs so close to the mission."

"Not even if it provides work for the people in the area and improves their standard of living? That was an important purpose of the mission, you know, to teach the natives how to live better by providing them with a trade of some sort. You are aware of the tallow vats and the candle- and soapmaking facilities?"

"Of course, and I'm familiar with the wool-dying vats and the tannery, as well as all the craft shops—blanket weaving, shoemaking, hat blocking. I know about all those things."

"Then why do you object to what I'm doing? The mission has always been craft-oriented."

"Craft-oriented—that's the key word. I hardly think the shops in your mall will be craft-oriented."

"That remains to be seen, doesn't it?"

"Not really. I know enough about you to venture an educated guess."

"Somehow I don't think you do, and it's much too beautiful a day for such deep thoughts, but I will tell you this. I've bought the antique shop and the entire mall. I'm going to close everything down right after Christmas; then I can rebuild the plaza the way I want it to be. And that's going to have to satisfy you for now, because we've arrived at our destination."

Karin had been so involved in trying to explain her position that she hadn't realized they had left the freeway.

"The food here is very good," Lucas said as he

pulled into the parking lot of a restaurant that looked like an old Victorian mansion. It was painted gray with white gingerbread trim and shutters. The cliff on which it was built towered above the gently lapping waves of a small cove. A waiter led them to a terrace overlooking the water. As they walked to their table, two middle-aged men waved to Lucas. He waved back, but didn't introduce Karin or stop to talk to them.

"Business associates," he explained. "If I stop by their table, they'll start talking deals." He smiled and held out her chair. "Right now, I'd rather be talking to you." He pushed her chair closer to the table, then let his hand drift lightly to her shoulder before taking his own seat.

Once again his touch caused the strange tingling sensation and Karin swiftly spread the bright red napkin in her lap, hoping her outwardly calm movements hid the nervous tension his contact had created.

Lucas seemed unaware of Karin's distress as he ordered for both of them: a large platter of cracked Dungeness crab on a bed of ice, a fresh green salad and a basket of hot French bread. She sipped pale Chablis and watched as the waiter added freshly ground black pepper to the salad.

"What do you think?" Lucas asked when the waiter bowed and moved away. "Isn't this the perfect place for a beachcomber's lunch?"

"It's lovely. I've never been here before." She turned and looked down to the water where two gulls swooped low, skimming the tops of the waves.

Lucas reached across the table and took her hands in his. "And I thought you knew everything about this area." He smiled warmly. "But since you don't, I'm going to share a very romantic story with you." His fingers stroked lightly against hers. "This house was built at the turn of the century by a wealthy sea captain from Massachusetts. His wife's health was failing and the doctor recommended a milder climate, so they moved here. The weather was warmer and he was still close to the sea. There's even a small widow's walk up there." He motioned to the upper stories of the house. "In New England the women would look out to sea hoping to sight their husband's ships when they returned, but out here the captain himself scanned the waters, pretending the perch was the deck of his ship."

"That's a beautiful story and this is a lovely old house. It has character."

"Not like the houses built today? The houses I'm building?"

"It would be a shame to tear down something like this and replace it with a housing tract."

"Or to tear down something like Casa del Mar?"

"You own Casa del Mar. I no longer have any say in what happens to it. I'm only concerned about my father's health."

"No problem. Your father can stay as long as he likes, and since that's all settled, I think it's time for you to start making some plans of your own. You're much too lovely to be living in the past."

His gaze met hers and she lowered her eyes, but not before she had seen the beginning of that faintly curving smile she was coming to know so well. The past, indeed! If Lucas had his way there'd be no reminders of the past anywhere, and the future would consist of a lot of American International bungalows by the sea.

He signed the check and took her hand. "Let me show you the rest of the house. All the rooms have been converted into dining areas, but the owners have tried to preserve as much of the original craftsmanship as possible." He led her through the restaurant and pointed out the hand-carved doorframes and banisters, the plank floors and etched-glass windows, and the large stone fireplaces in each of the rooms. In some places old headboards had been converted into the backs of benches for cozy little dining booths surrounding cloth-covered tables. Dressers from the former bedrooms were now used as serving buffets.

"They've done a wonderful job. They've saved everything they could. What marvelous atmosphere this place has." Her gaze swept the room, admiring the individual beauty of each rare object.

"You still haven't seen the best part." Taking her hand, he led her up the narrow stairway and onto a small balcony. "Well, what do you think?"

"What do I think?" She looked out over the water. The view was even more breathtaking than the one from Casa del Mar because that house was set back amid a forest of trees while this one had been built right over the ocean. The balcony curved out over the water and Karin felt as if she were standing on the prow of a ship. "I know exactly how that sea captain felt. I've never been in a house like this. It's a totally new experience."

"Is it?" Lucas' arm settled on her shoulder, drawing her closer. His fingers feathered the base of her neck. "This seems to be a day for new experiences; let's not stop now." His warm breath caressed her ear as he turned her slowly into his arms.

"Lucas?" She placed her hands on his chest.

"Mmm . . ." He moved them to his shoulders and tilted her lips toward his.

His heartbeat hammered against hers and she felt her legs grow weak. Her fingers curled into his shoulders, seeking the support of his inflexible strength. With consummate expertise, his lips parted hers and their warm breath mingled with the lingering traces of Chablis.

His muscles rippled beneath her fingers while his hands explored her body, urging her hips toward his, and Karin turned her head, gasping for breath, when his raw sexuality reached out to claim her. Her hungry fingers combed through his black hair while his mouth seared across her arching neck. Karin moaned as the fiery passion flaming deep within her sought to escape between her sensuously parted lips.

Lucas' huge frame shuddered beneath her touch and his body grew rigid as he set her away from him. "That's enough for now." His voice was husky, his breathing ragged. "This place leaves a lot to be desired"—his eyes searched her face—"for what I have in mind." Drawing her to his side, he led her down the stairway.

"Wait here. I'll get the car." He brought her hand to his lips as he spoke.

Karin nodded; she couldn't speak. He squeezed her hand gently. "Don't go away. I'll be right back."

She watched him stride swiftly into the parking area. She wasn't going anywhere, at least not without him. The intoxicating ride he had just taken her on had left her physically drained, but her nerves were clamoring, seeking a fulfillment they hadn't even known existed. Somehow she had to regain control of her senses. Restlessly she surveyed her surroundings, searching for some mundane activity which would take her mind off Lucas.

A stained-glass window at the side of the house caught her interest. She walked over to examine it and was running her fingers over the colorful leaded glass when the restaurant door opened and she heard a masculine voice ask, "What do you think of McKay's latest charmer?"

Karin's attention was caught by the mention of Lucas' name as well as the offhand reference to herself. She took a few steps forward, peeked around the corner of the building and saw the two men Lucas had referred to as business associates.

"Looks a bit naïve for our boy, wouldn't you say?

I've always thought he was addicted to actresses and models."

"My thoughts exactly. But I'm sure he has his reasons. Maybe she has a piece of property he wants to get his hands on."

"You're probably right, but while he's about it, knowing McKay, he's sure to get his hands on the girl, as well. I doubt she'll be able to resist. Not that she's not pretty, mind. . . ."

Both men laughed and walked into the parking lot, their voices fading. Karin was burning, from what she had heard as well as from the shame she felt about her own reactions to Lucas' intimate caresses. Irresistible, was he? Well, not to her. Not if she could help it. She would never give him the chance to boast about an easy conquest. Remembering her passionate response on the balcony, she flushed and dismissed it as a moment of weakness, one that would never happen again. He might be buying Casa del Mar, but he definitely was not going to own *her*, and she intended to let him know that right now. She walked down the steps as he drove the car up to the entrance.

He got out and opened her car door. Bringing her hand to his lips, he caressed her palm with the tip of his tongue. "We'll go to my place." His seductive voice promised fulfillment.

Shivers of desire ran through her body, but she remembered the men's laughter and forced herself to pull her hand away. "I really have to get home," she said coldly. "The only free time Jenny has is on weekends, when I can stay with my father."

"Your father said he was going to rest. I don't think you have to hover over him while he sleeps. He's not an infant, you know."

"I'm well aware of that, Mr. McKay. After all, he is *my* father. And just remember, I didn't want to go out at all today. *You* were the one who insisted. Now we've had our lunch and I want to go home. What's so unusual about that? We're only business associates, after all. Don't try to make our relationship into more than it is." She tried to sound calmly detached, but her heart was pounding so violently that she could hardly catch her breath.

"You came to lunch with me out of a sense of duty? Is that it? Now you can't wait to be rid of me. I must be like my houses: too brash and unrefined for your delicate taste. You must have really hated it when I kissed you." His dark piercing eyes reflected the violence he was holding tautly under control. "Well, did you? Answer me."

Karin turned away and faced the front of the car. She couldn't lie, but she would rather die than admit the truth. "I'm not interested in pursuing this conversation. Please take me home."

"Not until you tell me what happened. We've spent the last hour or so getting acquainted—some people might even call it more than that—then I leave you alone for two minutes, and when I return, my soft kitten has turned into a snarling tigress." He put his hands on her shoulders.

She shrugged them off. "I'm not *your* anything—kitten or tigress—and I never intend to be. Now, are you going to take me home or shall I call a taxi?"

"Get in," Lucas snarled as he flung the car door open. "I suppose you think I should apologize for forcing my attentions on you, but you can forget that. I'm not going to bother saying anything to you until you come to your senses—and I certainly don't intend to apologize when you're the one who's behaving like a fool."

She could feel him looking at her, but she kept her eyes facing straight ahead until she heard the motor start up and felt the car move rapidly out of the parking lot.

Chapter Four

$\mathcal{L}$ucas took Karin directly home. Neither one attempted to make conversation, and when she left the car and he sped down the road, she still hadn't recovered from her angry embarrassment.

In her heart she knew that what hurt most was the fact that if she hadn't overheard the two men, and if, while she was in his arms, Lucas had asked her, she would indeed have become his latest girlfriend. It was futile to deny, to herself at least, the intense attraction she felt for him, an attraction which she now realized had started the first time she saw him in the Sacred Garden of the mission.

Karin watched him go and wished she had been calm enough to choose her words more carefully. Obviously she meant nothing to him, just an amusing footnote to one of his many business deals, but she had been so enraged by the conversation she had overheard that she hadn't even considered the possible consequences of her actions. It certainly wasn't very smart to antagonize the man who owned both the home where she lived and the shop where she worked.

But the events of the next two weeks proved that her concern was baseless, because all through November the shop operated as usual, the only difference being that their paychecks now came from American International. Every so often some new piece of furniture or an interesting accessory would arrive to replace something they had sold, and Karin did think it odd that the company should be replenishing the merchandise of a store it intended to close.

Karin knew that Lucas was staying at the cottage occasionally, because she sometimes saw lights in the evening. Still, he kept his word about respecting their privacy and never came near the main house.

On the morning of Thanksgiving Day Karin accompanied her father on a leisurely stroll around the grounds. The warm sun had taken the chill off the nippy fall weather and Dr. Stevens had said that walking was the best exercise her father could get. Grasping his elbow, she guided him away from the sharply slanting driveway where it curved to avoid a towering palm tree.

"We should cut down that tree and straighten out this road. It's dangerous the way it is, especially when it rains and you can't see the dip."

Karin smiled and squeezed her father's elbow affectionately. "You'd never do that. These trees are like your children."

Her father stopped walking and turned to look at her. "Not at all, Karin. I enjoy their beauty, but I've never thought of them as my children. I have only one child—you—and your happiness means more to me than anything else in this world. Do you understand that? More than anything."

Karin stood on tiptoe and kissed his cheek. "I love you, too, and I'll never do anything to hurt you." She felt proud satisfaction in the way she had solved their financial problems without involving him. Everything would be perfect if only she could stop thinking about Lucas. . . .

Evenly thudding footsteps moving quickly up the driveway caught her attention, and taking her father's arm, she moved to the side of the road just as Lucas rounded the bend, jogging steadily toward them.

He was dressed in a dark blue exercise suit trimmed in red and white stripes, and his lean, athletic body covered the space between them effortlessly. Karin felt an unwelcome fluttering in her stomach as his vibrant masculinity once again began its silent assault on her senses. Then, as he came closer, the colors of his outfit flared into prominence and she remembered American International—what it represented and what Lucas represented. She balled her fists into her sides as she reminded herself that Lucas was a dangerous man, both in his business dealings and in his affairs with women.

Paul Andrews didn't share Karin's misgivings, so he smiled broadly and offered his hand to Lucas, but Lucas only shook his head and kept jogging in place.

"Can't stop now," he said breathlessly. "Too sudden." He waved and continued swiftly up the drive.

"What do you suppose that was all about?" Paul Andrews' face wore a hurt expression.

"I think his body was geared to the pace of his running and he couldn't make a sudden stop to speak with us."

"Oh." Paul Andrews nodded understandingly. "Well, I hope we see him later. I'd like to get his ideas about the house."

"Don't worry; I'm sure he likes it."

"Of course. It's a beautiful place; you can't help but admire it. But I was speaking as an architect. I'd like to know his thoughts from that point of view."

"He's probably very busy."

"Probably, but I did think he'd show me his designs. Somehow, the last time we spoke I got the feeling that he respected my ideas."

They rounded the corner and the house came into view, along with Lucas' well-muscled form leaning against one of the arches. The even rise and fall of his broad chest showed that he had slowed his body's momentum enough to stop and wait for them. He came forward and held his hand out to her father.

"Sorry I couldn't stop before. I know it seemed rude, but I have to wind down slowly."

"No problem," Paul Andrews said. "I just wanted to ask how things were going. Any new ideas?"

"A few. In fact, I intend to put them on paper this afternoon."

"On Thanksgiving?" Paul Andrews asked.

"It's just another day for us lonely bachelors." There was mischief in his eyes as he glanced over at Karin.

"Well, then, you'll have to join us," Paul Andrews insisted. "Karin, tell Jenny to set an extra place."

Karin's mouth fell open as she tried to protest, but she realized that would only arouse her father's suspicions, so she clamped her lips together angrily and started up the steps. But not before she saw the mockery in Lucas' eyes turn to the gleam of victory.

Jenny prepared their dinner, then left the serving to Karin and went to spend the holiday with her sister. Karin was stirring the mushroom soup when the doorbell rang. It had to be Lucas. The tempo of her heartbeat increased as she went to answer it.

"Hello, Lucas." She stared at the knot in his tie, unwilling to risk an encounter with his eyes.

His thumb caught her chin, raising her troubled eyes to his steadfast gaze. "You didn't want me to come, did you?"

"It's my father's house. . . ." Lucas raised an eyebrow and Karin realized her mistake. "I mean he lives here. . . ." She stopped in midsentence, too flustered to continue.

"I know what you mean, and I'm not going to use my ownership to force my presence on you. Do you want me to leave?"

Karin shook her head. "No, of course not. My father is looking forward to seeing you."

"Well, I'm happy to hear that, but I'd feel even better if his daughter shared that sentiment."

"His daughter isn't your concern."

"Really?" His hand cupped her chin, fingers stroking down the curving lines of her neck. "What if I want to make her my concern?" His eyes probed hers for an answer.

"Then I'd say you were wasting your time."

He grinned and brought his lips lightly against hers. "I've never backed off from a challenge."

His touch sent shivers racing up her spine and she pulled away. "My father's waiting for you." Her legs trembled as she led Lucas to the library before seeking her own safety in the warmth of the kitchen.

She busied herself with last-minute preparations for dinner, but all her thoughts were centered on Lucas. What had he meant when he said that he wanted to make her his concern? She knew that he was attracted to her, just as he was to numerous other women, women much more beautiful than she. So why was he so determined to make her fall in love with him? She couldn't solve that riddle, but she had no intention of providing him with an easy victory.

She stayed hidden in the kitchen for as long as possible, but finally she had to start serving dinner unless she wanted to risk burning all of Jenny's carefully prepared food. Her father sat at the head of the table, Lucas and her on either side of him.

Lucas and her father kept up a lively conversation, but Karin didn't join in. She kept her eyes fastened on her plate, unwilling to raise them to where Lucas sat directly across from her. Even so, she knew he was looking at her, and the unseen intensity of his gaze sent a warm flush into her cheeks.

At one point, at her father's urging, she had to pass

the warm dinner rolls to Lucas. Reaching for them, he covered her hand with his and held it there until her eyes met his in a startled gaze.

"Hi." His fingers curved around hers, sending small flashes of warmth surging through her body. "I was afraid you'd fallen asleep. All this architectural talk must be boring you."

"Not at all," Karin said. "I heard every word you said." She tried to pull her hand free, but Lucas had it tightly imprisoned.

"I'm glad, because I want you to enjoy my company as much as I do yours," he whispered.

Karin tugged her hand free, and the rolls slipped, falling over the damask tablecloth. "I'm sorry. I'm not usually so clumsy." She began gathering them up.

"It was my fault," Lucas said as he helped her. "My mind wasn't on the rolls. I was hungry for other things."

Paul Andrews laughed. "I know just what you mean . . . no sense filling up on bread with all these other delicacies to feast on." He handed Lucas a platter of turkey.

"Exactly," Lucas said. He took the turkey, but his eyes never left Karin's face.

She picked up the candied sweet potatoes and, holding them toward Lucas, fought down an urge to mash them into his grin. She had understood his double entendre even if her father hadn't, and she hated the fact that Lucas was enjoying her embarrassment. "Would you like some potatoes?" she asked.

"Of course," Lucas said. "I'd never refuse anything you offered." He smiled angelically, but a demon winked deep in his eyes.

"Cut it out," she hissed.

"What did you say?" Paul Andrews asked.

"Nothing," Karin said. "I was just repeating Jenny's

favorite maxim. You know, the one about your eyes being bigger than your stomach. And some men are like that, just greedy little boys." She smiled sweetly at Lucas.

"And greedy little boys don't give up until they get what they want." Lucas returned her smile. "Sometimes there's no limit to what they can handle."

"Everything is on the table. Don't expect more." Karin couldn't control her anger.

"Not even dessert?" Lucas teased.

"You know what I mean," she said grimly.

"Karin, what's wrong with you? I've never seen you behave like this." Paul Andrews was annoyed.

"I'm sorry, Dad." The last thing she wanted was to upset her father. "Perhaps I'd better concentrate on eating." Picking up her fork, she toyed with her food until dinner was over and she could begin clearing the table. "I'll get the pie and coffee." She rose from her chair and gathered some dishes before heading for the kitchen.

She was too edgy to eat any dessert and just sipped nervously at her coffee while Lucas and her father enjoyed Jenny's delicious pumpkin pie. When the men retired to the library for some of her father's expensive Napoleon brandy, she breathed a sigh of relief and carried the remains of the turkey into the kitchen.

She was wrapping the thinly sliced meat in foil when the door swung open and Lucas entered, carrying the leftover rolls and candied sweet potatoes.

"Thanks. You can put them down there." She turned back to her packaging and waited for him to leave.

"Your father's resting. I told him I would help you."

"I couldn't allow that. You're a guest. Besides, I'm sure you're not used to working in a kitchen."

"And you are?"

"Of course. Why shouldn't I be?"

77

"Come off it, Karin. You know less about kitchen work than I do. Don't pretend that you haven't been pampered by servants all your life."

"What do you know about my life?" She dried her hands and, still clutching the towel, turned to face him.

"Quite a bit—but not as much as I'd like to." His warm gaze moved over her body.

"Well, the feeling isn't mutual." She turned away, grasping the sink with her trembling hands. Why didn't he leave before she lost her tenuous grip on reality?

"Isn't it? Methinks the lady doth protest too much." He lifted her hair and began massaging her shoulders in small, erotic circles.

She closed her eyes and leaned back as the spicy scent of his cologne surrounded her. Every inch of her flesh responded to him, wanted him: the touch of his hands, the caress of his lips, the promise of more. She smiled contentedly as he nuzzled her neck and let his hand fall to the curve of her breast.

"Let the dishes go. I have more interesting things on my mind." His husky voice couldn't disguise the arrogance of his words as he turned her slowly into his arms. "I'd much rather hold your warm, lovely body than some cold china plate."

The words she had overheard outside the restaurant flashed through her brain like a bright red danger signal. She pulled herself free and turned to face him. "It's bad enough that I was forced to sell you my house. You'll never get anything else from me."

"Who are you trying to convince? Me or yourself?" He gripped her upper arms angrily. "You're fighting to stop what you're feeling, but you're not going to win. I haven't lost a battle yet." Cupping her chin, he bruised her lips with the demanding harshness of his.

She struggled against him for a few fleeting moments, then the sensuous demands of her body overrode all other considerations. His lips softened as he tasted the sweet flavor of victory and her hands, which had tried to separate them, now toyed restlessly with the buttons on his shirt.

His arms went behind her back and brought her close, eliminating the inches between them. Opening a button, she slipped her hands beneath his shirt, her fingers brushing against his flaming skin. His swift intake of breath testified to the sensual impact of her explorations, and he released her lips, turning to whisper into her ear.

"Let's go someplace where we can be more comfortable." With one arm tightly encircling her waist he led her toward the door. His other hand traveled to her neck, then lowered to her breast, claiming the territory as his own.

She felt his experienced touch and was once again reminded of his friends' laughing prediction. She spun away from him and met the shock in his eyes. "I'm not going anywhere with you. I'm perfectly comfortable here. Now, will you please go? Our agreement gives you access to the property, but I'm not included. So do us both a favor and leave me alone. This is one battle you're not going to win."

"I could prove you wrong, but I don't think this is the time to try. Not with your father sleeping right next door. My best maneuvers demand privacy, and a good general knows when to retreat." He smiled smugly. "But I'll be back to enjoy the fruits of victory." He kissed her cheek and left the room.

Karin walked to the window and, edging the curtain aside, watched his retreating figure move toward the cottage. Despite all she knew about him, she couldn't prevent the surge of desire that tore through her flesh. He represented everything she hated in a person. So why did he attract her more than any other man she had known? She shook her head at the futility of trying to combat his magnetic appeal.

There was no denying that every fiber of his body was loaded with virile masculinity, and she had caught the message as well as any other woman. But somehow, somewhere, she would find the strength to block his signals and ensure that she was the one woman his acquisitive hands would never possess.

She finished the dishes quickly, but with Jenny gone and her father asleep, the house seemed too quiet and lonely to contain both Karin and her disturbing thoughts about Lucas. She looked in on her father to see that he was resting peacefully, then threw a jacket over her shoulders and headed out the door. A good brisk walk was just what she needed to rescue her from the helpless quagmire into which she seemed to be sinking.

The sun was even warmer than it had been that morning and she slipped off her jacket, casually flinging it over her arm. She walked through the trees, circled the tennis court and settled herself on a lounge chair beside the pool. The sky was a pale blue and the few fluffy clouds seemed like balls of cotton which floated through the sky, taking special care not to block out the soothing rays of the sun.

She closed her eyes and enjoyed the mild ocean breezes, realizing how much she had to be thankful for—her father's returning health, a job she enjoyed, and the right to stay on at Casa del Mar. Despite her ambivalent feelings about Lucas McKay, this Thanksgiving Day had turned out to be a far more pleasant one than she had ever thought possible.

The sun was stronger than she had expected; she soon felt warm all over and droplets of moisture began forming in the shadowed cleft between her breasts. She had opened her blouse to tissue them away when long, lean fingers closed firmly over hers, then blazed a path of their own, leaving the still-damp valley to open the front clasp of her bra and explore the flesh that was now burgeoning with pulsating sensitivity.

Karin's eyes widened in astonishment as she awoke from her relaxing lethargy and looked directly at Lucas. She tried to bolt upright in the seat, but the full force of his body came down on hers, pinning her back against the cushion and making it impossible for her to move. His lips met hers firmly preventing her from turning away and forcing her to exercise a maximum of will-power as she desperately fought off the mounting desire to respond to his touch.

Keeping her lips tightly closed, she tried to remain impassive, to think of other things, things which didn't involve Lucas McKay or his ability to arouse the erotic emotions that were seething deep within her body. But her efforts were in vain. Lucas had removed his shirt and the matted hair on his granite-hard chest was vibrating against her bare breasts and tantalizing them into an erotic reaction which no amount of hastily imposed self-control could hold under restraint.

Just when Karin felt that she was going to cry out from the sweet torment he was subjecting her to, Lucas lifted his head and ran the palms of his hands down the sides of her body, pausing to circle, massage and caress her breasts until she closed her eyes and murmured, "Lucas, please. . . ."

His lips moved to her temple. "Lucas, please what?" he whispered huskily. "Do you like what I'm doing?" His tongue circled a tantalizing path along the inside of her ear as he waited for her answer.

Every inch of her flesh reached out to him, aching for the seductive magic of his caresses. Yes, she liked what he was doing; in fact, she loved what he was doing, and every nerve in her body threatened to revolt if she said or did anything to stop him. "Oh, yes, Lucas, yes." She grasped his head and brought his lips back to hers, holding him with a desperate urgency while his hand circled her waist and prepared to travel downward.

She arched her torso, eagerly meeting his fingers. Her body yearned for fulfillment, and Lucas McKay was the only one who could assuage that need. The only invasion that mattered to her was the invasion his hands and tongue were making on her body.

Their fingers traveled to each other's waistbands as their bodies shifted savagely against each other, dancing to a tuneless melody that was as timeless as the ages.

Suddenly a distant sound broke into the melody and Karin tried to block her ears, willing it to stop, to go away. She wanted no interruption. She couldn't stand one—not now. Her hands clutched Lucas' shoulders tightly when he moved away from her, but he caught them up in his and kissed them gently.

"It's your father, Karin. He'll be wondering where you are." He moved away from her and started refastening her clothes.

She felt the heated embarrassment rise through her as he gently brushed one nipple before reclasping her bra. What on earth was wrong with her that Lucas had to be the one to remind her of her duties to her father? As soon as he stood up, she tried to race past him. But he held her hand, keeping her at his side. "It's not over, Karin; you know it's not."

"There's nothing to be over, nothing at all. I was just half-asleep. You caught me unaware, that's all. You took advantage of me. It won't happen again—not ever."

"Meet me at the cottage tonight. After your dad is asleep," Lucas said as if he hadn't heard anything she had said.

"No, never!" She ripped her hands from his and tore up the path toward the house. She didn't know who she hated more, Lucas McKay or herself, for the way she let him treat her.

That night Karin drew the drapes tightly across her window and snuggled deep beneath the covers of her bed. As far as she was concerned, nothing existed beyond the confines of this room, and there was no such place as a cozy little guest cottage down the road.

December started off rainier than usual, and by the middle of the month her father was constantly complaining about being confined to the house. They definitely needed a vacation in a warmer climate, he declared, and he even had a travel agent come to the house to discuss tours he thought they might enjoy. Now he spent most of his time studying the brochures and trying to decide on the best itinerary.

The inclement weather kept customers away from the antique shop, too, since people in Southern California tended to stay indoors when it rained, so Karin had been closing the shop early. One evening, after work, she came in cold, damp and barefoot, to find Lucas sitting in the library with her father. They looked up from the paper they had been working on.

"Still raining?" her father asked. "This weather is impossible; we've got to get away." He shook his head. "I'm glad you're home early; I've invited Lucas to stay for dinner." He pointed to the blueprint on his desk. "I've been showing him how the early Spanish settlers used thick adobe walls and wide verandas to keep out the sun's heat in the summer and the damp and cold in the winter. He thinks it might be useful nowadays, what with the energy crisis and the cost of heating and air-conditioning."

Lucas had looked up when Karin walked in, his eyes moving slowly over her body, evaluating her appearance, but other than that, he made no attempt to acknowledge her presence. She combed her fingers through her damp hair and wished Lucas wasn't seeing her like this. An overwhelming combination of hurt and indignation enveloped her. Since he was making such an obvious effort to ignore her, she felt under no obligation to greet him. Once again a flame of anger flared, making her forget how dependent she was upon him.

She realized that common courtesy required that she second her father's invitation, but she certainly didn't feel she had to be polite after the way Lucas had slighted her.

She retreated to her room, where, after fluffing her hair with the blow-dryer, she put on a long hostess gown with a dusty-pink velvet skirt and a white silk shirtwaist. A series of thin gold chains flipped beneath the collar and clustered in the open neckline. Black silk slippers matched the wide, pleated sash that encircled her waist.

She always dressed for dinner when she was eating with her father. It was one of the habits from his former life that he still insisted on. However, as she looked in the mirror, she realized that she had put more effort into her appearance than she usually did. She knew she was trying to impress Lucas, to show him that she could look attractive and that his callous attitude hadn't caused her any great pain. She walked downstairs, her heartbeat quickening at the thought of seeing him again.

Lucas and her father were still in the library, but the papers had been put away and they were talking quietly. They held ice-filled glasses and stood up as she walked into the room.

"Ah, Karin, you look lovely—well worth waiting for," her father said. "Now you can keep Lucas company while I get a fresh shirt."

"Can I fix you a drink?" Lucas asked when her father

had gone. His casual manner made Karin feel that he was her host.

"No, thank you." She walked around the room, rearranging some ashtrays and straightening the papers on her father's desk. Her nerves were so taut that she couldn't stay still.

"Your father invited me to dinner; in fact, he seemed eager to have me accept. I'm sorry if you find the situation so distasteful." He made no attempt to disguise his sarcasm.

She bent to fluff a sofa pillow but said nothing. She knew she was tidying up the already immaculate room just to avoid looking at Lucas. In spite of everything that had happened between them, and in spite of her fervent desire not to become involved with him, she still had to fight to control the intense attraction she felt for him—an attraction that was ridiculous, considering the way she felt about his life-style. Yet she couldn't deny the messages her body kept sending her every time he was near. She was silently berating her own vulnerability when his voice broke into her thoughts.

"I realize we've had some problems, but I don't think it would do your father's appetite any good to watch us snarling at each other over dinner."

"Then why don't you just leave? I'll explain to Father that you suddenly remembered a previous engagement."

"Will you stop this ridiculous behavior? Your father is practically a prisoner in this house. He needs to see people. Fortunately, I'm available and he enjoys having me here." He strode across the room and grasped her shoulders. "Answer me when I talk to you."

"I have nothing to say to you." She held herself stiffly and coldly avoided his gaze.

"Why? Are you so taken with your own importance that you can't bear the thought of speaking with me?"

"I don't have to explain my motives; I'm free to

choose my friends on any basis I please." She twisted her shoulders, trying to pull away from him.

"Fine. Then let's pretend we have an amicable relationship. I don't intend to stay away from here just to avoid you."

"Of course not. Why should you? After all, you do own this house," she hissed.

"That's not what I mean and you know it."

"Our agreement gave you the use of the guesthouse; it said nothing about having you as a dinner guest. I thought I made my feelings about you clear on Thanksgiving."

Lucas tightened his grip on her and inhaled deeply. She could tell that he was restraining his anger, not trusting himself to speak until he was in full control of his emotions. "I thought you did, too, but your biggest problem seems to be that you can't make them acceptable to yourself. And that's too bad, because you can pretend to be as icy as you like but I'm staying for dinner. Your father invited me."

"Then let him entertain you."

"I don't need to be entertained."

"Good, because I'm rather tired."

"You left work early."

"You can take it out of my pay, if that's what's bothering you. Now let me go." She tried to twist away from him.

His fingers tightened on her arm, preventing her from moving. "Not until you tell me why you're acting like this. I don't care about your pay, so forget that excuse."

Karin's angry eyes stared directly into his. "Why am I acting like this? You looked right through me when I came in. You deliberately snubbed me. How do you expect me to act?"

"Maybe I expected you to take the first step, to show

me that you'd gotten over whatever it was that had turned you into an icicle. I'm not in the habit of pursuing reluctant women."

"And I don't intend to be Lucas McKay's latest girlfriend." The angry words had slipped out before Karin even realized what she was saying.

Lucas looked momentarily startled, then he grinned. "You haven't even been asked," he said softly. "But the idea has definite possibilities."

Footsteps, slow and even, sounded in the hallway. Lucas dropped his hands and moved away from Karin.

"Well, now." Karin's father smiled at her. "I hope you've made Lucas feel at home."

"Karin is a charming hostess. She made me feel as if Casa del Mar belonged to me." A cynical smile curved the corners of Lucas' mouth.

Karin caught her breath and narrowed her eyes at him, but her father's presence prevented her from venting her anger. After taking a moment to regain her composure, she said, "I'm sure that Jenny has dinner ready. Why don't we go into the dining room?" Without waiting for a response, she began walking toward the door.

"Lucas is building some houses in Dana Point. He's asked me to help with the designs," Karin's father said over the meal.

"Tract houses?" Karin knew her father's views on the subject. How could he possibly be working with Lucas?

"I thought your father might have some ideas about how we could preserve the natural contours of the land while building affordable housing." Lucas smiled smugly, showing Karin that he had found a way to circumvent her father's prejudices.

"I thought you were opposed to large housing tracts." Karin looked directly at her father.

"I haven't changed my mind. You know how I feel about cutting the land into postage-stamp plots. But it's going to be done anyway, and at least this is a chance to try to make the place more aesthetically appealing. Besides, it will give me something to do."

"You're supposed to be resting."

"I feel fine, and there's nothing physical about this work; it will help keep my mind active."

Jenny cleared the table and told Karin that she had set the coffee tray in the library. Lucas moved quickly behind Karin to hold her chair away from the table and she felt the immediate charge of nervous tension that always occurred when he was near. Her breathing grew shallow and she held herself stiffly as she moved in front of him and walked through the arch leading to the hallway.

She had just entered the library when she heard her father's voice. "I believe I'll pass on the coffee. The doctor says the caffeine isn't good for my heart anyway." He smiled at Karin. "I'll say good night, but you two are a good deal younger. No need to cut your evening short." He held a hand out to Lucas.

Karin watched her father walk slowly down the corridor. Lucas slipped behind her and, his arm around her waist, guided her toward the sofa.

"I like mine black," Lucas said.

Karin looked at him.

"My coffee. We *are* having coffee, aren't we?"

"Yes . . . yes, of course." Karin moved away from him and seated herself on the sofa behind the coffee table. She tensed at the thought of being alone with him, but he was her guest and there was no gracious way to refuse him.

"You know," Lucas said, "when we first discussed the sale of this property and the fact that I would insist on having someone from my company stay here, you were concerned about the effect it would have on your father. It turns out that your father and I get along very well, but *you're* finding it impossible to be in the same room with me."

"That's not true."

"Isn't it?"

"You're sitting on the edge of your seat. You can't wait for me to leave."

She hesitated and looked down at the floor. "I'm tired."

"Of my company?"

"Why must you put words in my mouth?"

"Because I don't like dishonesty."

"Okay, I admit it. I don't like being with you. Is that what you wanted to hear? Now are you satisfied?"

"No, it's not what I wanted to hear—and I'm not in the least bit satisfied. What are you afraid of? Becoming my latest girlfriend? You didn't seem to mind the idea until that afternoon at the restaurant. What happened while I was getting the car?"

She shrugged. "Why did anything have to happen? We're just not compatible. Our values are totally different; we have absolutely nothing in common." She tightened her grip on the china cup. "Besides, I'm not interested in a romantic involvement with anyone, but if I were, it certainly wouldn't be you."

"Meaning I'm not in your social set."

"Meaning whatever you choose it to mean. I don't owe you any explanations." She put her half-empty cup on the table. "And now, since we're being perfectly honest, I really must ask you to leave. I have to get in early tomorrow . . . to make up for today."

"You won't let go, will you? I wonder who you're fighting, me or yourself?"

"Stop being ridiculous. I'm not fighting anyone; I'm just tired."

He watched her silently, then placed his cup beside hers and stood up. "You do know that the shop is going to close after Christmas?"

"Yes, I've heard." She planned on looking for a new job right after the holidays. All because of Lucas. Everything was because of Lucas. She pursed her lips in anger. "You just can't wait to rip down anything that's noncommercial. All you understand is money. You have no appreciation of grace and beauty."

Disdainful amusement flickered across his face as he tilted his head and stared at her. "On the contrary, I've always been attracted by grace and beauty. That's why I think of things in monetary terms. In this materialistic world most beautiful things cost money, and I enjoy having the power to buy whatever catches my interest, anything I want to have." He smiled, let his gaze move intimately over her body and walked slowly toward her.

His fingers slipped beneath her hair, stroked the soft silk collar of her dress and stole into the open neckline. He lingered at the center of her collarbone for a moment, letting his thumb draw small circles as he seemed to probe for the very core of her being. Then he lifted the thin strands of gold and let them fall lightly over his fingers.

"Everything costs money," he said. "This outfit you're wearing cost plenty, so don't pretend poverty with me."

She felt her breath catch in her throat just as it did each time his flesh touched hers. "It's an old outfit; I've had it for years." She tried to move away from him, but he caught her hand and brought her body back firmly against his.

"And you love old things, don't you? Things you've had for years. Maybe that's why you keep pretending that you're still a little girl with the same childish emotions you've had for years." His hands traced a path of ecstasy down her body as he watched her tongue slip between her teeth to moisten lips that had suddenly turned dry.

After watching for only a moment longer, his mouth came down on hers, trapping it, circling her tongue with his, teasing it, tantalizing it, proving that while her old clothing might still fit her needs her old emotions were no longer suitable—not suitable at all. A bitter-sweet yearning for fulfillment blended with pain as she realized how carefully he was manipulating her emotions to prove his power over her.

Yes, despite the warnings of her mind, her traitorous body still fitted itself closer to his as her fingers drew a languorous path from the strong base of his neck to his thick black hair.

His arms lowered, went beneath her knees and lifted her to his chest. "Where's your room?" He started toward the hallway.

Reality returned in a flash and she pressed her palms against his chest. "No, put me down! My father . . . Jenny . . . I can't do it."

He looked at her disdainfully for a moment. "Still worried about the proprieties. Always the constant deb. Well, you can't keep playing this game forever. Your body won't let you—and neither will I." He smiled smugly as he set her on the floor. "Don't bother seeing me out. I know the way." He tilted her chin up with his index finger and planted a light kiss on her still-parted lips. "Try to get a good night's sleep . . . if you can." He smiled at her seductively and left the room.

Karin's nails dug into the sofa's walnut arm as she listened to Lucas' footsteps move confidently across the tile entryway and she remained absolutely immobile until she heard the front door close with an oppressive finality that seemed to seal her fate. She took a deep breath, then exhaled slowly, as if the action could dissolve the paralyzing tension that Lucas had created within her.

Forcing herself to her feet, she gathered the cups, placed them on a tray and washed them without being really aware of what she was doing. Lucas' words filled her thoughts to the exclusion of everything else. He was blatantly taunting her with his power—his ability to dominate her—to get whatever he wanted. And what did he want? Her home, the antique shop, her father's friendship—everything that gave meaning to her life.

Not quite everything, she thought as she went upstairs. In a none-too-subtle manner Lucas McKay was diminishing the importance of all her other interests and filling the void with his own overpowering personality. Entering her bedroom, she stopped before the mirror and studied her reflection with troubled eyes. She remembered how he had looked at her just minutes ago, and the way he affected her senses, obvious in her flushed face and rapid breathing, bothered her almost as much as what he had said. She knew that her reaction to him was too intensely complex to be dismissed as mere anger and the attraction that tugged at her heart was based on something stronger than sex.

Slipping into bed, she thought about her feelings for Lucas. He represented everything she hated: his values were totally materialistic, he had no use for anything unless it could be bought and sold and he looked upon all the beauty in the world as just another commodity to be purchased with his enormous wealth.

Why, then, did she find him so fascinating? Was she so weak that his glance, his touch, could make her forget everything else she knew about him? Was his appeal so devastating that it could shatter the beliefs of a lifetime? She refused even to consider the possibility and, erasing his image from her mind, turned on her side and tried to fall asleep.

Chapter Five

Although he never left her thoughts, she didn't see Lucas again until the Saturday before Christmas, when he rang the bell just after lunch.

She answered the door and quickly turned away. "My father is in the library. I'll tell him you're here."

He reached out and caught her shoulder. "It's nice to see you, too, Karin." His voice matched the mocking glint in his eyes.

"I'm sorry. Lately I can't seem to remember my manners." And it's all your fault, she thought. "Please come in." She stepped aside to let him pass.

"You still haven't said that you were glad to see me."

She wasn't glad to see him. How could she be, when she was so unsuccessfully fighting the powerful attraction she felt for him? Without answering, she began walking toward the library. After a moment's hesitation he followed.

Her father's face brightened when he saw Lucas, and Karin became all too aware of how eager he was for the companionship of the younger man. She had been so concerned about his physical health that she hadn't even thought about the effect this enforced seclusion would have on a man who had been as active as her father once had been.

"I've been doing a lot of thinking, but not much work, I'm afraid," Paul Andrews said when he saw Lucas. "I've got nothing concrete to show you."

"No problem," Lucas said. "This is a purely social call. I thought you and Karin might enjoy coming back to Newport with me. The Christmas flotilla starts tonight; my house is on the bay, and we can get a good view of the decorated boats as they go by."

Karin was about to say that it might be too much activity for her father when he declined the invitation himself.

"I'm not ready for late-night festivities, but I'm sure Karin would enjoy going."

"That's all right, Dad. I'm pretty tired myself. I think we've both gotten away from evening activities. I'd better pass. It was nice of you to ask us, though, Lucas."

"Nonsense, I won't hear of it," her father said. "You've been staying home too much on my account. Go along with Lucas. Then you can tell me all about it tomorrow."

"I have a few things I planned on doing this afternoon," Karin said.

"No problem," Lucas said. "I'll wait." He sat down and began speaking to her father.

There was no way Karin could refuse without making a scene. She controlled her anger until she had left the room, but when she got upstairs, she took her shoes off and flung them down. She slammed the sliding door back as she opened the closet and looked for another outfit. She didn't feel like getting dressed up. It would serve him right if she went just as she was, but her father would think it odd if she went to Lucas' home in a pair of faded blue jeans, and she didn't want to do anything that would make him the least bit suspicious.

She knew she should refuse the invitation. It was madness to go to his home—to be alone with him—but she had no choice. No, difficult as it was, she would have to continue pretending that she and Lucas enjoyed an amicable relationship.

She sighed, walked across the room, picked up her shoes and put them in the closet. Then she changed into a mauve wool dress with a softly pleated cowl neckline, long fitted sleeves and a slightly flared skirt. Her heels clicked when she left the carpeted stairway and walked across the tiled hallway.

Lucas stood when she entered. "You look lovely," he said. "As always."

"Thank you." She turned to her father. "Are you sure you'll be all right?"

"Of course. I'll have a quiet dinner and watch some TV." He waved them away. "Now you two get going; enjoy yourselves."

"Why did you do this?" Karin asked when she and Lucas were in the car, heading north on the San Diego Freeway.

"Do what?"

"Force me into coming with you."

"I don't remember using force. I merely extended an invitation."

"You knew I didn't want to go."

"Then you should have said so."

She made a face. "How could I? With my father in the room, watching everything?"

He took his eyes off the road for an instant. "Since you expect me to be considerate of your father's feelings, I think perhaps you should try being a bit more friendly toward me. Being subjected to your childish tantrums wasn't part of our sales agreement and there's a limit to my patience, so I suggest you change your attitude if you want me to honor the terms of our contract."

Karin was silent. He hadn't even bothered to disguise his threat. If he decided to tell her father that they no longer owned Casa del Mar, there was no doubt that the older man would be upset. Perhaps she could use legal means to enforce their right to stay in the house, but that would involve a lengthy court battle and neither her meager finances nor her father's health was stable enough to cope with that situation.

Lucas made no attempt to break the silence until he began driving over the small bridge leading to Linda Isle. "My house is at the tip of the island," he said, pulling into the brick driveway at the back of a large French Normandy house. He came around to help her out. "The one thing we don't have here is land, but I enjoy being able to dock my boat in the front yard." He took out his key and unlocked the door, then he pressed a switch, making the house glow with softly diffused lighting.

Dark oak parquet covered the entryway floor; its waxed surface reflected the shine of the overhead candelabra. Lucas cupped Karin's elbow and led her down a step into a large living room which ran the length of the house. Oriental rugs blended with the parquet and the wall opposite the entrance was made entirely of glass. When Karin walked toward the windows she understood what Lucas had meant about docking his boat in the front yard; his front yard was Newport Bay.

A wide brick terrace covered the area from the windows to the bay, then there was a concrete retaining wall and a long wooden dock which extended into the water. A large yacht was anchored by the pier.

"This is beautiful," Karin said. "How can you bear to stay at the guesthouse?"

"I told you, I need a place near our construction sites. When I'm working I don't have much time to relax."

"That's terrible," Karin said. "I mean, being so busy that you can't even enjoy something like this."

"I'm not always too busy." He came to stand beside her. "I'm going to enjoy being here tonight. I hope you will, too." His hands moved slowly over her arms and she couldn't control the shiver that moved through her body. His fingers tightened momentarily, then released her. He walked toward a mirrored bar at the side of the room. "What would you like to drink?"

Karin shook her head. "Nothing, thank you."

"I thought I had convinced you to try to make things a bit more friendly between us. I was hoping for a pleasant evening. Don't spoil my plans." His statement was a command. "Now, what would you like to drink?" She didn't answer. "If you intend to keep up this antagonistic attitude, I'll take you home and we can play the game with a new set of rules."

"I'm not being antagonistic; I just don't know what you want from me." And I'm afraid to find out, she thought. I'm afraid because I don't think I'll have the strength to refuse.

He put his glass on the polished walnut bar top and walked toward her, placing his hands on her shoulders. His warm breath caressed the curve of her ear. "Don't you? Don't you know what I want? I thought I had made that very clear." He turned her in his arms and their eyes met as she looked up at him. "I want *you.*"

Before she had a chance to move, he lowered his head and caught her lips in a firmly demanding kiss. His arms encircled her possessively, crushing her against the hard lines of his body. His hands moved across her back and shoulders before lowering to languidly explore the gentle curve of her hip.

Karin felt her body arching toward his, all her vows to resist him forgotten. She had never been so overwhelmed by a kiss or an embrace. Her arms went around his neck and her fingers combed through his hair, pressing his lips closer to hers. He was like an aphrodisiac; she couldn't get enough of him.

He caught his breath and lowered his lips to the

throbbing pulse in her neck, pressing tantalizing kisses along her shoulder where the loose drapes of the cowl collar revealed the pale luminescence of her skin. Then he started to retrace his path, curving up to her chin and the finely carved outline of her jaw until once more his warm breath teased the inner shell of her ear.

"You enjoyed that as much as I did." His hands moved up, his fingers combing beneath her hair and softly massaging her scalp. "Why do you keep fighting me?"

Her mind was reeling in a sea of confusion, her mouth felt dry and she couldn't find the words to answer him. She let her head rest against his chest and savored the contented relaxation that was slowly flowing through her body.

Lucas gripped her upper arms and held her away from him. His dark eyes glowed with desire, but their depths still displayed the iron discipline that never seemed to desert him, and Karin was embarrassed by her own uninhibited response. Somehow she had expected his emotions to be in the same wild turmoil as hers. The fact that they weren't shamed her, forcing her from the security of his arms. She backed away, trying to free herself from his hands.

"I think I'll have that drink now. Do you have any Chablis?"

His eyes flicked over her face and he hesitated for a moment as if he were undecided about what he was going to do next. Then he released her and walked slowly toward the bar.

She ran her hands lightly over her hair and brushed down her dress, straightening the disarray his touch had created. Attempting to shield herself with an air of calm detachment, she walked toward the sofa by the window and sat down.

Lucas took a bottle of California Chablis from the

refrigerator below the bar and watched her silently while he removed the cork. He poured some wine into a glass that had been chilling beside the bottle, refreshed his own drink and walked toward her. He handed her the wine and sat down beside her.

"It's a beautiful view of the bay," she said.

His arm was stretched along the back of the sofa and his fingers reached down to stroke the nape of her neck. "I don't want to talk about the view, and neither do you."

His touch made her skin tingle and she shivered as his index finger languidly drew a small circle along the edge of her collarbone. "What do you want to talk about?" Her voice sounded tautly artificial, even to herself.

"Us. I've told you how I feel about you. I was hoping you might feel the same way about me." He shifted on the sofa, inching closer to her. His arm rested on her shoulder, his fingers drifting possessively along the curve of one breast.

"I can't lie to you." She shrugged. "It would be pointless. You know I enjoyed kissing you, but I'm just not ready for the relationship you have in mind."

"Meaning?"

She stood and walked to the window. "I know about you, your reputation with women, I mean. I'm not judging you, but you wanted an explanation. I'm afraid of the way you make me feel. Maybe that's why I've tried to convince myself that I wasn't really attracted to you. You say you want me, but you hardly know me. I'm frightened about what will happen when you decide you no longer want me."

She saw his reflection in the window as he moved beside her and placed his arm around her shoulder, drawing her to him. "That won't happen. You're special. I need you in a way I've never needed any other woman. But I understand how you feel. All I'm asking is that you let us get better acquainted. Forget everything you've ever heard about me and just think of me as a man who enjoys your company."

He turned her toward him, placed his hand beneath her chin and lifted it so she was looking into his eyes. "Can you agree to that?"

Her body trembled silently at the nearness of him. She took a deep breath and caught her lower lip between her teeth to still it before she trusted herself to speak. She nodded her head; her voice was a mere whisper. "Yes, I can agree to that." When he looked at her like that, she would agree to anything—regardless of the consequences.

"Good. Now that we've settled that, why don't we get something to eat? I took some T-bone steaks out of the freezer. Want to join me in the kitchen or would you rather continue studying the view?" His lips parted in a slow smile.

Karin smiled back. "I'll come with you. Somehow I can't imagine you preparing dinner. I'll never believe you actually did it unless I see it with my own eyes."

He laughed and bowed pretentiously, flinging out his arm and motioning her toward the kitchen. "Come watch."

A small dining area surrounded by an outer wall of bay windows adjoined the kitchen, and the round table with its floor-length ecru linen tablecloth, silver candlesticks and crystal bowl of red and white roses was set for two. Lucas motioned her to the tall stool beside the butcher-block island in the center of the kitchen.

Karin hesitated. "Shouldn't there be an extra place setting?"

"Should there be?" Lucas asked teasingly.

"You did invite my father."

"I suspected he might not come."

"I can see that," she said, glancing pointedly at the table.

Lucas laughed. "You see too much. Just relax and enjoy your wine. Maybe when you see that you're wrong about my ability to cook, you'll also realize that you're mistaken about everything else you believe about me."

He took two strips of bacon and quickly sauteed them. As soon as they were crisp, he crumbled them into some chopped hard-boiled eggs and toasted croutons and tossed them over some spinach leaves which he had previously mixed with oil and vinegar.

"Can I help?" Karin asked.

"Definitely not," Lucas said as he put the salad in the refrigerator. "You're my guest and I intend to do all the work." He put two potatoes in the microwave oven and turned on the charcoal grill that was built into the tile counter. "How do you like your steak?"

"Medium rare."

Lucas was quiet while he grilled the steaks. When they were done to his satisfaction, he placed each one on a plate next to a baked potato.

"Sour cream and chives?" he asked.

"Just butter, please."

"That's how I like mine," he said. "You see, we've already found something in common." A smile played around the corners of his eyes.

He placed the food on the table, lit the candles and held a chair for her to sit down. Her eyes moved over the table. "What would you really have done if my father had come?"

"I'd have set another place, but I'd much rather be alone with you." He dipped his head and lightly kissed the curve of her neck.

She bit her lip and hoped he wouldn't notice the trembling that ran through her body. Why had she come? Her flimsy defenses were no match for Lucas' sensuous assault. "Stop that."

"Why?" His lips were moving over her hair.

"I'm hungry." She picked up her fork, clutching it like a lifeline.

"I am too . . . but this meal isn't going to satisfy my hunger." He chuckled and moved to his own seat.

Karin tasted the salad. "This is very good." Food seemed to be the safest topic. Although she couldn't really be sure, since Lucas had a way of twisting her words to suit his needs.

"Of course. I told you I was a good cook. Now just sit back and enjoy the meal."

Lucas had opened a bottle of Pinot Noir wine at the start of their dinner, and after the meal he divided the small amount remaining between their two glasses. Karin sipped hers slowly and leaned back in the comfortable armchair. The food had been superb, the wine excellent, and most important, Lucas had been a charming host. The combined effect made Karin forget all her misgivings—everything she had disliked and feared about Lucas.

"That was perfect," she said.

"I'm glad you enjoyed it. I'm not much on desserts, but I got some petits fours from a pastry shop. We can have them with our coffee."

He stood up and walked into the kitchen. Karin felt so comfortable that she hated to move, but she forced herself to stand and begin stacking the dishes. Lucas was arranging a silver coffeepot and some white china cups on a tray when she walked into the kitchen. He looked at her and immediately came to take the dishes, which he placed in the sink.

"No dishes tonight." Then he walked back to the tray and picked it up. "We'll have our coffee in the living room. The boats should start passing by about now." He carried the tray into the living room and placed it on the round table in front of the sofa. "You pour." He motioned her to a seat and sat down beside her.

"You take it black, don't you?" she asked.

"You remembered," he said, reaching for the cup she held out to him. "I'm glad." He smiled and shifted his gaze to the windows. "The boats are starting to come."

Karin's eyes followed his. Colorful strings of lights twinkled from the masts and decks of sailboats and yachts, while brightly decorated houses blazed a response from the surrounding shores. The waters of the bay reflected the glimmering lights like the rippling surface of a darkened mirror as a long line of boats glided slowly past the window.

"I've heard about the Newport Harbor Parade of Lights, but I've never seen it before. We've never stayed down here during the winter. Father likes to follow the sun."

"Like the swallows?"

She looked at him and smiled. "That's what the natives used to call us: swallow people, because we came and went with the swallows."

"Not anymore?"

"Not anymore. I'm just grateful that we're able to stay at the house."

"How grateful?" He put his cup on the table, then reached over and did the same with hers. His empty hand cupped her chin, turning her face toward his, and he kissed her, gently at first, then with more intensity as he lowered his hand and drew her body closer to his. Slowly he forced her back until she was lying against the seat of the sofa. Her lips parted beneath his and she tasted the lingering traces of coffee and wine.

Shifting his mouth, he moved it to the corner of her lip and across the curve of her cheek until he caught her earlobe lightly between his teeth. She turned her head and pressed kisses into the strong brown column of his neck. His hand moved behind her and expertly eased down the zipper of her dress, then he parted it and slipped it off her shoulders, revealing a lacy bra which gave his lips free access to the swelling curve of her breasts and the tantalizing valley between them.

"I've wanted to do that for so long," he murmured against the warmth of her skin. "Tell me that you want me, too. Say it. Admit what we both know is true."

The huskiness of his voice and the erotic explorations of his hands and lips sent an uncontrollable shiver of delight surging through her body, and she sighed with the joy of the emotions he had released within her. "Yes, Lucas, I want you. I want you so much it hurts." Her moist lips parted with a passionate longing she couldn't control.

As the quiver of her responsive flesh passed through to him, he raised himself on his elbows, his face just inches above her own. Triumphant satisfaction vied with a gleam of dominating male supremacy as his eyes studied the languid look of total surrender softening her features.

His voice purred with the velvety ease of a sleek panther. "I want you more than I've wanted any other woman." Once again his lips sought the sweetness of hers.

Karin shivered and the heated desire which had raged through her body only moments before was replaced by the icy chill of reality. His words had conjured up a picture of the other women he had known and wanted, forcing her once more to face the fact that she was just one among many and that she, too, would be discarded when he had grown tired of her.

The unexpected pressure of her hands forcing his chest away from her startled him, and the passion in his eyes was quickly replaced by a look of disappointed confusion. A shuddering wave of self-contempt swept through her body when she realized how wantonly she had responded to his caresses. She was thankful that she had had the strength to push him away before she had succumbed to his seductive expertise.

She sat up and tried to pull her dress back over her shoulders. He reached out and gripped her upper arms, imprisoning her hands within the power of his. His gaze darted over her face, forcing her to turn away from him.

"What's wrong? What happened? Why did you do that?"

"I want to go home."

"Not before you tell me what caused all that fire to turn to ice. I'm not going to allow you to do this to me again. You're not going anywhere until we've talked this out. No more walls of silence."

"I don't have to explain anything to you."

"Why, Karin? Why?" His voice was a rasping whisper as he pulled her against him. "You wanted me as much as I wanted you. I could tell. You admitted it. So why did you push me away?"

"Because I'll still be wanting you long after you've stopped wanting me." Salty tears trickled between her lips as she murmured her words into his beige silk shirt.

His hand came up and caressed the top of her head, smoothing back the hair he had tousled in the passion of their kisses. "How can you be so sure of that? Do you really know how long I've wanted you or how long I'll go on wanting you?"

Still clutching the neckline of her dress, she took a deep breath and leaned away from him, trying to gather as much control as she could. "I don't want to be hurt and I know I won't be able to live with the arrangement you have in mind." She sniffed and choked back the lump that was rising in her throat. "Please take me home."

"Not yet. I haven't said everything I want to say. Look at me. Forget everything you've ever heard or read about me. None of it matters anymore. All that matters is us. You can't deny that you enjoy being with me or that my kisses excite you. I'm asking you to marry me. Is that so repulsive?"

"You can't be serious." Karin was so shocked that she let go of her dress, parting the back and letting the neckline fall to her waist.

He laughed, turning her away from him. "You'd better let me do that." She felt the zipper glide slowly up her back. "I've never been more serious about anything in my life. I want you for my wife."

"But why? We hardly know each other."

"Must you keep saying that? Maybe it was something I felt the minute I saw you. I can't explain it. I don't even want to try. I know everything I need to know about you and I'm certain I want to marry you." Turning her into his arms, he traced a finger across her parted lips before dipping his head to cover them with his own. His arms crushed her against him in a possessive demand which clouded her senses in a swirling mist and made her body mold itself to the strength of his desire.

His breathing was ragged, but his iron control was still firmly in place as he set her away from him. Taking her hand, he led her to a small Queen Anne desk at the side of the room. He opened a drawer, took out a small black velvet ring box and flipped it open to reveal a sparkling pear-shaped solitaire flanked by two slender baguettes.

"This is for you." He took out the ring and tried to place it on her finger.

She stiffened and drew her hand away. "You *are* serious." She looked down at the ring and backed away. "I can't. I mean, this is too sudden for me, Lucas. I don't take marriage lightly, and I can't tell you I'll marry you. I never expected anything like this. I need more time to think about it."

"I don't take marriage lightly either. Do you think I propose to every attractive woman I meet? Well, you're wrong. You're the only woman I've been sure of . . . the only woman I've wanted for my wife." His voice softened and his eyes met hers in a tender caress. "But I'm not going to rush you into something as important as this—much as I'd like to. I just want you to know what my intentions really are. You're more than just another girlfriend to me."

He replaced the ring in the box, shut the drawer and bridged the distance she had opened between them. "Don't turn away from me, Karin . . . give us time . . . try to let me convince you of what I know to be a fact: that we were meant for each other." He retrieved her hands and held them tightly between his. "I'm willing to wait as long as it takes for you to reach that conclusion." He lifted her hands to his lips, caressing the curve of each finger. His voice was soft and husky as he murmured against her skin, "You will marry me, Karin . . . never doubt that."

She stared at their hands, her senses reeling. Was this the president of American International? The land-grabber? The man she hated? It couldn't be. She didn't want it to be. Her words took shape in her heart before they left her lips. "Yes, we can keep seeing each other." She looked up at him and their eyes met; she saw her own confusion reflected in the clear determination of his. How could he be so calm and sure of himself when everything was happening so quickly? Much too quickly, as far as she was concerned. She had been upset when she thought Lucas had just wanted to have an affair with her; why was she so unsure of his motives now that he had asked her to marry him?

"That's enough for now. No more hostility, no more running away?"

"No more running away," she agreed, and her eyes moved over his face, examining each feature until she realized with a sudden surge of emotion how deeply attracted to him she was.

He smiled and ran his hand lightly over her hair. "It's like molten copper. It always was." He kissed the tip of her nose and then her eyelids. "Come on. It's time I took you home."

Chapter Six

*K*arin spent a restless night thinking about Lucas and his proposal. Impetuous romanticism flooded her senses when they were together, but in the privacy of her room she remembered his sordid business methods and his jaded view of life—and love. *Love!* What bothered her most was that Lucas had never said he loved her. He had proposed to her, but he had never mentioned love. Was that part of his philosophy? Marriage without love? If so, it was a relationship she couldn't share; the disturbing implications of this realization kept her awake hours after she had gone to bed.

When she came down to breakfast the next morning, her father announced that Dan Robbins, a former client, had invited them to spend the Christmas holiday at his home in Palm Springs.

"It's a two-hour trip," Karin said. "I'll have to check with the doctor."

"I already have. He said the warm weather would probably do me good . . . get me away from all this rain."

"I don't know," Karin said. "I'm not sure I can go. I have things to do." Something stopped her from telling her father about Lucas' proposal. She wasn't sure of her feelings, but she knew that she didn't want to be parted from Lucas even for a few days.

"Nonsense, you can use a change of scenery. Start getting your clothes together."

"What about Jenny?"

"I've spoken to her. She's been anxious to visit her sister, but she didn't want to leave if we needed her. Now she's free to go. So you see, everything is working out perfectly. Go upstairs and pack."

"I'll have to think about it. I told you, I can't just run off." She sat down and poured some coffee into her cup. "At least let me have my breakfast." Her father was probably right. The warm weather would be good for him. But what about her? What about Lucas? She couldn't go. Not now. Not until she knew how she really felt—and how he really felt.

"Very well, but I want to leave tomorrow, so try to get everything under control by then." He passed her the buttered toast and orange marmalade. "Did you enjoy yourself last night?"

Karin nodded. "Yes, Lucas has a lovely home. It's right on the water."

Her father watched her silently for a moment. "I wasn't asking about the house, and I don't think Lucas' only interest in Casa del Mar is the architecture. Do you like him?"

"Very much." Her fingers tightened around her cup and her body trembled with the remembrance of Lucas' touch. She liked him too much to discuss it with anyone—even her father.

Her father grinned. "When I think about your usual reaction to potential suitors, I'd say that's most encouraging."

The doorbell rang and her father raised his eyebrows. "I wonder who that could be." He smiled.

Placing her napkin on the table, Karin went to answer the door.

"Good morning. I know it's early, but I couldn't wait to see you." Lucas pulled her into his arms and kissed her forehead lightly. "Have you had time to make up your mind?"

Karin laughed, but made no attempt to leave his arms. "I said I wanted us to get to know each other better. We haven't been together since you brought me home last night."

"I never should have taken you home. I spent a sleepless night reaching for you and finding that you weren't there." His lips moved across her forehead and down her cheek until he captured her mouth, then he pulled her tightly against his body, shattering her senses with the demanding force of his kiss. Her reaction was automatic, her hands curving over his shoulders and caressing the column of his neck. She heard his swift intake of breath as the kiss deepened and a strange yearning awoke within her, hungering for greater intimacy. She was breathless by the time he released her and she rested her palms against the rough fabric of his tweed jacket, not really wanting to move away from him.

His warm breath feathered her hair. "I think I could have convinced you to stay, but I want you to be as sure of me as I am of you. I want you for my wife, not my mistress. Once you agree to marry me, I'll have everything I've ever wanted."

His bold assumption brought Karin back to reality, reminding her of Lucas' insatiable desire to possess. "I want you," he had said, not "I love you." Did he view her as just another acquisition? This chilling possibility cooled her flaming passion, and lowering her palms, she pressed them on his chest and backed away from him. "My father will wonder what's taking us so long."

His hand curved around her waist, bringing her against his side. "Perhaps we should tell him." He smiled down at her.

"Not just yet."

"Soon?"

"Yes, soon, very soon." She smiled back at him and he tightened his grip on her waist before leading her into the dining room. She couldn't deny how comfortable she felt with Lucas, how much she was beginning to look forward to seeing him, touching him, just being with him. But why did she have these nagging doubts, this relentless suspicion that he wasn't being truthful with her, that she still had more to learn about him, that there were things he wasn't telling her?

"I thought it might be you," her father said, smiling at Lucas when they entered the room. "Join us for coffee?" He motioned to the seat opposite Karin.

She poured some coffee and handed it to Lucas.

"Did Karin mention that we were going to Palm Springs?"

Lucas put down his cup and looked at Karin. "No, she didn't." His voice held an undertone of pained surprise.

"I just found out myself. I didn't have a chance to tell you," Karin said. "Besides, I'm not even sure I can go. I have to check the schedule at the store."

"I don't think the store will present any problems," Lucas said, and Karin realized that he was telling her that he, as the owner, would have no objections.

"You want me to go?" Karin felt a dull pain move down her throat and press against her heart. Just minutes ago he had been the eager pursuer, and now that she was beginning to respond, he was telling her that not seeing her for several days didn't matter to him. How could he act this way, especially when he claimed to be more certain of his feelings than she was of hers?

"Of course. Why not? Palm Springs is delightful this time of year." His entire attitude was one of relaxed amusement, reflecting none of the depression that was nibbling at Karin's soul. "In fact, I couldn't be happier to hear about your plans. My brother and I spend the holidays in Palm Springs every year." He hesitated for a moment, letting his eyes rest on Karin's astonished features. "I thought that more serious commitments might keep me from joining him this year." His lips parted in an intriguing grin; his dark eyes met hers and seemed to reassure her. Then he turned his steady gaze to her father. "You've solved my problem. Thank you."

Her father glanced slowly from Lucas to Karin, then lifted his cup in a toast. "My pleasure," he said, smiling broadly.

Lucas insisted on driving them to Palm Springs and Karin was grateful both for his company and for the careful attention he paid to her father's health. He drove slowly, the solid steel frame of his dark brown Corniche cushioning any bumps he couldn't avoid.

Dan Robbins lived in a country-club community which had been built around the edges of a sprawling golf course. The guard recognized Lucas and raised the gate blocking the private road. Each house they passed was entirely different from the others, and Karin could tell that they had been individually designed to meet the particular needs of the owner.

Lucas was familiar with the area and drove through the winding streets without hesitation until he pulled the car into the circular driveway of a sprawling white brick house, starkly modern in design.

"Not quite in keeping with your ideas of traditional architecture," he said, turning to her father.

"No, but it isn't a cheap box either," Paul Andrews replied. "The lines are there."

"Dan Robbins is a wealthy man. He doesn't have to live in what you call a cheap box." Lucas smiled to soften his pointed remark. "But everyone needs a place to live, even people without Dan's wealth, and there's nothing wrong with a small, utilitarian house that's been tastefully designed."

"Tasteful is the key word," Paul Andrews said,

getting out of the car and moving toward the front door. "Most housing tracts have about as much aesthetic appeal as a pile of cardboard cartons." His voice reflected his scorn.

"I'm afraid Dad and I tend to cling to traditional values," Karin said as Lucas held the car door open.

Lucas reached out to help her and his hand caught hers, drawing her closer to him. "That's nice. I always wanted to marry an old-fashioned girl." He spoke for her ears only, and looked into her eyes.

She blushed and turned away. "I meant we're fond of old houses, antiques and things like that. It has nothing to do with anything else."

"I see," Lucas said. "Not meek and obedient?"

"You know I'm not." She slipped out of his grasp and went to join her father.

The front door opened and Dan Robbins came down the stairs to greet them. He shook her father's hand and kissed Karin on the cheek. Then he noticed Lucas, who had just taken the luggage out of the trunk.

"Good to see you again," he said, grasping Lucas' hand. "I didn't know you two knew each other." Dan looked at Paul.

"He's a friend of Karin's," Paul explained, smiling as he glanced at his daughter.

"Oh?" Dan followed his glance and smiled conspiratorially. "Come in for a drink. I'm sure you could use one after that drive."

Lucas came up behind Karin and rested his hand on her shoulder. "I hope you won't think we're rude, but I promised Karin I'd show her some of the local scenery and I want to do it before it gets too late. We'll take a rain check on your offer."

Dan waved them off. "No problem. Paul and I have enough catching up to keep us busy for hours. We'd probably only bore you. Cocktails at seven, dinner at eight. You'll join us, Lucas?"

"My pleasure, Dan." Lucas shook hands with Dan and Paul before leading Karin back to the car.

"You never mentioned anything about sight-seeing," Karin said as the Rolls passed through the gate.

"I didn't? Hmm . . . it must have slipped my mind." For one brief moment his gaze left the road and their eyes met. His smile was so warm and gentle that Karin felt herself melting beneath his intent observation. "Actually, I wanted to be alone with you. Do you mind very much?"

Karin felt the tingling warmth rise slowly into her cheeks but she answered truthfully. "Not at all, I enjoy being with you."

One hand left the wheel, moved to her lap and began stroking her palm in a slow, massaging motion. He lifted her hand to his lips and caressed her fingers, curving their tips around the gentle warmth of his kiss. "I'm glad." His voice was a seductive murmur.

She tried to mask the thundering crescendo beneath her breast, but her husky voice gave her away. She could never stay calm in Lucas' presence. "Where are we going?"

"To my house. My brother's family arrives tomorrow and I want to show you the place before his two children rip it apart."

"You're an uncle?"

"Do I detect a note of disbelief in your voice?"

"I can't imagine you in the role."

"My brother never asked my preferences. I had no choice in the matter." His mouth widened in a broad grin.

He seemed to be driving out into the desert when suddenly Karin saw a huge expanse of green encircled by a wrought-iron fence. "What's that?" she asked.

"An oasis, solitary, peaceful, away from civilization." He pressed a button on a brick post and the black gates swung open. Palm trees swayed above rock gardens and cacti bloomed amid free-formed circles of sand. Tall square columns created a veranda around the house, blocking out the scorching rays of the hot desert sun while letting in the soft glimmers of daylight.

Lucas stopped the car in front of some small shrubs which had been trimmed into the shape of animals. It seemed as if the topiary cats, dogs and rabbits were guarding the entrance to the house. He came around and helped Karin out of the car.

"Welcome to Sunrise, winter home of the McKay clan."

"A fitting name," Karin said. "It's very beautiful."

"I told you. I'm a lover of beauty—beautiful things and beautiful people." He drew her into his arms and kissed her, gently savoring the softness of her lips while his hands made small circles across the width of her back. There was no passion in his caress, just an overwhelming tenderness, as if he hungered for the touch and the taste of her.

Letting herself drift across the peaceful sea of relaxation that had engulfed her, she shaped her lips to his. Her hands moved up his back, palms stroking, fingers probing, seeking the sinewy muscles that were hidden beneath his light blue silk shirt.

Her eyes few open when he lifted his head and held her at arm's length. She felt hurt and deserted. She wasn't ready to be separated from the security of his arms.

His whole face seemed to be smiling at her, his eyes as well as his mouth. "Am I right in believing that you're becoming more receptive to advancing our relationship?" He rested his hands on her waist.

She freed her hands and ran her fingers up his arms. "I like you a lot. Surely you know that." Her voice was a mere whisper.

"Enough to wear my ring?" His fingers tightened.

She lifted her palms and shrugged, a helpless expression etching her features. "I think so. . . . I just don't know . . . a little more time, please?" She knew that she wanted to be with him, so why did she keep holding back? Why couldn't she say yes? What made her so uncertain?

"Is that a definite maybe?" He grinned, put his arm across her shoulder and pressed her to him. "Come on. Let's go inside."

"You have no luggage?"

"I make it a point to keep enough things at each of my homes so I don't have the hassle of packing."

"How nice to be rich."

"You should know."

"What does that mean? You of all people should realize that I'm anything but."

"Paul Andrews' daughter, the darling debutante, I wouldn't say that your childhood was exactly deprived."

They had entered the house and were now standing in a cathedral-ceilinged entryway. Colorful panels of stained glass framed the entire area, but Karin's thoughts were not on her surroundings.

"How do you know about my childhood? Did we know each other?"

"Not exactly, but you were so pampered and charming that it was hard not to be aware of you."

"Aware of me? How?"

"Like I am now. Every time I see you I want to take you in my arms, kiss you, make love to you." Slowly, lingeringly, his finger traced the oval of her face and he kissed her forehead, the corner of her eye, the tip of her nose. "Now will you please stop asking so many questions, or I'll do just that and make you forget everything."

Somehow Karin found that idea very appealing, but

the hint of amusement in his voice made her move away from him. A disturbing murmur at the back of her brain insisted that he hadn't answered her question. How had he known her? She silenced herself. What difference did it make? She relaxed again and smiled. "Okay, lead on. You promised me a tour of the house, and I'd love a cool drink. My throat is parched."

"Let's go. I'll take care of that right now."

The living room was two steps down from the entryway. Oriental rugs in muted tones of beige and powder blue covered all but the edges of the white marble floor. Rattan chairs and small brass cube tables formed little conversation groups in several areas of the large room. Lucas led Karin to the beige linen modular sofa which flanked the fieldstone fireplace.

"Sit down. What would you like to drink?"

"Anything cold."

Lucas laughed. "That thirsty, are you? I'll make you my specialty."

He busied himself at the bar, which was built into one of the bookcases that framed the fireplace. Ice cubes clinked, liquor splashed, the blender whirled, and in a few minutes he handed Karin a tall frosty glass filled with a foamy beverage that reminded her of chocolate milk.

"Umm, this is delicious," she said after taking a sip. "What is it?"

"I don't usually give out the recipe, but since you're going to be a member of the family . . ." He smiled and ran his fingers up her arm. They were cold from holding his glass, but she was sure that the shivers tingling through her body weren't caused by that. She was becoming all too aware of how his lightest touch could raise or lower her body temperature with equal ease.

"It's a combination of shaved ice, crème de cacao and coconut milk. I'm glad you like it."

"Where does your brother live?" Lucas seemed to

know so much about her, while she knew hardly anything about him.

"Rancho Santa Fe, but he spends his winter vacations here, and most of the summer in La Jolla." He hesitated for a moment, as if he were going to say something else about his brother, then he seemed to change his mind and he rose, placing their empty glasses on the bar. "Would you like to see the rest of the house? I did tell Dan that I was showing you the sights, so I feel obligated to make the effort. He might ask questions." The edges of his eyes crinkled as he smiled. "And you really should see my bedroom; you might want to make some changes. I want everything to be exactly the way you want it."

Karin stood up and walked toward him, but before she could reach the hand he held out to her, they both turned in the direction of a grating sound at the back of the room.

The sliding glass door was open and a tall brunette was leaning against the frame. Her white bikini concealed only the most intimate parts of her well-tanned body.

"Lucas," she said. Her voice was soft, with a deep breathless quality, and she glided toward him without even glancing in Karin's direction. "Tom said you wouldn't be here until tomorrow. I came early to get a head start on my suntan." Standing on tiptoe, she flung her arms around his neck and raised her lips to his.

Karin stood transfixed, held in bondage by a stab of despair that pressed painfully into her heart. She was too breathless to even whisper, but her mind was shrieking in protest and an emotion she had never before experienced was gnawing at her insides like a green-eyed cat. Ignoring her completely, the other woman continued to embrace Lucas, urging his lips down toward hers.

Before she could complete the kiss, Lucas reached

behind his neck, caught her hands and removed them. He stepped away, casually resting his hand on her bare shoulder. "Danielle, I don't believe you know Karin."

Karin stared at the hand, the shoulder, the relaxed intimacy, and her heart began a slow descent to agony. Danielle was definitely not the housekeeper.

"Is she staying here?" Danielle ignored the introduction and addressed her question directly to Lucas.

"No. She and her father are visiting a friend at the country club."

Danielle smiled up at him, then turned to Karin and let her gaze run slowly down the other girl's figure. "I see."

Karin suspected that what Danielle saw didn't impress her in the least. Her agony became a death knell as she prayed for some simple explanation. Was the woman his brother's wife? Was she merely observing an expression of brotherly love? Impossible. That seductive figure had never nurtured two children. She let her mind go blank and waited for the worst.

Danielle walked to the bar and placed some ice cubes in a tall glass. "Didn't Tom tell you I was coming?" She poured some gin over the cubes, added a touch of tonic and walked slowly to the sofa, her languid movements highlighting everything the bikini was supposed to conceal.

Lucas closed the distance between him and Karin and placed his arm around her waist. She was too tense to relax and her body stiffened at his touch. His casual familiarity with Danielle had made her feel like an intruder and she wanted to leave as quickly as possible.

As if sensing her discomfort, Lucas tightened his grip around her waist, drawing her to him possessively and silently telling her that he had no intention of letting her leave his side. "I understood you were in New York."

"A dreadful place in December." Danielle reached

over with her free hand and took a cigarette from a lacquered box on the small table in front of her. Then she placed it between two fingers, held it toward Lucas and tilted her head expectantly.

Lucas took the cigarette lighter from the table and bent closer to Danielle. She cupped his hand with hers and raised it to her lips. Karin watched them and thought despondently that the flame coming from the lighter was a mere flicker in comparison to the inferno that Danielle was trying to ignite.

"Thank you, darling." Still holding Lucas' hand, Danielle turned and exhaled a puff of white smoke in Karin's direction. "Besides, my show closed, so I had no reason to stay away any longer. I spoke to Tom and decided to surprise you—sort of a live Christmas present. Aren't you glad to see me?" Her low throaty voice softened to a contented purr and she rubbed her thumb along the edge of his wrist.

Karin's fingers curled into fists as she repressed an urge to strangle the voluptuous brunette. Why was she so angry? It was as if Danielle was violating her domain, trespassing on her property. Oh, no, she was beginning to sound like Lucas. But that was just how she felt. Lucas belonged to her and she didn't like Danielle playing in her garden.

"Of course," Lucas replied. "I just wish that Tom had told me you were going to be here."

Danielle shrugged and looked at Karin again. "It didn't seem important at the time, but perhaps things have changed."

"Nonsense, nothing's changed. If Tom invited you, then I'm delighted to have you. You just caught me by surprise." Lifting her hand, he kissed it and placed it gently in her lap.

"Obviously," Danielle purred. Her eyes never left Karin's face.

Karin forced her body into rigid immobility. If she

moved, she would claw, stomp, scratch and do some other very unladylike things she couldn't think of right at this moment. But she was sure they would come to her, because she had an irresistible urge to destroy the other woman's alluring elegance, which seemed intent on making her feel about as glamorous as the before picture in a beauty product advertisement. For the present she contented herself with a hostile glare, which didn't seem to bother Danielle at all. Her disdainful attitude implied that she found Karin about as threatening as a newborn baby.

Lucas returned to Karin's side. "Karin, I'm sure you've heard of Danielle Matthews. Her last show ran on Broadway for nearly two years." He tried to lead Karin to the sofa and was surprised when she resisted.

Karin knew all she wanted to know about Danielle. She couldn't care less about the actress's career; it was her relationship with Lucas that was tearing Karin apart, and she wasn't interested in watching any more of this intimate performance. "I'm tired from the ride down, Lucas. I'd like to go back to Dan's and rest for a while before dinner." She had to get away before she exploded and abandoned all pretenses of polite behavior. Could the virago seething in her breast really be a part of her?

"Sure, I understand." He turned to Danielle. "I hope you don't mind."

"Not at all." Her eyes were still on Karin and her lips curved in a smug little smile. "Just try to hurry back. It does get lonely here and we have so much catching up to do."

Karin's eyes widened. Danielle made catching up sound like a party—a very private party—one with just two guests, and Karin wasn't one of them. She turned to Lucas, searching for his reaction, but his face was blank, as if this little charade didn't concern him at all.

Danielle sipped her drink. "It was nice meeting you, Karin." Languidly she waved the hand holding the cigarette. "I don't suppose I'll be seeing you again; you'll probably be busy with your host." Her sultry eyes flickered to Lucas. "And I'll be busy with mine."

Karin forced herself to smile and reply, "I expect so. Enjoy your vacation. I won't keep Lucas too long; Dan's house is only a few minutes from here." How was that for cool, calm and disinterested? she thought. Danielle wasn't the only actress in town. She turned and left the room, her emotional state a depressing mixture of anger and embarrassment. Without waiting for Lucas, she stormed out of the house and settled herself in the passenger seat of the Rolls. She waited silently while he let himself out and walked to the car. Without saying a word, he started the engine and began driving. The fact that Karin was upset didn't seem to disturb him at all and she was too proud to ask for an explanation.

After driving only a short distance, Lucas stopped the car, still within the boundaries of his estate. He got out, came around, opened her door and held out his hand.

Karin didn't move. "I'd like to go home; I'm really very tired."

"We have to talk, then I'll take you home." He caught her hands in his, drew her out of the car and led her to a circular redwood gazebo in the middle of a small grove of Mediterranean palm trees.

They sat on a padded bench which overlooked a water fountain and a carefully mounded rock garden.

"I didn't know Danielle was going to be here," Lucas said.

"Obviously!" Her voice was cold and clipped as she repeated Danielle's word. She couldn't look at him. She didn't want him to see how deeply he had hurt her.

"Just what is that supposed to mean?"

"She said she wanted to surprise you. She was sure you'd be delighted to see her."

"Well, I'm not. I certainly wasn't planning a secret tryst. Not with you here." He grabbed her chin in his hand and forced her to look at him.

Moisture glazed her eyes, but she controlled her voice and made it sound calm and unaffected. "Of course not; it is a sort of sticky situation—having the woman you've just proposed to meet your mistress." She clenched her fists and felt her nails cutting into her palms. "And she *is* your mistress, isn't she?" She scanned his face, desperately hoping for a denial.

"I don't see where that's any concern of yours. I've always enjoyed the company of attractive women; surely you didn't think I'd been leading the life of a celibate?" He reached for her hands, lacing his fingers into hers.

Karin felt all the fight go out her. She couldn't confess her thoughts; they were too painful. She pulled her hand free. "And that's your explanation. Just that . . . that you aren't a saint?" Her lips curved in a contemptuous sneer. "I didn't need you to tell me that. Some things I can figure out all by myself."

"Then why are you carrying on like this?" He recaptured her hand and pulled it toward him possessively. "Just what do you think is happening?"

"I don't know what to think. I don't understand the entire situation. None of it makes sense; it never did." She pushed his hand away from her but continued to stare at him. "I can't imagine why you asked me to marry you. I'm nothing special. We haven't even known each other very long." She smiled cynically. "And it's all too evident that you aren't starved for female companionship."

"To me, you're special. I asked you to marry me because I want you for my wife, and although I won't deny that I've had affairs with other women, I've never proposed marriage to anyone else." His harsh words grated against her ear, but she refused to be intimidated.

"Then why me, someone you hardly know? Did you think I was so childishly naïve that I wouldn't object to Danielle? Was I meant to fill in while she was busy on Broadway? Is she too caught up in her career to be the kind of wife you want? Do I fit your image—the old-fashioned girl you want to marry? Well, forget it. I may not be as sophisticated as Danielle, but I'll never agree to the arrangement you have in mind."

"What arrangement is that? Marriage? You find that insulting? You don't understand why I want to marry you? Is that your problem? Well, I can solve that very easily."

A throbbing muscle worked along the side of his jaw and his eyes narrowed, their gaze piercing hers. A deep guttural sound that was almost a growl escaped his clenched lips, and without warning, he dipped his head, catching her lips beneath the force of his. She struggled, placing her palms against his chest, trying to twist out of his arms and free herself.

His hand came up and cradled the back of her head, forcing her mouth against his. In the brief instant when their lips were apart she heard his husky voice murmur, "Don't fight me. I want you too much."

She tried to ignore his words and pull herself free, but his grip was too tight and there was no escape. His lips pressed against hers, moving persuasively against them until they parted to his demands. His hand slipped beneath her sweater, stroking the bare skin of her back, then edging slowly forward to probe beneath the lacy bra and intimately explore the rounded softness of her breast.

A fiery warmth consumed her flesh, melting all thoughts of resistance. She shook from the emotional charge his caress had generated and a barely audible gasp passed from her lips to his. When he drew his head back and released her, she didn't want to leave him. She kept her eyes closed and ran her hands along the silky fabric of his shirt, letting her fingertips trace his flexing muscles.

He lowered his head and kissed her shuttered eyelids, moving gently from one to the other until at last she opened them and he could see the clear reflection of her surrender.

"Does that explain why you're special, why I want to marry you? Are you convinced? No more fighting?" His voice was muffled as he pulled her to him and whispered into the curve of her ear.

She leaned against him and shook her head. "No more fighting." She sighed with both exhaustion and pleasure as she voiced her agreement. What had they been arguing about anyway? Her mind was so saturated with sensuous delight that she just couldn't remember.

She felt the rumble of his silent laughter as he held her from him and looked down at her in self-satisfied triumph. "Good. I'll take you home so you can get some rest before dinner." He cupped her elbow and led her to the car.

On the ride back to Dan's house Lucas began telling Karin about the dry climate of the area. He mentioned that it would be especially beneficial to her father and that perhaps he should consider moving from San Juan Capistrano.

A red, white and blue American International sign flashed before her eyes. "I won't let you tear down Casa del Mar while my father is alive."

Anger froze Lucas' features, but his voice was tautly controlled. "How can you even think that? I wasn't trying to get you off the land. I was just thinking of your father's health."

Karin felt like an ungrateful shrew. Two minutes ago

she would have done anything Lucas wanted and now she was storming at him like a waspish old woman. Why did she have to keep challenging his motives, trying to find a flaw in everything he said and did? What was the matter with her? She shook her head in bewilderment and fought to regain her self-control. "I'm sorry, Lucas. I guess I'm just overtired. I was wrong to snap at you. Lately I can't seem to do anything right."

Lucas smiled. "Oh, I wouldn't say that. You knew exactly what to do when we were in the summerhouse a few minutes ago."

"I wish you wouldn't mention that."

"Why not? Are you ashamed of what we feel for each other?"

"It's all physical . . . not enough to form the basis of a marriage."

"Maybe not, but I'd hate to think of a marriage without that attraction. People get married for a lot of different reasons, and what seems important to one person might be irrelevant to another. So let's not probe too deeply into our motives. All you need to know is that you're special to me and I'm determined to have you as my wife. I'll give you some time to get to know me better, but don't take too long; I'm not a very patient man." A smile quirked the corners of his mouth, but his voice was emphatically insistent.

"People get married for a lot of different reasons." Lucas' simple statement sent her thoughts racing in circles. Didn't he remember how she felt about marriage? She recalled the day he first came to see Casa del Mar and the drive back to town when she told him that she would only marry for love. How could he have forgotten? If he really cared about her, wouldn't he be aware of how she felt? Wouldn't he remember?

Involved in her own private thoughts, she chewed her inner lip and mused silently. Other people might marry for a variety of reasons, but for her there was only one—love, true love—and if she couldn't be certain she felt it for Lucas, she would never marry him, no matter how special he insisted she was. But right now she couldn't think of a sensible reply, so she remained silent until he parked the car in Dan's driveway. She waited while he opened the door.

"I won't come in. I know you're tired and need to rest." He bent his head and kissed her on the forehead. She didn't answer and heard the car move away even before the maid had let her into the house. Was it her imagination or was Lucas awfully eager to get back to Sunrise? Danielle's svelte image loomed in her mind and she knew that if Lucas *was* eager to return home he wasn't planning on spending his time with the topiary animals.

Her father and Dan were out walking on the golf course, so Karin followed the maid to her room, grateful for the chance to be alone. Her thoughts were too painful to be shared with anyone.

Stripping off her clothes, she changed into a robe and stretched out on the bed. How easy it was for Lucas to make her forget everything just by taking her in his arms. Not once during the ride home had he offered any further explanation of his relationship with Danielle. He had kissed Karin passionately and declared that she was special, the only woman he had ever wanted to marry, yet when they had arrived at Dan's house, he hadn't been able to wait to return to Danielle.

Images of Lucas kissing and caressing Danielle tormented her musings and she closed her eyes tightly in an attempt to banish them. Why torture herself? Lucas didn't love Danielle. He loved her. Or did he? He had never said so. But why else was he marrying her? He had to love her. Wasn't that what he had meant when he said she was special? There was no other explanation. But what about Danielle? Was she really in the past? Only Lucas knew, and Karin needed an answer.

She must have dozed, because the next thing she knew the maid was tapping at the door and telling her that cocktails would be at seven and dinner at eight. She sat up, switched on the bedside lamp and checked the time. She had one hour to get ready. After showering quickly, she took out a long brown silk jersey dress which was styled like a Grecian toga, baring one shoulder completely while covering the other with a wide pleated strap. Matching high-heeled sandals completed the outfit. A narrow gold serpentine necklace and a bangle bracelet were the only jewelry she wore.

She checked her appearance in the mirror as she brushed her hair. She knew she had never looked more attractive and she was suddenly eager to see Lucas. She hoped he'd be early so they could have some time together before dinner. There were so many things she wanted to ask him, things she needed to know about his past before she could believe what he was planning for the future. But most of all she just wanted to be with him. She could no longer deny that she missed him desperately whenever they were apart.

Leaving her room, she walked down the hallway in the direction of voices and soft music. Dan came forward to greet her when she entered the library. There were several other people in the room besides her father, but she didn't see Lucas.

Dan followed her eyes around the room. "Lucas couldn't make it; something unexpected came up. He called while you were napping and told me not to wake you. He sent his apologies."

Karin felt her energy drain to the pit of her stomach and settle there like a heavy iron ball. If Lucas wasn't here, he was home—with Danielle. Something unexpected indeed! Some*one* was more like it! Someone with sensuous lips and a figure to match. Someone

Lucas couldn't resist. The thought made her sick. She wanted to be angry, but a nauseating feeling of nothingness smothered her rage.

"Now, what will you have to drink?" Dan's voice seemed to come from a distance and she felt numb as he hooked his arm through hers and signaled for the butler.

Sipping the chilled Chablis gave Karin an excuse to remain silent. She had never before considered that Lucas wouldn't come to dinner that night, and now she was annoyed at her own naïveté. How stupid she had been not to have realized that Lucas hadn't known that Danielle would be in Palm Springs when he had accepted Dan's invitation. When he had taken her home that afternoon, he had never said that he would see her at dinner; in fact, he had practically fallen over his feet in his rush to return to Sunrise. How foolish she had been to behave like a lovesick schoolgirl, pining over Lucas when he could only think about being with Danielle. Of course he would want to spend the evening alone with his mistress before the arrival of his brother brought more people into the privacy of their secluded little love nest. So now one of her questions was answered, and she hadn't even had to ask Lucas. His actions told her more than any verbal explanation ever could. Whatever his motives for wanting to marry Karin, they did not include depriving himself of Danielle. His past continued to be a vital part of his present, and that realization shattered Karin's crystal dreams of the future.

Dinner was an absolute blur. She had no idea what was served or what she discussed with the two older men who were seated on either side of her. Everything that had happened in the summerhouse was meaningless. Lucas was an exciting man, virile and attractive enough to appeal to a beautiful, sophisticated woman like Danielle Matthews. There had never been any plausible explanation for his whirlwind courtship of Karin, and now that he had chosen to spend his first evening here with Danielle, she realized why she had been so afraid to accept his proposal. He might claim that she was special, but in her heart Karin knew that she wasn't special enough.

Not once had he said he loved her, and he probably never would. Love didn't enter into their relationship, not into his side of it, anyway. He had his own mysterious reasons for wanting to marry her, reasons she might never learn about, reasons that no longer mattered to her, because she would never agree to marry him now that she knew about his continuing intimacy with Danielle. And this time she wouldn't allow his kisses to change her mind.

Chapter Seven

She spent the next morning by the pool. Her father and Dan played backgammon while she tried to concentrate on the plot of a new novel she had brought with her. But it was hopeless; Lucas' face leaped from the pages, making it impossible to think of anything but him. The situation had been disturbing enough when he had the power only to orchestrate the passionate responses of her body, but now his domination was complete: he had taken control of her mind. Yet, she had been right about him all along. He was a brigand who took what he wanted—anything at all—and for some mysterious reason, he wanted her for his wife. Well, this was one time when he wasn't going to have things his way. She was not about to enter into a marriage which would make her part of a cozy threesome with Lucas and Danielle.

Yet, even as she tried to cloak her misery with anger and indifference, she knew that she was desperately hurt and disappointed to find that Danielle meant so much to Lucas that he couldn't stay away from her when he knew she was waiting for him. Karin had been expecting some explanation, some apology, some lie, no matter how feeble. But apparently Lucas had no intention of asking for her forgiveness. Her feelings probably weren't important anymore. Now that Danielle had come back into his life, no one else seemed to matter to him. She snickered under her breath. And he had called her special. Ha! She was special all right—special in a dumb sort of way, dumb enough to believe all the lies that Lucas had been feeding her; well, not anymore. She didn't need a Ph.D. to understand what was going on between Danielle and Lucas.

After a while she put the book aside and lay on one of the rafts that were floating in the large pool. The warm sun was so thoroughly relaxing that she was almost able to forget Lucas and enjoy a lazy reprieve. She sighed blissfully. How could anyone be miserable on such a sunny day? This was her vacation and she wasn't going to let Lucas ruin it. She had been right about him in the first place; he was cold, heartless, a totally ruthless person—and if she never saw him again, it would be too soon for her.

Every time the raft nudged the side of the pool, she reached out and pushed it back toward the center in a lazy, almost automatic motion. That was about the only exercise she felt like doing. Her eyes were closed and her head rested on her folded arms.

She felt the raft bob against the side of the pool once more and she reached out to push it away, but her hand was grasped and she opened her eyes, to see Lucas kneeling at the edge of the pool. His other hand kept a firm grip on the tow cord of the raft.

"I thought I was going to have to swim out to get you." He steadied the raft and pulled her toward him. Then, releasing the raft, he used both hands to lift her over the edge of the pool. Holding her slightly away from him, he let his gaze roam slowly over her body. "You look very nice." Drawing her closer, he cupped her chin and raised her lips to his, catching them in the light promise of a kiss. "Mmm . . . you taste good, too. I'm sorry I didn't get to see you last night."

His words released her from the mesmerizing effect

of his kiss and she pulled away from him. "It doesn't matter." She wasn't going to let him know how upset she really was. "I'm sure you had better things to do." She walked to the padded lounger, picked up a towel and threw it around her back. She absently noticed that Dan and her father had gone.

He followed her and curled his hands over her shoulders. "Danielle didn't feel well; I couldn't leave her alone." His fingers probed the flesh beneath the towel.

I'll bet you couldn't leave her alone, she agreed silently. "Nothing serious, I hope." Or contagious, she thought, because I'm sure you were close enough to catch whatever she had.

"I doubt it. Just too much sun and alcohol. She's better today."

"So you were able to come and see me. How nice." She twisted her shoulders in an attempt to pull free of his grasp.

"I told you, I couldn't leave her alone."

"Apparently you couldn't."

"That's not what I mean and you know it."

"I don't really know what you mean; that's the problem."

"Only because you insist on making it one," Lucas said. "Danielle was too sick to be left alone. That's all there is to it . . . nothing more. Now let's leave it. I don't like making explanations."

And I don't like being played for a fool, Karin thought. "What about the servants?"

"She asked me to stay."

"And you did? Just like that? Did you ever stop to think that maybe I wanted to see you?"

He turned her toward him and studied her face. Amusement crinkled the corners of his eyes. "You're jealous?"

"That's ridiculous. Why should I be jealous?" So much for cool and disinterested. She was no competition for Danielle on or off the stage.

"Because you enjoy being in my arms and having me kiss you. And you don't want to share me with anyone else—any more than I want to share you." He let the towel drop to the ground and ran his hands across her bare back. "Danielle is a very good friend and I don't intend to have my friendships questioned by you or anyone else." His features softened and his eyes met hers with a probing intensity. "But I will tell you this: I didn't make love to her last night." His fingers slipped beneath the edge of her suit, making it hard for her to concentrate on what he was saying. "You believe me, don't you?"

"I don't know what to believe." It was happening again. Lucas was making her forget everything except the way his hand moved across her body.

"You can believe that I want to marry you and that *nothing* and *no one* is going to prevent that from happening." He tightened his arms around her and held her quietly against him. "Now, get dressed; I told your father we were going out for a while."

"Oh, really? You spoke to my father and settled things, did you? Well, what if I don't want to go? If you didn't care about seeing me last night, I don't see why I have to drop everything and run off with you today."

"Then I'll just have to spend more time convincing you. I don't mind doing that at all, but you might find it embarrassing." He dipped his head and began nuzzling her neck. She tensed and tried to move away. A low rumbling chuckle escaped his lips and he nudged her toward the house. "Come on. Get dressed. Nothing fancy . . . take a heavy sweater; we're going mountain climbing."

"In the desert?"

"Have I ever lied to you?"

She tilted her head, meeting his gaze in a slow, cynical glance.

"I guess I haven't convinced you." He began walking toward her, a comically exaggerated leer on his face.

She laughed and ran into the house. Maybe Lucas was telling the truth. Maybe Danielle really had been sick. After all, he wouldn't be spending the day with her if he loved Danielle. He had told her that she was special—she, not Danielle. That meant something, didn't it? She smiled as she changed her clothes and got ready to meet Lucas.

He was waiting at the car when she came out, dressed in navy corduroy pants and a matching sweater, and carrying a lightweight white jacket, which was the only thing she had with her to combat the chill mountain air. They drove through the desert and she could see that they were getting closer to the mountains looming in the distance.

"You're not serious?" she said.

"Deadly serious." He took his eyes off the road and smiled at her.

"I meant about mountain climbing."

"I'm serious about everything I've told you." He shook his head. "You've really got to start believing me."

He turned the car into Chino Canyon at the foot of the San Jacinto Mountains and she understood what he had meant. "The tram! Why didn't I think of it?"

"It *is* mountain climbing." He smiled innocently.

"I suppose it is."

"See, I told you I never lie."

He parked the car and they boarded the tram at the Valley Station.

Karin had been on the tram before, but she never lost her sense of awe at the spectacular views the aerial ride offered. The changes in scenery were breathtaking. Bright green golf courses dotted barren desert sands and the date and lettuce fields of the Coachella Valley loomed in the distance. Midway through the trip she slipped the jacket over her shoulders. When they arrived at Mountain Station, they had climbed nearly six thousand feet and the temperature had dropped about forty degrees.

"Hungry?" Lucas asked, leading Karin off the platform past the gaily decorated Christmas tree and toward the small cluster of buildings built along the mountaintop. "That's a man-made tree," Lucas said as Karin stopped to admire it. "Every time they tried using a live one the wind blew it over, so now they use one made of metal pipes and just string it with lights."

"It's very effective," Karin said.

"It is, isn't it?" He tightened his hand on her waist. "Come on, we can stop at the restaurant before exploring the trails."

He led her to the rustic wooden building and chose a table by a window which overlooked the tramway so they could watch the cable cars moving slowly up the mountain. He ordered a carafe of Burgundy and two hot roast-beef sandwiches.

"Your father looked good this morning," Lucas said. "He seems to be enjoying himself."

"Yes. The warm weather is good for him."

"Maybe he ought to stay here for the rest of the winter."

"That might be too much of an imposition on Dan."

"He's welcome to use my place. After Christmas, my brother and I only come for an occasional weekend."

"Jenny will be back next week."

"Let her stay at her sister's awhile longer. I'm sure she'll appreciate the extra time."

Karin nodded. "She probably would." She looked across the table at Lucas. "You're sure it wouldn't be too much trouble?"

"Hardly." He smiled and reached for her hands. "We're going to be family, remember? I'll enjoy having your father depend on me." His words sounded strangely self-satisfied, almost triumphant, as his dark eyes studied her face intently. "Come on, let's get out of here. I want to show you the trails before it gets too late."

The trails wound through the mountains, but they were all well-marked and patrolled by guides so there was no danger of getting lost. Karin looked at the tall pine trees perched along the slopes of snow-covered peaks and found it difficult to believe that directly below them was a hot desert community of sun-baked sand and tropical palms.

They came to a clearing in the trees and Lucas led her to a flat rock in the midst of some orange wildflowers. He sat and pulled her down next to him, then his hand moved over her shoulder, drawing her to him and caressing her upper arm. Lifting her hair, he bent to kiss the side of her neck.

She felt her flesh tingle as she tried to fight the tiny shivers that began moving through her body. Turning her to him, he stretched out on the smooth surface of the rock and pulled her alongside him. Shifting his weight onto one elbow, he looked down at her and raised his other hand to gently trace a path across her lips with the tip of his index finger. He probed the parting of her lips softly, but with an intense firmness that made her answer his quest with a nibbling, teasing kiss of her own. Her tongue came out to meet his finger, circling it, tantalizing it, seductively guiding it toward the warm moisture of her mouth. With an agonizing groan of surrender he ran his finger along her lower lip and pressed his open mouth against the welcoming warmth of hers.

Then, with an abruptness that stole the breath from Karin's lungs, Lucas' gentle entreaty became a tumultuous demand as his mouth covered hers, grinding against it with a tempo that spread throughout their bodies. His fingers slipped beneath her sweater, frantically searching, finding and caressing her breasts. They blossomed beneath his touch, quivering tremulously and then burgeoning with such force that she thought they would burst with their wildly pulsating desire.

He shifted his body, moving it fully over hers, and she could feel the strong muscular vibrations of his flesh affirming both his desire and his power to answer her needs. The rock was hard against her back as his lean masculinity pressed firmly against her; unconciously she began to arch herself against him. His mouth traveled to the shell of her ear while his finger tugged at her lower lip, urging it gently away from her teeth.

Desperate with her ever-increasing need for him, she turned her head toward him, once again seeking out the excitement of his lips. "Lucas, please . . . please kiss me . . . I need you so." Her passionate words came from the depths of her heart; she no longer had any control over her actions.

His voice was as breathlessly husky as hers, but he seemed in full control of his emotions as he traced an erotic circle around her tongue. "Christmas would be a good time to announce our engagement. I'm still carrying your ring." His finger left her lips and began moving over her chin, lightly caressing the side of her neck before drawing small circles across the edge of her collarbone. "Besides, this way we could tell everyone at once. It would make things a lot easier."

The word "everyone" flashed through Karin's mind and she had the unwelcome vision of Danielle, leaning against the sofa and ordering Lucas to hurry back. She pushed him away and stood up. "How do you think Danielle is going to take the news?"

"I wasn't thinking about Danielle. I was thinking about our families." He followed her up and grasped her shoulders, turning her toward him. "Can't you forget about Danielle?"

Karin looked at him with a cool indifference she didn't feel. "I can forget her very easily, but what about you?"

"My feelings for you have nothing to do with Danielle. How many times do I have to tell you that? I want you for my wife; whatever else there was between us, Danielle and I never discussed marriage."

"Why me? You hardly know me. Why the overwhelming urge to marry me? I'm nothing special."

"To me you are. I thought we settled all that yesterday. Why do you still need an explanation?" He ran his hands up her arms and over her shoulders. "Why can't you just accept that we enjoy being with each other, that your skin comes alive under my touch and that your lips fit against mine like the missing piece of a puzzle." As if in slow motion, he bent his head and kissed her, moving his mouth seductively until she had parted hers in answer to him. The kiss grew stronger and her entire body began arching toward him as she succumbed to an uncontrollable desire to merge with him.

Finally he set her away from him. His breathing was as uneven as hers, and when he spoke, his voice was husky with unsatisfied desire. "That's why I want to marry you. I've wanted you for my wife from the first time I saw you." He groaned and pulled her back against him. "I can't wait much longer."

She tensed as he reached out to claim her. His eyes flickered over her startled face, then he released her and, turning away, walked to the edge of the trail. Raking his fingers through his hair, he was kicking idly at the pebbles lining the ground when a large clump of earth suddenly gave way beneath his feet and he slid down the embankment, disappearing from Karin's view.

Helpless panic enveloped her as she stared blankly at the place where he had been standing only seconds before. "Lucas!" Terror gripped her as she visualized him lying broken at the bottom of the towering mountain. In that endless moment of insurmountable loss Karin knew the truth of what she had been trying so hard to deny. She couldn't bear the thought of anything happening to Lucas. She loved him and wanted to spend the rest of her life in the firm security of his arms.

How could she have been so foolish? If only she had admitted her love for him, this would never have happened, and Lucas would be standing here next to her, holding her, caressing her. Instead, because she had been too blind to heed the messages of her heart, he was injured, or perhaps even dead. The thought was so frightening that she dismissed it and ran quickly to the place where he had fallen.

A small spark of relief banished the icy chill of her fears when she saw that the edge of the trail sloped to a flat wide area not more than five feet below her. But the spark was quickly extinguished when she saw that Lucas was lying on his stomach—*motionless*. Lowering herself, she slid down the incline and ran to his side.

"Lucas! Lucas!" She shook his shoulder, begging for a response. "Lucas, please say something! Anything! Please! I couldn't stand it if anything happened to you." Her sob-choked voice reflected the tears in her eyes as she tried to wake him.

With an unexpected burst of energy he rolled over, caught her in his arms and pulled her down on top of him. "That's all I wanted to know. Now will you stop fighting what we both want?" Framing her face with his hands, he urged her lips down to his and explored the sweetness that she now offered willingly.

Still claiming her mouth, he turned and rolled her beneath him. Encircling his neck with her arms, she pressed his face against her body and sighed contentedly as his lips softened and moved to the corner of her mouth, then followed the curve of her jaw and explored her arching neck.

"I was so worried, Lucas. You're not hurt?" She lifted his face as she searched his eyes for reassurance. "Why did you frighten me like that?"

He smiled, a slow, comforting grin. Then he ran his hand over her cheek, caressing it lightly, cherishing the smooth softness of her skin. She smiled back at him, warmed by the glow his fingers were creating deep within her body. His hand grasped hers as he moved away and sat back, looking down at her.

"I'm fine, Karin, better than I've ever been. I'm sorry I frightened you, but I just had to know how you felt. Now that I do, there's only one thing missing in the perfection of this day." He reached into his pocket and drew out the ring. "Put it on. Tomorrow is Christmas and you're the only present I want." Without waiting for her answer, he slipped the diamond on her finger, sealing the sanctity of the moment with the firm pressure of his lips.

She leaned against him when he released her, and she meekly let him pull her to her feet. He reached up and brushed some wisps of hair off her face. "We ought to be starting back. I think your father should be the first to know."

Nodding mutely, Karin followed him up the slope and along the trail leading to the tram. Much as she still questioned Lucas' motives, at this moment she wanted to be his wife more than anything else in the world.

Dan was inside making a phone call and her father was seated alone by the pool when they returned to the house. The news of their engagement made him look happier than he had in years. Karin was reminded of the vibrant, enthusiastic man he had been before his heart attack, before her mother's death, and she was grateful that she had been able to provide him with this moment of joy.

When Dan returned, her father told him the news in a voice filled with proud delight. Dan poured some drinks and Karin clung to Lucas as the two older men toasted their happiness.

"You'll all come to dinner tonight. We always have a Christmas Eve buffet." Lucas kept his hand on Karin's shoulder, stroking her arm possessively as he spoke. "I'd better get home now and make sure my nephews haven't torn the place apart looking for their presents." He reached out to shake hands with Dan and her father. "You'll walk me to the car?" he asked, turning to Karin.

She nodded and let him lead her away.

"Happy?" he asked when they were standing in front of the Rolls.

"I think so."

"You *think* so? Hardly the enthusiastic response one would expect on such an occasion." His voice was cynical, but there was a teasing look in his eyes.

She smiled back at him. "You're right. I *am* happy. . . . I know it's crazy, but I am happy—deliriously so."

He pulled her to him and looked down at her, his dark eyes caressing her features. "It's not crazy. It was meant to be—always." He bent and kissed her lightly on the forehead. "Remember, you're definitely happy." He ran his index finger across the tip of her nose. "Don't think of anything but me and how happy we are together." He kissed her again, then waved as he got into the car and drove away.

Her father and Dan were still on the patio when she excused herself and went into the house. She needed time to rest and prepare for the evening, not to mention time to think, to think about everything that had happened—was happening—happening all too fast. It *was* crazy, no matter what Lucas said. They had met through an arrangement that was purely business. He didn't know her. How could he be asking to marry her? And why was she suddenly so overjoyed at the thought of being his wife? She had always believed him to be a heartless businessman, but now his lightest touch was enough to make her knees weak and watery. How could a heartless man have such an effect on her?

She looked down at the ring which signified her intention to marry him. It was just a piece of jewelry, yet it made her feel like a beautiful storybook princess. But fairy tales always had happy endings. Why did she continue to fear that her relationship with Lucas would not run quite so smoothly?

Then she remembered his parting words to her: "Don't think of anything but me and how happy we are together." She smiled as his image flashed into her mind and she forgot the annoying doubts that had been clouding her bliss.

When they arrived at Lucas' house, the long driveway was lit by *luminarias,* flickering candles in sand-filled paper lanterns, and Karin thought it was a beautiful variation of "Las Posadas," the Mexican custom where children carried similar lanterns in a procession to the village church each Christmas Eve.

A butler opened the door and took their coats, and they were immediately enveloped by the noisy shouts of children scrambling to get the contents of a broken red and white Santa Claus *piñata.* Karin hesitated, watching the scene before her. Lucas was standing by the window, a drink in his hand. Danielle, in a form-fitting, strapless silver lamé gown, stood next to him, one hand resting languidly on his shoulder, the sleek lines of her body melting effortlessly against his. Suddenly Karin's brown silk toga, which had seemed so chic the night before, felt about as elegant as a faded cotton bathrobe, and she fought back an urge to turn and run out the door.

Lucas glanced in their direction and his relaxed demeanor disappeared when he noticed Karin. He straightened away from Danielle and she followed his gaze. Her eyes narrowed angrily and she clutched at his white dinner jacket, but he bent over, whispered in her ear, released himself and walked toward the entry. Every muscle in Danielle's face was taut as she watched his movements. He put his drink on the tray of a passing maid, shook hands with Dan and her father and, placing his hand possessively around Karin's waist, kissed her lightly on the cheek.

Karin held herself stiffly. Although Lucas hadn't been touching Danielle, he had seemed quite content to have her clinging to him. In fact, his placid look had changed to one of annoyance only when he had seen Karin, and Danielle's furious expression left no doubt as to the effect Karin's appearance had had on her. Once again she got the feeling that she was the outsider, breaking up the cozy relationship which existed between Lucas and Danielle—a relationship Lucas insisted she had no right to question, a relationship he described only as a friendship. But there were varying degrees of friendship and Lucas was entirely too ambiguous about the extent of his association with Danielle.

Yet she was the one he wanted to marry. *Why?* The question kept whirling through her mind, threatening the happiness Lucas was offering her. Did he love her? If so, why hadn't he ever told her so? She flipped through the pages of her memory, trying to find one instance when he had uttered those words, and despair shaded her features when she realized that he had never even mentioned them.

Lucas guided them toward the bar, and after getting

something to drink, Dan and Paul joined a group of men seated by the fireplace. Danielle was watching Karin, a sulky pout on her face.

Lucas didn't seem to notice. "Come on, I want you to meet my brother."

"I thought you said that he had *two* children." She looked at the noisy group of boys and girls. "It looks like at least twenty."

"Some of our friends have children. We invite them to the party, too. It's just not Christmas without children." He stopped walking and looked down at her. "What's wrong? Don't you like children?" His dark eyes held a hint of laughter.

The amusement deep in his eyes didn't detract from the intensity of his gaze and she felt unbidden warmth stealing up into her cheeks. "Of course I like children. I was just surprised to see so many. I didn't think . . . you only mentioned two." She was so nervous that she couldn't stop talking, yet all her explanations only made the situation worse.

His mouth widened into a grin. "Okay, okay, I believe you. It's just something I had to ask." His hand reached up and his index finger tapped lightly against the tip of her nose. "Since we're getting married . . . and I do want a family . . . eventually." His arm drew her to him as if to reinforce the protective tone of his voice, then he continued moving across the room until he stopped before a man and woman who were trying to divide the last of the *piñata*'s candy between six shouting children.

The man, who looked vaguely familiar to Karin, gave some chocolate bars to a small boy. "Okay, that's it. Now you kids disappear into the game room." He motioned to the teenager who was apparently baby-sitting. "This part of the house is off limits for the rest of the night." He looked up as the children ran off.

Karin watched him inquisitively. She was sure that

she had met him before, but she couldn't place him immediately. She needed a few more moments to sift through her memories and find the exact time and place.

"Don't tell me that we're going to have peace and quiet from now on?" Lucas said.

"Stop complaining," the dark-haired woman said. "You're the one who keeps saying it wouldn't be Christmas Eve without the children. If not for that, I would have had them tucked quietly in bed by now."

The man laughed. "Come on, Linda, you know Lucas enjoys our children so much because he only gets to see them a few times a year. The rest of the time he's an uncommitted bachelor."

Karin's eyes studied the man's face. She couldn't repress the disturbing impression that she had met him before—that she knew him—but before she had a chance to ask any questions Lucas' words cut into her thoughts.

"Not any longer." Lucas smiled. "Karin, this is my brother, Tom, and his wife, Linda." His arm tightened around Karin's waist and drew her closer to him. "Karin and I are going to be married." He smiled down at Karin. "You'll have to excuse me for keeping it a secret, but I wanted Karin with me when I told you."

Tom laughed and took Karin's hands between his. "Well, you've certainly surprised me. When is the happy event going to take place?"

Before Karin could say anything, Lucas answered. "As soon as possible. I'm not going to give Karin a chance to change her mind." His hand slipped from her waist and moved along her upper arm. "Now, come on, let me take you two over to meet Karin's father. After all, it's only a matter of time before we'll all be one big happy family."

Paul and Dan stood when Lucas introduced them to Tom and Linda.

"Paul Andrews," Tom said slowly. His eyes narrowed, and his forehead furrowed as if he were traveling deep within his memory to grope for some long-forgotten piece of information. A slow smile spread across his face as he seemed to remember.

"Paul Andrews . . . Karin . . . you wouldn't by chance have a summer home in San Juan Capistrano?"

"We live there year round now," Karin said. "But when I was younger we used to stay for just the summer."

"The swallow people. I thought your face looked familiar. Karin Andrews . . . you don't remember me, do you?"

Karin shook her head and smiled, her memory suddenly clear. "Yes, I do. Of course I do. You're Tom McKay. I knew we had met before. We used to go surfing." Her amber eyes widened dreamily. "We had so much fun together. I wish those days had never ended," she said truthfully. "They were the happiest times of my life." Jenny had been right. Lucas *was* related to the McKays who had owned the nearby farm. Each moment she looked at Tom brought back stronger memories and increased her feelings of familiarity.

"We used to meet on the beach," Tom continued as if he hadn't heard her. "It must have been about seven years ago. I was nineteen." He smiled. "You were sixteen. Yes, I remember it very well. You had quite a birthday party."

"You were at my birthday party? I remember asking you, but I don't remember seeing you there. In fact, I'm sure you're not in any of the pictures."

Tom smiled. "You invited me." His glance flickered to her father. "But I wasn't able to attend." A tight harshness had crept into his voice. Then he seemed to collect himself and he laughed lightly, almost cynically. He reached out and patted Lucas on the shoulder.

"Well, well, so you're marrying Karin Andrews. Now isn't that a pleasant surprise?"

"Somehow I get the feeling that I don't quite understand what's going on," Linda said. She looked at her husband quizzically. "Don't tell me Karin is an old girlfriend of yours?"

"No," Tom said, putting his arm around his wife. "We were just beach buddies." He smiled at Lucas. "Old friends who used to surf together." He kissed Linda on the cheek. "There's no need for you to be jealous."

Linda nudged Tom with her elbow. "Don't be silly; I'm not jealous. It's just that everything seems so mysterious. I'd like to know what's going on."

"Nothing too mysterious, as you put it," Tom said. "We had a small farm near the big house on the hill where Karin's family spent the summers. I used to meet her on the beach. That's all there is to it . . . except that *now* Lucas is marrying her." Once again his glance drifted to Karin's father and he smiled sardonically.

"I realized I knew you as soon as Lucas introduced us," Karin said. "But when I met Lucas I never would have thought that he was your brother. He's so different." She looked from one man to the other, comparing Tom's fair complexion and light sandy hair with Lucas' darkly compelling features. Then she noticed their eyes—that was why Lucas had looked so familiar to her. Their eyes were the same inky brown, and when Lucas smiled, his emitted the same warmth as Tom's, although Tom now seemed to be enjoying some secret amusement. "I had no idea that Lucas was your brother." She turned to Lucas. "Why didn't you tell me?"

"This is a Christmas party, not a class reunion. Some things are better left unsaid. You two will have plenty of time to reminisce after we're married." Lucas smiled at his brother, but Karin knew him well enough to detect an undercurrent of annoyance in his voice. "Now, if you'll excuse us, there are some people I'd like Karin to meet."

Lucas walked Karin through the room, introducing her to his friends. Karin noticed that he deliberately avoided Danielle, although she felt the other woman's gaze following them closely wherever they went. The sensation made her nervous and she kept glancing surreptitiously sideways, hoping that Danielle had turned her attention elsewhere.

Lucas followed her gaze and tightened his grip on her shoulder. "You must be getting tired. I guess I've been so eager to show you off that I haven't considered how exhausting all this must be for you." His hand slipped to her waist and pressed warmly against it. "I know a nice quiet place where we can rest for a while." He led her through the door opening onto the patio. Karin shivered. Warm as it was during the sunny daytime hours, the desert evenings were always cold.

They walked quickly across a narrow brick path which bisected the lawn, separating the pool from the tennis court. A small house with a glass roof and walls stood at the end of the path and Lucas led her to it. The floor was made of brick and large clay pots overflowing with greenery covered most of the area.

"This is an all-purpose shed," he explained as they waded through a sea of ferns. "It serves as a greenhouse, a sauna"—he indicated a door to the left—"and a quiet place to relax after swimming or tennis." A glass sliding door opened onto a large interior room with a massive fieldstone fireplace. Deep brown carpeting covered the floor and the two sofas and chairs were upholstered in muted shades of beige. Lucas led Karin to a sofa which looked out onto an atrium stocked with desert plants and illuminated by the soft glow of multicolored Malibu lights.

"Would you like something to drink?"

Karin shook her head. "Why didn't you tell me Tom was your brother?"

"It didn't seem to matter."

"But it would have made everything so different. I mean, you really did recognize me that day in the Sacred Garden."

"You didn't give me a chance to explain."

"But later, when we became more friendly . . ."

"I was waiting for the right moment," Lucas said. "Besides, we'd never been formally introduced. I'd seen you in town once or twice, and Tom was quite taken with you." He stopped and smiled at her. "But our life together began that morning in the Sacred Garden. A beautiful beginning, don't you agree?"

He settled himself into the seat beside her. She closed her eyes and leaned her head against his shoulder. His hand began moving along her upper arm, his fingers stroking lightly against her skin. Everything felt so right, so in place.

"Do you want a big wedding?" He bent his head to hers; his voice was husky, his breath warm against her ear.

"I hadn't thought about it. Do you?"

"No. I don't want to wait for all the planning. I thought perhaps something small in church, then a reception at Casa del Mar. Just the family and some close friends."

"I don't know if Jenny can manage all that. It might be too much for her."

"Don't worry. She won't have to do anything. I'll call in a caterer; they'll take care of everything. You just pick out a dress." His hand went beneath her chin and lifted her face to his. Their eyes met for an instant before he lowered his lips and caught hers with a demanding urgency.

His arm still circled her body and supported her

151

when he tipped her back until they were stretched along the length of the sofa. She felt her flesh responding to his with a will of its own and she reached up to encircle his neck. His hands moved down her body, touching, probing, making her writhe ecstatically in his arms as she tried to fit herself closer to him.

She uttered no words of protest when his hand slowly stroked the pulse of her neck and lowered to her shoulder, slipping beneath the wide pleated strap of her toga. Her lips shifted to the side of his mouth and she murmured incoherent words of contentment as her body anticipated the pleasures that only Lucas' touch could bring.

She gasped with delight as his hands traveled down her back, circling gently in the direction of her breasts. Her mouth moved across the length of his as she parted her lips and revealed her overwhelming need for him.

The party was completely forgotten as her hands moved between them and began unbuttoning the pleated front of his white silk evening shirt. It was as if she and Lucas were the only two people in the world and she couldn't wait to slip his shirt off his shoulders so she could feel the hairy roughness of his flesh against her softly swelling breasts.

She lowered her shoulder, giving his hand more room, impatiently urging him to remove her dress so that their bodies could unite as one. But his hand still kept moving slowly, exciting her, delighting her, but taking no rapid action toward the fulfillment she so fervently desired.

She caught his lower lip between her teeth and her breath whispered against his. "Make love to me, Lucas; please make love to me. I love you so much."

His hand stilled for a moment as if he were considering what to do. Karin panicked. What could it be? Was it possible he didn't love her? Had her words frightened him and cooled his ardor? Impossible. She refused even to consider the idea as her fingers combed through his hair and dug into his flesh.

Suddenly she felt him stiffen and move away. She moaned in protest and tightened her arms, trying to bring him back to her, but he reached up and gently pulled her hands apart, releasing himself from her grip.

She felt empty, deserted, and somehow ashamed as he sat up and held out his hand. Her eyes filled with tears as she watched him, but she accepted his hand and let him pull her up beside him. Her eyes moved over his face and she saw that despite the wildly erratic emotions that were surging through her body, his feelings were totally under control and he had not lost the cold composure that seemed to dominate his personality.

He stroked back her hair and kissed each eye, tasting the salty tears that were pooling within their depths. "That lock's been broken for years," he explained, looking at the door. "It's never made any difference until now." His hands smoothed over her cheeks, down her neck, and curved onto her shoulders. "Anyone could walk in here. I want to marry you; I don't want you embarrassed." He cupped her chin. "And you would be, wouldn't you?"

Karin nodded. He looked so cool and in control of himself; his thoughts were so practical and realistic. How could she tell him that a few minutes ago she hadn't really cared about anything except the way his body felt against hers? Yet, he was able to think about mundane things like broken locks. None of the reckless passion which dominated her whenever she was around him ever seemed to cloud his clear thoughts or to loosen the tight rein he held over his emotions.

Taking his hand away from her chin, she stood and ran her hand along her hips, straightening out the creases in her dress. She tried to make herself seem as calm as he was, but her words sounded artificially brittle as they echoed in her ear. "Perhaps we should be getting back to the party. After all, you do have other guests."

He stood and came up behind her. "I'd rather be here with you." His fingers stroked the nape of her neck. "We can just sit and talk for a while." His hand slid over her shoulder and moved lightly down her arm.

His touch made her shiver and she realized just how much she was affected by being close to him. He might be able to sit and talk, but she couldn't; talk wouldn't satisfy the passions he had aroused. Being alone with him was both a temptation and a torture that her senses could no longer endure. She brushed his hand away and caught it with hers. "I'd like to get back. It's late; I think my dad should be getting home."

They began walking back toward the house. "There's no need for you to leave. Dan can drive him."

"I'm tired, too." She smiled up at him. "Just being with you is an exhausting experience. I don't know if I'll be able to keep up the pace."

Turning her to him, he looked into her face. "I'm not worried about that. You'll do everything I want you to." His smile was warm, but his voice was coldly assured.

The party seemed to have settled down and people had broken into casual groups. Karin looked for her father and saw that he was still talking to Dan and the other men he had been with when she and Lucas had gone outside.

"I'll say good night to Tom," Karin said, taking Lucas' hand and walking toward his brother, who was seated on the sofa next to Danielle. The actress's eyes lifted and she glared at Karin as they approached.

"Karin's leaving," Lucas explained. "I'll get her coat." He left them alone.

Danielle leaned back, flicking her cigarette and studying Karin through thick false eyelashes. Karin felt as if she were being dissected by an ice pick. "Enjoying yourself?" Danielle smiled sweetly.

"Yes, and you?" Tension knotted Karin's stomach, but she tried to appear pleasantly amiable.

"I always enjoy Lucas' parties." Danielle snickered. "Especially when we're alone—like last night. Too bad you have to leave so early." Her snide tone insinuated that she wished Karin had never come at all.

Karin refused to let Danielle intimidate her. After what had happened outside she was sure that Lucas loved her, and she was going to let Danielle know it. "I spent the day with Lucas, and he's been with me all evening." Her voice sounded as cold as she felt.

Danielle laughed. "Of course. There wasn't much else for him to do. I was so exhausted after last night that I slept the day away. I got up just in time for the party. And as for him being with you tonight . . . as I said, the night's still young, even if it is past your bedtime." She ground her cigarette out in the ashtray. "I've been having a lovely chat with Tom and I assure you I don't intend to go to bed until Lucas feels the same way." She blinked demurely and Karin wanted to scratch her eyes out.

Lucas returned with Karin's coat to find Danielle relaxing politely on the sofa. "Ready to go?" he asked Karin. "Have you said good night to everyone?" He glanced at Tom.

Tom stood up. He held a nearly empty liquor glass in his hand and he swayed, unsteady on his feet as he clutched the arm of the sofa for support.

Lucas reached out, caught his arm and took the glass from his hand. "I think you've had too much to drink." He looked around the room. "Where's Linda? It's time you went to bed."

Tom pushed Lucas' hand away and retrieved his glass. "Actually, Lucas, I was just toasting your engagement." He looked down at the sofa. "And explaining the situation to Danielle."

Lucas grasped his arm again. "I'll take you to your room myself. You're making a fool of yourself."

Tom's voice had been so loud that all other conversation in the room had ceased and everyone was watching the two brothers. Karin moved back toward the wall. She wanted to escape this tense scene which she didn't quite understand, but which frighened her with its dangerous undertones. Tom's slurred voice called her back.

"Don't go, Karin. You are absolute living proof that Lucas always keeps his word; he always gets what he wants."

Karin looked from Tom to Lucas, searching for an explanation. "I don't understand."

Tom grinned crookedly. "You invited me to your sixteenth birthday party, but when I showed up at the door, the butler refused to let me in. Seems I was good enough for the public beach but not for the privacy of your home. Lucas was wild when he heard about it—swore that someday he'd have it all: money, the house, and the girl in it." He lifted his glass. "And Lucas always comes through. So tonight I drink a toast to a marriage that I played an important part in bringing about."

Karin put her hand to her throat. Her skin felt taut, as if the blood in her veins was draining away. Lucas pushed Tom down on the sofa and went to Karin. She felt stunned, unable to say anything, just wanting to escape from this scene which was taking on all the dimensions of an unbelievable nightmare. She looked to where her father and Dan were standing. Ripping the diamond ring from her finger, she threw it at Lucas and rushed out the door. She heard Lucas calling to her and his footsteps following after her, but she didn't stop. She wanted no more of his lies. Now, at last, she had the explanation she was seeking; her doubts had been well-founded and all she could feel were a mortifying shame and an awful pain, thorough and irreversible.

She stopped at the front of the house, breathing deeply of the cold night air in an attempt to regain control of her senses. Her father's voice, precise and authoritarian, drifted through the open door. "You, sir, will let my daughter alone. We are leaving your home."

Within seconds he was at Karin's side. Dan quickly brought the car and they drove down the winding driveway.

Chapter Eight

$\mathcal{K}$arin was grateful that her father and Dan were understanding enough to remain silent during the ride back to the house. She knew that if either of them had said anything to her she would have burst into tears. She felt both used and abused. It had been bad enough when she had thought that Lucas' interest in her was purely physical. Now she realized that he wasn't even attracted to her in that way. He wanted to marry her because of some childish desire for retribution, to fulfill a vow for vengeance that any normal person would have forgotten long ago.

But Lucas McKay was not just anyone. She was all too aware of his inflexible will and rigid determination. Obviously he hadn't planned to be inconvenienced by his marriage to Karin because he hadn't intended to let it stop him from seeing the woman he really loved; Danielle's behavior had convinced her of that. How sweet Lucas' revenge would have been when, after making Karin his wife, he had shamed her by continuing his affair with Danielle. And she had no doubt that he had planned on doing just that. After all, hadn't he told her that Danielle was his very good friend and that she, even as his future wife, wasn't to question that friendship?

How could she have been so naïve as not to know what he really meant? Lucas had been telling her, in no uncertain terms, that Danielle was a very important person in his life and that he had no intention of altering that situation merely because he was getting married. She pressed a fist against her mouth as an even more disturbing question forced itself into her mind. The declaration of love that she had never heard—had Lucas whispered it to Danielle? Had he held her tightly in the dark intimacy of passion and spoken the words that she had been yearning to hear? She couldn't bear to think about it.

Now she knew what Lucas meant when he said she was special, and it had nothing to do with love. No wonder he had been so agreeable to her terms for the sale of Casa del Mar. She had walked right into his trap. How could she have been foolish enough to think that Lucas was in love with her, when all along he had been coldly pursuing a course of action he had drawn up seven years ago?

Karin was glad to be in the privacy of her bedroom when this last thought finally released the tears that she had been holding back. At least she had spared her father the pain of her anguish. Thinking of her father made her remember that Lucas now owned Casa del Mar. Although the sales contract gave them the right to remain there, it also gave Lucas the right to stay on the premises, and there was no way she intended to be that close to him ever again.

Somehow she would have to tell her father the truth and hope that he was strong enough to cope with the situation. She would try to make the move as easy on him as possible, but they would have to find another place to live, so her immediate need was to return to San Juan Capistrano and review their finances. Finances . . . her job . . . she would have to find a new one. Working for Lucas was out of the question, and he was closing the store after Christmas anyway. Suddenly the loss of her job and Casa del Mar seemed very unimportant when compared to the loss of Lucas' love—a love she had never really possessed.

How could she have been so naïve? But then, how could she have realized the truth? She had never known that Tom had been barred from her party all those years ago, and when Jenny had mentioned the possibility, she had refused to consider that Lucas might be related to the McKays who had once owned the farm below Casa del Mar. Even if she had, she would never have believed that any man could be vindictive enough to go to such lengths to avenge a ridiculous incident that had occurred so far in the past. Well, at least she had found out about him before she had married him.

Closing her eyes, she thought about how much she loved him and how he really felt about her. Hatred, vengeance, these were the words to describe his emotions, certainly not love, and if Lucas loved anyone, it was the beautiful Danielle, who had probably spent the rest of the evening nestled in his arms. Karin was now determined to do everything in her power to erase him from her life.

This vow was easier made than kept, and if she slept at all that night, it was for brief periods only; she seemed to hear every little click of the digital bedside clock until at last it was dawn. Her father and Dan were at breakfast when she came into the dining room, but after wishing her good morning, Dan excused himself, saying he had some things to take care of, and Karin realized that he was giving her the chance to speak privately with her father.

"Lucas phoned last night," her father said. "He wanted to talk to you."

"I have nothing to say to him."

"That's what I told him." Her father looked at her thoughtfully. "Somehow, I feel responsible for all this.

If I hadn't been so wrapped up in myself, I would have had his background investigated, found out who he really was. Money is so easy to come by these days that you can't use it as a guide anymore."

Karin put down her coffeecup. "Will you stop talking about money? That's what caused all this trouble in the first place!"

"Nonsense! I never would have let McKay into the house if I had known how he was using us." He shook his head. "What a smooth talker . . . he had me convinced that he was trying to build tasteful housing, that he valued my opinion, but we were both deceived. Look what he's done to you; no gentleman would behave that way."

Karin laughed, but there was no humor in her voice. "You're right about one thing: Lucas McKay is no gentleman." She pushed her chair away from the table and studied her father. "But you can't continue behaving as if time stopped twenty years ago. Things are different now, and you can no longer control other people with just a flick of your finger." She watched his reaction to see if she should continue. As eager as she was to rid herself of Lucas McKay, she was not about to sacrifice her father's well-being to do so.

"What do you mean?" Her father drew himself up in his chair and it suddenly appeared that he had regained all his old strength and dignity. "I believe you'd better tell me what's been going on while I've been ill."

Karin shook her head and turned away. Determined as she was to release herself from Lucas' debt, she was still too unsure of her father's health to risk telling him the truth.

"All right." Paul Andrews' voice sounded vigorous and healthy. "I've been doing some careful thinking about this entire situation. Would you like to hear my conclusions?"

Karin turned to him and nodded.

"I think we've been having some financial problems and you asked for Lucas' help. Am I right?"

Again Karin nodded.

"I thought that might be it." Paul Andrews still sounded completely calm. "Well, you'd better tell me everything. It will be a relief to know what's been going on in my own home."

Karin sighed and told him about their money difficulties, the sale of Casa del Mar and the arrangements she had made with Lucas concerning their right to remain in the house.

Her father's voice was firm and unemotional. "You should have discussed it with me before you sold. There might have been another solution."

"I didn't want to upset you." She got up and walked around to his chair. "You're more important to me than any house."

"As you are to me. I thought I had made that clear to you. I'm sorry that I put you through all this. It doesn't make me feel like much of a father . . . or much of a man. But things are going to be different from now on. I can promise you that." He pressed his lips firmly together before continuing. "We'll let Mr. McKay have the house, since he already owns it. I'm sure we can find another place to live. As you've said many times, Casa del Mar is too big for us anyway. Even Jenny will be delighted. You've told me often enough that she wants to retire."

"Lucas is on the phone," Dan interrupted, standing in the doorway and looking over at Karin. "He wants to talk to you."

"Dan, I hate to put you on the spot, but will you say I can't speak with him right now?" Karin's eyes pleaded with her father's friend, begging him to understand how she felt. Hearing Lucas' voice would be like pouring alcohol over the incision he had made in her heart, and there was nothing he could say to heal the wound.

Dan hesitated for a moment, looking steadily at Karin. "I think you're making a mistake, but if that's what you want . . ."

It wasn't what she wanted, but she couldn't have what she wanted and this was the only thing she could do to retain her pride and her sanity. "It is, Dan. Please?"

Dan shook his head. "All right." He turned and left the room.

"You're making the right decision," her father said. "He's nothing but a fortune-hunter."

Karin smiled. "But I don't have a fortune. Remember? I just told you that."

"Maybe so, but you have breeding and McKay is well aware of that."

Karin shuddered inwardly. Her father's words might be old-fashioned and out-of-date, but they were a painfully accurate description of why Lucas had wanted her for his wife. He wanted to possess everything that had once belonged to Paul Andrews: his house, his daughter—everything.

"He's coming to see you," Dan said as he walked back into the room.

Karin pushed her chair away from the table and stood up. "I don't want to see him." She held on to the back of her chair and tapped her fingers against the frame. "What a horrible way to celebrate Christmas. I'm sorry, Dan."

Dan waved his hand. "No need to apologize. I feel terrible about what's happened." He cleared his throat and paused. "It's none of my business, but your dad is my friend and I've always considered you the daughter I never had. I've known Lucas McKay for a long time, both in business and socially, and I've never known him to behave in any way that wasn't absolutely decent. I think you're wrong about him. At least see him, give him a chance to explain."

"No. I can't do that." She walked to the window. "And I can't stay here. Not now." She turned back to Dan. "May I borrow a car? I want to go home; there are a lot of things I have to do."

Dan reached into his pocket. "Yes, of course. Take the BMW; I haven't been using it much lately." He removed one key from a large key ring and handed it to her. "But I still think you're making a mistake."

Her father pushed his chair away from the table and stood up. "I'll go with you."

Karin walked quickly over to him and placed her hand on his shoulder. "No, Dad; please stay here. I need to be alone for a while. I have so much thinking to do, so many things to straighten out. I'll feel better if I know you're resting."

Reluctantly her father agreed, and in a short while Karin had packed and was on her way to Casa del Mar. A slight drizzle had begun to fall by the time she reached the Capistrano exit, and when she parked in the driveway, it had turned into a downpour. She ran into the house, but even that short distance was enough to get her clothing wet and she found the chill dampness of the interior only a bit more comforting than the storm outside had been. Remembering that she had turned down the heat before they left for Palm Springs, she went to raise the thermostat.

She turned the dial and immediately heard a click, but there was no accompanying hum from the furnace. Holding her hand to the vent, she waited to feel the surge of warm air, but nothing happened. She went down to the basement to check the furnace; the mechanism was dead; the light that indicated when it was on had gone off. She made a fist and banged the cold metal box, hoping it was just a loose wire, but still nothing happened. It just wasn't working, and no repairman would be willing to come out on Christmas Day. Quickly she went upstairs and checked the log box, but found it empty, and she knew that the wood on the pile outside would be too wet to burn, so the fireplace was out of the question.

She would just have to make the best of it, and the first thing to do was to get out of her wet clothing. But once she went upstairs and began changing, she realized she couldn't stay here. Although she was now wearing her heaviest sweater and slacks, she was still shivering and her teeth were beginning to chatter. The only thing to do was to spend the night in a motel and get the furnace fixed in the morning. She threw a nightgown and fresh underwear into her overnight case, grabbed a book from the library and left the house.

The car was still warm and she welcomed the stream of heated air that began flowing out of the vents when she started up the motor. She drove slowly down the old cobblestone driveway, peering carefully through the heavy veil of rain. The surroundings were so much a part of her life that she scarcely paid any attention to them and didn't notice the deep puddle that had formed where the driveway curved and dipped. By the time she was aware of it the car had already passed through the middle of it and was making strange choking noises. Then it stopped—stopped completely.

Karin tried several times to restart it, but nothing happened. She could have kicked herself. Now she was stranded here. Why hadn't she concentrated on the road? Looking around, she saw the guest cottage a short distance in front of her. She could stay there. Why hadn't she thought of it before? Lucas had casually mentioned that he had had the plumbing, heating and electrical systems checked out when he first moved in; she would have no trouble starting the furnace there. And as for Lucas himself, he was in Palm Springs and she would be gone by the time he returned.

Afraid that the book and her overnight case would

get soaked, she left them in the car and ran to the cottage, but by the time she reached the door, the rain had seeped through to her skin. She shivered as her slippery fingers groped for the key. It was still above the doorframe, and after using it to let herself in, Karin replaced it, so Lucas would never know she had been there. She immediately went to the thermostat and the furnace came on instantly, filling the small rooms with a steady gush of warm air. Sighing in relief, Karin removed her sweater and walked into the kitchen. Every inch of her felt cold and soggy. She boiled some water for tea, and as the house began to get more comfortable, she discarded the rest of her wet clothing.

Thinking of staying in the guesthouse had been a marvelous idea. Tomorrow, if the rain stopped and the car started, she would get the furnace repaired and begin going through the bank statements in the main house. She intended to have everything sorted out by the time her father returned. Taking a spare blanket from the linen closet, she wrapped it around herself and settled down on the sofa with a hot cup of tea. The snug security of the cottage was a welcome change after a sleepless night and the long car ride. She placed the empty cup on the floor in front of her and before long she was asleep.

As difficult as it had been to keep Lucas out of her waking thoughts, it was utterly impossible to dismiss him from her dreams—dreams in which she felt the warmth of his lips against hers, dreams in which she tried to forget the painful realization that he didn't love her . . . had never loved her.

A loud noise shattered the tranquillity of her sleep, and half-raising her head from the sofa, she turned in the direction of the door. "Lucas!" She stumbled to her feet, and the blanket slipped to the floor, revealing her nudity. She bent to retrieve it, but her fingers felt like a clumsy wooden sticks when she tried to pull it back over her shoulders. Her dream had become a nightmare.

Lucas' eyes widened when he looked at her, and a strange expression seemed to darken his face. Then, just as quickly as it had appeared, it vanished, replaced by a coldly incomprehensible mask of detached arrogance. Droplets of rain glistened in his hair and moistened his forehead. Raising his hand, he wiped them away with a gesture of annoyance, then tossed his tan raincoat on the Windsor chair by the door and stood before her in the same casual outfit he had been wearing that day in the Sacred Garden.

"Yes—Lucas. Did you think I wouldn't come after you?" He twisted his mouth cynically and strode toward her. She could feel his eyes traveling over her body, studying, evaluating, deciding. Finally, his hands reached out, moving toward her breasts, and she jumped back, unwilling to have him touch her flesh. He laughed at her as if she were a foolish child, and his fingers moved lightly over her shoulders. "Here, let me do that; you're still half-asleep." He took the edges of the blanket and tucked them above her breasts, swaddling her in a tight, restrictive cocoon. "What happened to your clothes?" he asked, lifting her in his arms and setting her in the easy chair beside the fireplace.

"They got wet."

"Not very surprising in this weather. And the car?"

"I didn't realize the puddle was so deep. I guess some wires got wet. How did you know where I was?"

"Just a lucky guess." He made a wry face. "Where else would you be? Although I did expect to find you in the main house."

"The furnace is broken. I was on my way to a motel when the car stalled; I had nowhere else to go."

"No matter. This is a cozy, private place to have our little discussion." He knelt by the hearth, holding a match to the logs in the fireplace.

"I have nothing to say to you." She tugged at the blanket and tried to shift herself against the back of the chair. Wavering shadows crept along the walls, muted reflections of the flames now flickering in the fireplace.

"Did you really think I was going to let you run off without getting some explanation of your childish behavior?" He stood and placed his hands on his hips as he turned to her.

"Childish?" She tried to stand up but found her movements impeded by the blanket and sank back on the chair. "You were actually planning to marry me because of some ridiculous vendetta, and you call *me* childish!" She shook her head in disbelief. "Get out of here. We have nothing to discuss." She turned her face away.

He came swiftly toward her, grasped her bare shoulders and pulled her to her feet. His hand came up and cupped her chin, turning it painfully toward him. "Don't ever talk to me like that. I'm not some simple farmboy you can dismiss by tossing your head." He bit off the words in a sharp, angry staccato rhythm.

"Get your hands off me!" Karin's request was icy.

"Don't tell me what to do. You're in no position to make any demands. You belong to me, and you always will. Don't ever tell me to take my hands off you again." His cupped palms traced the contours of her body, making her fully aware of his totally possessive attitude. "Touching you gives me pleasure, and as you well know, I don't deny myself those things I enjoy." His fingers tightened, burning through the blanket, making her feel naked and helpless in his arms. He raised her chin and lowered his head until their lips met.

The brutal force of his actions made Karin twist in his arms as she tried to free herself. Her lips remained closed, cold and unresponsive. She held her breath until her bones turned to steel and her entire body went rigid. She didn't belong to him—she didn't belong to anyone. She was a person, not an object, and that was something Lucas couldn't seem to understand. She loved him more than she cared to admit, even to herself, but if he couldn't return that love, she would rather never see him again than have him think of her as just another acquisition.

He raised his head, grasped her upper arms and set her away from him. His eyes narrowed as they flicked over her face and his mouth whitened at the edges; he was seething with suppressed anger. Lowering his arms, he placed one around her shoulders, the other beneath her knees, and lifted her off the floor. With the blanket still wrapped tightly around her, he carried her to the sofa and sat down, holding her imprisoned on his lap.

His arms encircled her and his face was only inches away. "I could shake you until you come to your senses." His voice was low and terse, little more than a whisper. "Or I could put you over my knee and treat you like a child until you decide to grow up." He stopped speaking and pressed his lips together, the small muscle in his jaw pulsing.

His eyes devoured her and pierced hers as if he were trying to read her thoughts. "But that's not the answer, is it? There's another, far more pleasant way to convince you not to fight me." The corner of his lip lifted, curving up in a cynical smile.

Karin struggled to free herself but found she was helplessly entangled in the snug folds of the blanket, the only shield between Lucas and her bare skin.

His smile widened as he watched her pointless efforts. "I told you not to fight me." One large hand curved around both her wrists and held them against his chest.

He bent his head, dropping a kiss on each eyelid; she closed her eyes, as if not seeing him would stop the devastating effect he was having on her senses. His marauding lips caressed her cheek and she held her breath, trying to maintain her frail resistance against his erotic assault.

Her efforts were in vain, and as his lips moved slowly along the curve of her chin down to her bare shoulders and the deep valley between her breasts, she found her body melting into his until the only reason she wanted to free her arms was to throw them around his neck and draw him closer to her. Lucas and the blanket still prevented any bodily movement, but her lips parted under the gentle pressure of his, returning his kiss with a passion that left no doubt as to her hunger for his touch.

When he lifted his head and drew away from her, she was breathlessly exhausted but by no means satisfied. She rested her head against his chest, gratified to hear that his heart was racing as wildly as hers.

She felt his warm breath move lightly through her hair when he bent to kiss the top of her head. "Now, you're going to forget all this silly nonsense and come back to Palm Springs with me." His voice, though soft and husky, was permeated with a self-controlled arrogance that made her remember the words he had spoken before kissing her—a smug promise to find an easy way to subdue her.

As if he could read her thoughts, he continued speaking. "You'll put my ring back on and we'll be married as soon as I can make the arrangements." He shifted in his seat and reached into his pocket.

She took advantage of her freedom to roll away from him but slipped and fell to the floor instead. Instantly, Lucas was down beside her, lifting her to her feet.

"Are you okay? What happened?"

"I'm fine; I just wanted to put a little space between us."

"Why?" His voice indicated his shocked disbelief.

"I didn't want you to get the wrong impression. I have no intention of marrying you."

He smiled and the worried look vanished from his eyes. "You need more convincing, and it will be my pleasure."

She tried to move away from him, but he followed her and moved her to the floor until they were stretched fully beside each other, only a few feet from the flickering hearth.

His fingers went to the tuck in the blanket, toyed with it for a moment, then released it and spread the edges apart so that her entire body was fully exposed to his view. His hands followed the path of his eyes, caressing her breasts, massaging her waist and stroking the inner sweetness of her thighs.

"You look beautiful in the firelight." His hands moved through her hair, brushing it back from her face. "Coppery hair, golden skin. You're the wife I've always wanted."

His hands left her hair, moved behind her hips and then curved slowly over her abdomen, hesitating only momentarily before teasing her flesh as he traced a steady downward path. Karin felt as if her skin was on fire. She knew she had to stop him, her mind told her to stop him, but her body just kept wantonly responding to his touch.

Suddenly a log flared brightly and popped, sending a cascade of cinders onto the rug just beside them. Lucas stood quickly and began stamping out the sparks.

Karin knew she had to stop him *now*, while his hands and his lips were not caressing her and her mind was in full control of her senses. Before he could reach for her again, she stood up and stepped back. Her voice was as softly controlled as his. She lifted her hands to the blanket that she had just resecured around her and held them as if she was debating whether or not to release the snugly tucked covering. "There's no need to play games. I won't deny that you can arouse me when you make love to me, but that doesn't mean we have to get married. Our physical needs can be satisfied without that formality." She tried to make her gaze as seductive as possible. "We're both adults. I'm sure you must have felt this way before. Lust is a fairly common passion, and you've already admitted that you haven't led a celibate life."

His face was contorted with anger and he came toward her, flexing his fingers with a violence that made her fully aware of his rage. Pulling her hands away, he resecured the edges of the blanket. "Stop acting like a tramp. I'm not looking for a cheap affair; I want to marry you."

"How do you know I'm acting? Maybe this is the real me. After all, you know very little about my morals or anything else. Most of what you feel for me is based on some misguided image that's been fermenting in your mind for seven years."

"Stop that!" His fingers bit into her shoulders and she felt his muscles strain to check the force of his fury. "I know everything there is to know about you . . . morals and all. So don't play games with me. I've never lost yet." His clenched fingers slid down her arms, making her aware of his power to dominate. "And forget about my previous life-style, because it has nothing to do with you. Lust and celibacy are equally meaningless where we're concerned, because I intend to get everything I want from you. You're the woman I'm going to marry."

"Of course you want to marry me, and we both know why, don't we? Tom told everyone. Well, forget it; you can make my body do anything you want, but I'll never marry you. That's one satisfaction you're not going to have, Mr. Lucas McKay!" Her gaze met his with a fierce determination and she refused to drop her eyes.

"Well, what's your answer? I'm sure you wouldn't refuse Danielle."

"You're not Danielle! If I had any sense at all, I'd carry you into the bedroom and see how far you'd be willing to go. But there's always the chance that I might not feel like stopping when you did, and I'm just not willing to take that risk."

His eyes raked her body like tiny razors slicing through her skin; then, growling with disgust, he grabbed his jacket from the chair. "I can't stay here any longer. I don't trust myself when you're acting like this. We both need some time to cool down, but don't think it's over. I'll be back, and I'm going to get what I want." He strode through the door, slamming it closed with a violence that made the tiny cottage shake.

Karin listened to the sound of his car starting up. She heard the tires bite into the gravel and take off in a screeching roar; she let her body go limp and slumped down on the sofa.

It was just as she had thought: Lucas didn't love her, and even the physical attraction he felt for her was subservient to his inflexible willpower; he only wanted to marry her to fulfill some irrational vow. Unless she would agree to be his wife, he wanted nothing to do with her. Obviously he had intended to keep Danielle as his mistress even after he had made Karin his wife. The shame of that would have been more than Karin could bear.

Much as she loved Lucas, she still had her pride and she could never marry him now that Tom had revealed his true motivations. She closed her eyes and took a deep breath, grateful that he had left her alone. But an apprehensive chill ran up her spine when she visualized what might have happened if he had carried her into the bedroom. She remembered the caressing warmth of his hands against her flesh. Would she have been able to stop him? Would she have wanted to stop him? Fortunately Lucas had no interest in her outside of marriage, and the decision had been taken out of her hands.

It was the most miserable Christmas Karin had ever spent, but somehow she got through it. The next day the car had dried out, she had the furnace repaired and reviewed the bank statements to get a better understanding of their financial situation. As it turned out, things weren't as bad as she had thought. She had been so busy worrying about the mortgage payments on Casa del Mar and all their other debts that she had been positive there would be no money left after the house had been sold and the debts taken care of. But, much to her delight, she was mistaken and the sale of the property had left them with enough money to buy a smaller, less expensive house.

She approached Jim Simpson and told him of her decision.

"If you're willing to move now, that changes the conditions of the sale. Let me talk to McKay; I'm sure I can get him to pay you something extra for leaving early. He's probably very eager to get his hands on the property."

Karin smiled wryly; Jim would never know just how eager Lucas really was. "Under no circumstances are you to discuss this with Mr. McKay until after we've left the house."

Jim shrugged. "If you say so, but I think you're being foolish. Where are you planning to move?"

"I was hoping you had some suggestions."

"Yes, of course. Let me check my listings." He reached for a thick book at the side of his desk.

The house Karin finally decided to buy was part of an adult community which had just been built. It was small and easy to maintain, with a modern kitchen that even her father could learn to use. All the yardwork was done by the homeowners' association and the financial upkeep would be minimal.

A previous buyer hadn't been able to get a mortgage commitment, so the builder was anxious to make a sale, giving Karin favorable terms which permitted them to move in immediately.

Karin told her father to stay in Palm Springs because she didn't want him exerting himself with the move, and in order to keep expenses down, she decided to do the packing herself. Her sales agreement with Lucas had included most of the furniture, so it was only a matter of going through her personal belongings and discarding those things for which she no longer had any use.

Househunting had occupied most of the week after Christmas and New Year's Day found her sitting on her bedroom floor, watching the parade on TV and looking through some old photograph albums. When she heard the front door slam, she left the room and walked to the top of the stairway.

"Lucas! What are you doing here?"

"Just checking over my property." His eyes moved slowly down her body with an intimacy that left no doubt as to what he considered the extent of his possessions. "It's in the contract, remember?" He glanced past her, his gaze taking in the cartons she had moved into the hall. "Doing your spring cleaning early?" He began walking up the stairs.

"I've found another house. There's no reason to stay here any longer..Thanks to you, Dad knows the truth about our financial problems."

"I never said a word and you know it." He reached the top of the stairway and gripped her arm with his hand. "Why are you moving? You don't have to. I don't want you to go."

"I don't care what you want. I don't need this house anymore. Jenny is staying with her sister and Dad accepts our situation. I should have told him about it from the beginning, then none of this would have happened."

"None of what? You mean you never would have come to me?"

"That's right."

"You would have had to sell anyway."

"Yes, but I could have listed the house openly. There would have been no need for all this secrecy. No need for any special conditions."

"You were happy enough with the conditions before. And with me."

"We had a business relationship; I was foolish to let it turn into anything personal. And now, if you'll excuse me, I have work to do." She began walking away.

He caught up with her at her bedroom door and turned her toward him. "We never had a business arrangement and you know it. Do you think for one minute I would have bought this property on those terms if it had been anyone but you?"

"So you admit that this was all part of some scheme to get back at my father?"

"Your father had nothing to do with it. I never would have signed a contract with him. You were the one I saw in the Sacred Garden—the one who came to my office. Everything I did was because of you, and until Christmas Eve you were as satisfied with our relationship as I was."

"Then you were getting even with *me*. I didn't know the truth."

"And now you do?"

"What do you think?"

"I think you're behaving like an idiot."

"Then you're well rid of me." She shrugged herself free, walked into the room and began stacking the albums in a carton.

Lucas picked one up and began thumbing through it.

"This is the crowd you used to hang out with. Spoiled brats with flashy cars—swallow people. A farmer's son still isn't good enough for you; that's it, isn't it?" He slammed the book closed and threw it on the bed.

Karin looked at him and shuddered. There was pain in his eyes, pain that made her want to go to him and comfort him. But there was also scorn, an unyielding contempt that made her cringe in fear. She represented a part of Lucas' past that he wanted to avenge. Everything Tom had said was true; just looking at the expression on Lucas' face convinced her of that.

"Lucas, please go. We really have nothing to say to each other."

Her words seemed to bring him out of his reverie. "You're right. For once I agree with you; all this talking only gets us into trouble. We have a better means of communication." He walked toward her and drew her into his arms. "You can't deny that we're in complete agreement when it comes to our physical needs."

Karin forced herself to stand rigidly. "I'll never marry you, Lucas, and you won't settle for anything less."

One hand supported her head while the other caressed her back; his lips traveled from her ear to her neck. Karin felt her harsh resolve melting beneath the warmth of his kisses and she edged away, trying to avoid the pressure of his lips. The back of her knees hit the side of the bed and Lucas pressed forward, forcing her down on the mattress.

Karin's breath was coming so quickly that she couldn't hide her emotional involvement from Lucas. He lifted his head, moved away from her and rested on one elbow; his other hand stroked the side of her cheek and his gaze dropped to study the swift rise of her breasts. Languidly he trailed his hand down to trace light circles around one peak.

"This is much better than talking." He dipped his

head and ran the tip of his tongue lightly over her lips. He took in the sudden intake of her breath and she detected a glimmer of amused arrogance just before he parted her lips with his own.

She wanted to put her hands around his neck and draw him to her, but she closed her eyes and made herself lie perfectly still. Her body seemed as lifeless as a limp rag doll. Her lips denied him the response he seemed so confident of achieving.

He grew still for a moment, then moved away from her. She kept her eyes closed but could feel his unwavering gaze burning through the lids. When he spoke, his warm breath caressed the curve of her ear.

"You know I can put an end to this little charade of yours." He laid his palm against her cheek. "Even now you can't stop the heat waves I feel flaming through your body."

She felt the mattress tilt as he shifted closer, captured her hands and imprisoned them behind her back so her body arched toward his. Her eyes flew open and the complacent grin on his face enraged her more than anything else he had done. She tried to pull away from him, but his hand tightened around hers.

"We both know how your body responds to mine."

Karin turned her head to the side as if she could dispute the truth of his words by removing him from her sight. His hands left hers and moved up to cup her face, turning it back toward him. His thumbs curved under her chin and his index fingers pressed into her temples.

"It's just going to take me some time to overcome the opposition of your fanciful little mind." His tone of voice indicated the assurance he felt. "No matter how much you hate the thought of marrying me, I'm going to keep after you until you have no choice. I was a fool to refuse what you offered at the cottage and I intend to remedy that mistake right now."

His hand moved to her breast, cupping it, stroking it, tantalizing it into an erotic peak of unconcealed desire. He lowered his lips to her cheek, kissed it softly and whispered into her ear, "I accept your terms, but can you really go through with this? As long as we're going to sleep together, wouldn't you rather be my wife?" His flattened palm drew circles on her abdomen and moved steadily downward.

To herself, Karin admitted that what Lucas had said was true. She wouldn't be happy as his mistress—nor would she be happy as his wife. She needed his love, and that belonged to Danielle. One hand was at the belt of her jeans, while the other stroked her inner thigh. She felt her heart begin to race and knew she had to escape before she succumbed to the demands of her body. Rolling away from him, she leaped to her feet, put her hands on her hips and glared down at him. "Fanciful, is it? Tell me that you never promised Tom that someday you would own everything my father had: his land, his home, his daughter."

Lucas stood up slowly and put his hands on her shoulders. His relaxed demeanor made her own anger seem foolishly childish. "I don't intend to discuss that with you. However, I will tell you this: I usually get what I want." He broke off and let his eyes wander slowly down her body. "And I want to marry you. I won't leave you alone until you see things my way." He bent down and kissed her, his hard, demanding lips emphasizing the strength of his determination. "And as for that little discussion we had about your morals the other day, I think this incident confirms what I've always believed. You were meant to be a wife—my wife—and the mother of my children." He smiled smugly. "These little tantrums of yours are only postponing the inevitable. But I'm not opposed to showing you what our married life is going to be like. I'm sure you won't be disappointed."

His hand slipped beneath her waistband, moving casually under her jeans, gently stroking the rounded flesh that was now openly responsive to his touch. He urged her toward him, grasping her hands and placing them on his belt buckle. "Come on, help me out. I'm not at my best with all these clothes between us."

She looked up at him. How could she tell him that more than anything she wanted to be in his arms, naked, with not even a few inches of cooling air separating their heated flesh?

His eyes met hers, melting her with the demanding desire that was blazing deep within them. "Come on, sweetheart; the house is empty, the bed is waiting. This moment is ours. I'll be as gentle as I know how, and once you've felt the joy I can bring you, you'll want to marry me as much as I do you. There are some things in life that can't be changed, that were always meant to be, and our marriage is one of them."

Once again Karin saw Lucas as the arrogant, self-assured businessman who would stop at nothing to get what he wanted, whether it was land or a wife. They were both the same to him: pieces of property, things to be owned, won by any means at his disposal. This was the part of Lucas she hated, the part of Lucas she wanted nothing whatever to do with. She pushed herself out of his arms.

"It's a new year, Lucas. I've got a new home, a new life which doesn't include you. Once I move out of this house, you'll never see me again."

Lucas studied her for a moment. "You don't really believe that, do you?" He reached for her again.

She picked a paperweight off her desk. "Don't come any closer, Lucas, I mean it."

He watched her for a moment. "Surely you know me well enough to understand that I won't be threatened." His voice was tautly controlled. "Put that down or I won't be responsible for my actions."

Karin's fingers tightened around the smooth glass semicircle. She knew she couldn't throw it, knew that no matter what had passed between them she could never do anything to hurt Lucas. She pressed her lips together angrily and slammed the paperweight down on the desk.

"That's better. Don't ever try anything like that again. Unfortunately, your childish little outburst has destroyed the romantic flavor of the afternoon." Turning, he began walking toward the door. "I'll be back to see you when you're in a more receptive mood."

"I'll never be receptive to you!"

Lucas was nearly out the door, but he turned back and grinned complacently. "Care to bet on that?"

Karin reached down and pulled a pillow off the bed. She threw it at his mocking features, but he ducked and kept smiling as he left the room. She could hear him whistling contentedly as he ran down the stairs, and she knew he felt much more confident about his prediction than she did about hers.

Chapter Nine

Jim Simpson helped Karin with the paperwork and the move went smoothly. She had taken some personal furnishings from the house, supplementing them with several items purchased from a neighborhood furniture store. Fortunately the new house was so small that she didn't have to buy very much.

A friend of Dan's drove the BMW back, and since January threatened to be as rainy as December, Paul Andrews decided to stay in Palm Springs. Karin was relieved that her father had accepted their move so easily, because selling Casa del Mar seemed to solve all their immediate financial worries. Most of the money left over from the sale had been reinvested in the smaller house, but at least she no longer had to be concerned about meeting huge mortgage payments. The only problem she had now was finding another job, and since her father knew the truth about their financial situation, it wasn't necessary to deceive him about her need to work.

Even if the antique shop in San Juan Capistrano hadn't been closed, she wouldn't have considered working there because she had meant what she said about never seeing Lucas again. Seeing him only made her ache for what might have been, so she paid no attention when Stephanie called to say that American International intended to continue paying their salaries even though the store had been closed. The last thing she wanted from Lucas McKay was charity, and she had no intention of remaining on his payroll while there was any chance of getting another job.

Most of the other really fine antique shops were in Newport Beach, and because of her experience and knowledge, Karin was hired at the second store she visited.

It was her third week on the new job, and all the other salespeople were busy with customers when Danielle came into the store. The icy chill that enveloped Karin lasted longer than the gust of wind that whipped through the open door, and her eyes darted around the room, searching for a place to hide. It had been over a month since she had seen Danielle at Lucas' Christmas party and she still didn't feel recovered enough to indulge in another sparring match with the beautiful actress. But while she was wondering how she could avoid this confrontation, she saw the owner look at her and nod toward Danielle. Now she had no choice, not if she didn't want to risk losing her job. So, although it was the last thing she wanted to do, she approached the tall brunette. "May I help you?"

Danielle turned away from the crystal vase she was fingering. Her eyebrows lifted and a condescending smile curved her lips. "Well, well, how the mighty have fallen." Her green eyes flicked over Karin disdainfully.

Karin took a deep breath, held it and exhaled slowly. Anger smoldered within her, but she couldn't do anything to release her seething emotions, not when she was supposed to be keeping her customer happy. "Are you interested in anything in particular?" Outwardly she tried to be as cool and businesslike as possible, but inside she was wondering whether she could trip Danielle and claim it was an accident. She frowned and dismissed that course of action. It would never work. She just wasn't the type to get away with anything that devious.

"Odds and ends," Danielle replied, shrugging indifferently. "I've just returned from a skiing trip to Tahoe and I'm staying at Lucas' house. It's beautifully furnished, but it does lack the personal touch a woman likes. . . . Of course, it was different when Lucas was there alone; men don't seem to notice these things."

The icy chill surrounding Karin became the Arctic Ocean, freezing every muscle in her body. So Danielle had moved in with Lucas. She smiled grimly. Her former fiancé had certainly made a rapid recovery from the heartache of their broken engagement, which wasn't very surprising, since Danielle had always seemed very capable of consoling him. Picturing the beautiful house on Linda Isle, Karin found herself wishing that a convenient tidal wave would remove Danielle from the scene. Not a very charitable thought —still, that was how she felt. But why should she care who Lucas was living with? Hadn't she known all along that he really loved Danielle and had proposed to her only to satisfy an egotistical boast he had made years ago? She shuddered as she envisioned how miserable she would be if she were married to Lucas and then found out that Danielle was feathering their little love nest.

Danielle's dulcet tones broke into her gloomy thoughts. "Why don't we just walk through the store? I really have nothing specific in mind, but I'll know what I want when I see it." She turned to Karin and smiled sweetly. "I'm that way about everything. I can always tell when something is right for me, whether it's a piece of furniture, a dress"—her smile broadened—"or a man. There's just that certain something when it's right. We seem to reach out to each other, then nothing and *no one* can tear us apart." Her cold eyes dared Karin to challenge her statement.

She paused for a moment, and when Karin didn't reply, she continued, "You were smart to get out when you did. The marriage never would have worked, you know. You're much too simple to keep the interest of a man like Lucas and I've been around enough to know that there's nothing more pitiful than a neglected wife."

Karin felt the blood drain from her face, leaving her skin with the chill of lifeless marble. She was only too aware of the hostility behind Danielle's supposedly consoling remark. Perhaps Danielle expected her to react with anger. Perhaps she would have, only a short while ago, but as of now, her anguish was so overwhelming that she couldn't say anything. She didn't want to fight with Danielle; she just wanted to curl up in some corner and cry.

But she wasn't about to let Danielle know how she felt; self-pity was just one more luxury she could no longer afford, so she clenched her fists and dug them into her thighs, rubbing them against the soft gray wool of her skirt. Danielle was watching, waiting for her reaction, and Karin was determined to deny her any satisfaction. Taking a deep breath, she compressed her lips and decided on a course of action.

"I'm glad you agree with my decision, but I'm sure you didn't come here to talk about my personal life—especially something that's such an unimportant part of my past." She ran her tongue over her lower lip. "Now, then, let's discuss those antiques you wanted to buy." Her voice sounded hollow, as if she were speaking into an echo chamber. Praying that her depression wasn't apparent to Danielle, she forced herself to continue. "I suppose you're most interested in seeing accessories, those little things that express a person's individuality and make a house a home."

"Exactly. Lucas wants me to be as comfortable as possible." Danielle smiled. "He's such a thoughtful man."

I'm definitely going to strangle her, Karin thought as she pasted on her salesgirl's smile and glanced around the store. Apparently Danielle wasn't content with the incision she had made in Karin's heart; she was determined to keep twisting the scalpel until the pain had destroyed her completely. She searched for a suitable means of retaliation and silently snapped her fingers as she thought of one. "I think we have precisely what you're looking for. Follow me." Enough is enough, she thought. Even employees have some rights. And I'm not doing anything wrong, am I? I'm only trying to make a sale.

She led Danielle to the back wall where two old Greek-style theatrical masks were displayed. The comedy mask was painted white and the tragedy mask black, but the features on both were carved in such a monstrous manner that they could only be described as grotesque—evil.

"Don't you think these are just the thing to make you feel at home? I mean, you being in the theater and all." Karin unclenched her fists and the relaxing warmth of mischievous delight spread through her body. She smiled sweetly.

She heard the swift intake of Danielle's breath, but that was the only indication that the other woman had been affected by Karin's little ploy. Whatever else Karin might think about Danielle, she had to credit her with being a superb actress.

Danielle glanced at the masks and then at Karin. "These aren't at all what I had in mind. When I'm with Lucas I never have time to think about the theater. He keeps me *much* too busy." Her lips parted in a feline smile. "I'm looking for something delicate, soft, romantic . . . in keeping with the way Lucas and I feel when we're together." Her long black lashes lowered and her gaze drifted disdainfully over Karin. "It's obvious you just don't understand. I'll have to look elsewhere." She turned and left the store.

Karin watched her walk down the street and open the

door to a brown Corniche. Lucas' car, the one he had driven to Palm Springs. No wonder Danielle said he was thoughtful. Ski trips, houses, cars, shopping sprees —he couldn't do enough for the woman he loved. The beautiful actress would have a different opinion about Lucas if he had been as cruel to her as he had been to Karin. But had he really been cruel? She thought about the way he had been so careful of her father's health on their trip to Palm Springs and how gentle his hands could be, how sweet his lips. She caught her breath as the vivid memories sent a yearning warmth rushing through her body. Then she remembered Tom's words and the languor slipped away as quickly as it had come. She meant nothing to Lucas, nothing at all, and he wasn't being thoughtful, he was being devious. He was using kindness to lull her into helping him achieve his goal.

The appearance of another customer brought Karin's reflections to an end, but throughout the day, whenever she had a moment to herself, she found herself visualizing Lucas and Danielle together and that same painful cord began knotting around her heart.

Somehow she got through the day and had just opened the door to the condominium when the telephone began to ring. It was Jim Simpson. "I've just closed a big sale. How about joining me for dinner to help me celebrate?"

Karin hesitated for only a moment. She really felt like getting out of the house and the last thing she wanted to do was spend her evening alone, brooding about Lucas and Danielle. "I'd love to."

"Great. Will an hour give you enough time? I've got some paperwork to clear up."

"I'll be ready when you get here."

The Capistrano Depot was a restaurant operating out of the old Capistrano train station, and silvery new passenger trains still picked up and discharged passengers on the platform beside the tracks. But the old enclosed station had been carefully restored to retain the flavor of the past while keeping pace with the present in its country western music and well-prepared food.

Karin walked beside Jim, pausing every so often to admire a touch of nostalgia: an old scale, the shoeshine stand, posters advertising products that could no longer be purchased, large fans revolving lazily above etched-glass chandeliers. They weren't expensive like the antiques with which she worked, but they, too, were a link with the past, a link that could never be reforged if things like this were destroyed.

The hostess showed them to a table which overlooked the track and Karin smiled when she saw the menu. All the dinners were listed in railroad terms. She ordered the Orange Blossom Special—filet of Dover sole—and Jim ordered the Great Northern's Empire Builder—roast prime rib.

After the waitress had served them with garlic bread and fried zucchini to accompany their Chablis, Jim began to speak. "I'm glad you were able to find another job so easily. You know, the entire arcade where you used to work is being remodeled, including my office."

Karin glanced at the blackboard listing the train schedules to Los Angeles and San Diego and nodded. Stephanie had told her about the remodeling. American International continued to pay Stephanie's salary and they apparently wanted her to work in the shopping complex once construction was finished. Karin shook her head. There was no fighting progress or people like Lucas McKay. She and her father had been forced into a condominium and the quaint gallery of shops would soon be replaced by a huge concrete monolith. She was thankful for small favors, like this restaurant, and the mission itself. Even Lucas McKay couldn't destroy the heritage and traditions of the mission.

"It's still early," Jim said as he signed the check. "But I don't think we can stay at the table any longer. There's probably a crowd waiting to be seated; the waitress keeps glancing in our direction. Why don't we sit in the lounge for a while?"

They found a small round table in the corner, not too close to the combo that was playing near the door. Jim ordered two Irish coffees and Karin excused herself to go to the ladies' room. When she returned, the drinks were on the table but Jim was gone. She sat down and let her gaze drift slowly over the room, trying to find Jim, but the people standing around the bandstand and swarming around the bar made that almost impossible. She had just about given up any hope of finding him when a darkly attractive man edged his way toward her table. Karin closed her eyes; her imagination had to be playing tricks. It just couldn't be—but it was.

"He's out in the reception area," Lucas said, placing his drink on the table and taking the seat opposite Karin. "He saw someone walking by and apparently wanted to chat with him. But don't worry, I'll keep you company."

"Don't bother. I'll be fine until Jim gets back and I wouldn't want to take you away from your friends."

"My *friend* hasn't arrived yet, so I'm just as lonely as you are."

"I'm not lonely."

"Nonsense, no woman likes to sit by herself in a bar."

"This isn't a bar, it's a cocktail lounge, and I'm selective enough to prefer solitude to just anyone's company."

Lucas sipped his drink and leaned across the table. "But I'm not just anyone. We were engaged to be married—remember? I hope you're not getting serious about Simpson. Nothing can come of it, you know. You belong to me, even if you're too upset to accept that right now." His deep voice caressed her ears and the flickering candle cloaked them in an atmosphere of intimacy.

Momentarily Karin felt that everything in the room had been blacked out except the two of them. Small, irrepressible trembles vibrated through her body and she hunched her shoulders, gripping her upper arms with her hands. "I don't belong to you; I don't belong to anyone. Jim is only a friend; our fathers have known each other for years."

"Good, because nothing has really changed between us."

"Oh, yes, it has. We have absolutely nothing in common. We haven't even seen each other since New Year's."

"You've been keeping track of the time. That has to mean something."

"It means that whatever was between us, if there ever was anything at all, is finished." She fingered the rim of her glass. "If I've kept track of time, it's only because of what I told you: a new year, a new life."

"Without me?"

Too choked to speak, she nodded.

"That can't be. We've gone too far for that. I know you were upset. That's why I've stayed away—given you time to think things over, to realize how much you've missed me." His voice was softly seductive yet firm with certainty. "You have missed me, haven't you?"

His eyes moved over her face and she felt that he was probing the depths of her mind, finding that she had indeed missed him, that, hard as she tried, she couldn't stop thinking about him. Her tremors turned into one huge shiver that she couldn't control.

"Cold?" Lucas shifted his chair, moving it next to

hers. His arm reached out and curved over her shoulder, drawing her closer to him. "Now, aren't you glad I'm here? Wouldn't want you catching the flu."

Karin turned her shoulders, trying to twist away from him. "I feel fine." At least, I would if you'd only leave me alone, she thought. She hated the way he continued to flirt with her, disregarding her words, acting as if she hadn't told him that she never wanted to see him again.

Lucas smiled and pressed her closer to him. "Good, I do too." His head dipped and she felt his lips moving over her hair.

"Stop that!" Every nerve in her body was exposed, eager to respond to his erotic teasing.

"I thought you said it felt good." Lucas lifted his head slightly, his voice mocking her.

"I said *I* felt fine."

"How true." He lowered his head once more and she felt his lips nuzzling the nape of her neck. "So Jim is only a friend, a member of an acceptable social class." His soft voice was threaded with the invisible strength of steel. "Unfortunately I own the building where he has his office and he's dependent on me for mortgage money—no realtor in this area can afford to antagonize American International. So if he really is your friend, stay away from him. I'd hate to destroy him, but I will if he comes between us. Nothing can come between us—ever." She could feel the piercing power of his gaze burning into her flesh as he repeated his resolute declaration.

Karin sat as stiffly as she could, but it didn't seem to matter to Lucas. "Why won't you leave me alone?" Her voice was more of a plea than a demand.

"You know why."

"I'm not going to marry you."

"Then I'll have to do some more convincing." He lifted her hair and began kissing the curve of her ear. "I told you, I'll never give up."

Karin blushed. "Stop it. Everyone is looking at us."

"Say you'll marry me."

"No!"

"Then I can't stop. And don't worry about anyone looking at us; this room is so dark that we can barely see each other, although I wouldn't mind moving to a more private place if you're going to take heavy convincing. Some of my most persuasive arguments are best done without an audience, no matter how inattentive they might be." He began moving his arm, letting his fingers curve lightly over her breast.

His grasp was so strong that Karin found it impossible to release herself. But she knew herself well enough to realize that she couldn't affect an attitude of indifference for much longer. Her response was automatic. She lifted her foot and drove her heel into the soft leather of his shoe. She heard his swift intake of breath as he released her and lowered his hand to rub his throbbing foot, but he gave no other indication of the pain she knew she had caused, and once again Karin marveled at the taut control he held over his emotions. She stood quickly and moved her chair to the opposite side of the table. He looked across at her and she met his gaze with a belligerent stare of her own.

"That wasn't very nice. But don't worry, you'll pay for what you've done—and I'm going to enjoy collecting."

"Remember, all's fair in—" Her voice stopped abruptly.

"Love and war," he finished. "Now, if we could only be sure which game we're playing at." His lips lifted in a quizzical smile.

"McKay, good to see you." Jim stood between them, offering his hand to Lucas. His voice was almost drowned out by the sound of the whistle from an arriving train. "I heard you were in Tahoe."

Karin felt as if she had been punched in the stomach. How could he? What a consummate actor he was, playing the loving suitor with her tonight when he had just returned from a tryst with Danielle. She felt totally defeated, so shaken that she couldn't decide whether she wanted to cry or to scratch his eyes out for making her feel this way.

"We're planning some condos; I just got back." He stood and grasped Jim's outstretched hand. "And was fortunate enough to run into Karin. We don't see nearly enough of each other lately."

Jim shook his head. "I saw a client, and I was talking to him longer than I expected. I feel bad about leaving Karin alone for so long." He looked at Lucas. "But I guess she wasn't alone, after all. Thanks for helping me out." He smiled down at Karin. "I hope you'll forgive me, but business comes first. . . ." He glanced back at Lucas. "You know how it is."

"Umm . . ." Lucas shook his head thoughtfully. "It takes a very special woman to make a man forget about business, but sometimes it happens and he'd have to be a fool to ever let her go." His gaze moved slowly over Karin's face. "And now, if you'll excuse me, I think my guest has arrived." He nodded to them and wove his way through the crowd.

Karin's eyes followed his retreating figure and saw Danielle standing at the end of the bar. At least four men were moving in her direction when Lucas came up, gripped her elbow possessively and led her out of the room. Seeing them together made Karin feel lonelier than she had all evening.

"I guess our coffee is cold," Jim said. "I'll order another round." He began looking around the room for their waitress.

"Please don't. I'd like to leave."

"You're angry with me." Jim looked at her dolefully.

"I guess I deserve that; I've behaved like a heel. Lucas was right; you are special enough to put ahead of business. What can I say to make you forgive me?"

"Lucas wasn't talking about me," Karin said. "And I understand what happened; there's nothing to forgive. I would have felt terrible if you had lost a sale because of me."

Jim flashed a broad smile. "You're wonderful, Karin. Just the sort of wife to help a man move up in his profession."

Yes, Karin thought wryly as she stood away from the table. I'm everyone's idea of the perfect wife. But just once I'd like to be described as the kind of woman who could make a man forget about everything else—a woman like Danielle. The minute Lucas saw her he had lost all interest in Karin. Danielle was right; no matter who Lucas married, he would always be in love with her. Lucas himself had just admitted that he'd never let her go. She was his special woman, and no one, least of all Karin, would ever come between them. The realization pressed against Karin's heart like a heavy lead weight.

Jim took her home and asked to see her on Saturday night, but she told him that she would be visiting her father for the weekend, so he said he would phone her when she got back.

Palm Springs was basking in sunshine and Karin found the dry warmth a welcome change from the gray dampness of San Juan. That was one of the marvelous things about living in California, she thought; its unique topography provided a diversity of climates, each with its own exciting choice of activities. While some people were sunning and swimming in the desert, others were skiing in the mountains, just a short distance away.

The warm dry air seemed to be just the medicine her father had needed, and he walked toward her with the same firm assurance he had had before getting sick. He reached for her overnight case, but she held it back.

"You're not supposed to lift things."

The broad smile with which he had greeted her left his face. His voice was somber. "I had a heart attack, but I've recovered, and I intend to live as normally as possible from now on. Don't pamper me."

Karin smiled, but still held on to her case. "I'm not pampering you. It's just silly for you to carry this when I'm perfectly capable of doing it myself. Women shouldn't be pampered, either."

Her father laughed. "You're just like your mother. I never could win an argument with her. Come out to the pool as soon as you've had a chance to freshen up."

The pool was too inviting to resist, and Karin lost no time in slipping into her bikini and joining her father outside. He was sitting at a large glass table covered with blueprints.

Karin looked over his shoulder. "Where's Dan?"

"In town. He had to attend to some business."

She bent down and fingered the papers. "What's this?"

"Plans for a new retirement community."

"You're working on mass-produced houses? I don't believe it!"

"Why not? I'm old enough to admit when I've made a mistake. This type of housing is here to stay whether I like it or not, so I might as well do my part to make it as aesthetically appealing as possible. There's a definite need for these units. Our own situation has shown me that all too clearly. Not everyone can afford to live in a mansion." He smiled at Karin. "Besides, it's time I got back to work."

"You've taken a job? You're being paid?"

"Of course. We need the money."

Karin nodded. "Are you sure you feel up to it?"

"Absolutely! Remember, Dr. Stevens said I was

almost completely recovered, certainly enough to draw a few lines on paper. Now, stop worrying and enjoy the beautiful weather."

Karin had just come out of the pool and was dozing in the warmth of the sun when the sound of voices made her lift her head. Instantly she put it down again and closed her eyes. Tom McKay was standing at the table speaking to her father. Well, it was Dan's house, and she had no right to tell him who he could have as a guest, but she certainly didn't have to welcome Lucas' brother. The less she had to do with anyone in the McKay family, the better she would feel.

The voices stopped and she heard footsteps moving away. Tom had apparently left. Someone was walking toward her—her father, she assumed—but when she looked up, she saw Tom. She sat up, swung her feet to the floor and began searching for her beach thongs.

"Wait. Don't go. I have to talk to you."

"Look, Tom, I don't want to be rude, but we really have nothing to say to each other."

"I can see where you might feel that you have nothing to say to me, but at least give me a chance to explain things to you."

"There's really no need. I understand everything perfectly."

"I don't think you do. I had no business saying what I did. It was just too much Christmas cheer."

"Don't blame yourself. It was better to learn the truth now, before I married Lucas."

"Then you would have married him?"

Karin shrugged.

"So I really did ruin things."

"On the contrary, you prevented a disastrous marriage from taking place."

"Why disastrous? You must feel something for Lucas if you were willing to marry him."

"Your brother is a very attractive man."

"Then you love him."

Karin ran her fingers through her damp hair. "He doesn't love me—that's the real problem."

"How can you be so sure? Because of what I blurted out, something that happened seven years ago?"

"That, and what's happening right now. Danielle is staying in Newport Beach . . . in Lucas' house." She shook her head as her eyes met Tom's. "I could never marry a man who loved another woman." She bit at her lower lip to prevent her emotions from breaking through her heavy shield of self-control. "Now, if you'll excuse me, I have to change." She snatched her towel from the lounger and ran toward the sliding glass door. As she crossed the entryway, heading for her bedroom, the front door opened and she almost collided with Dan.

"Whoa! What's the rush?" He caught her upper arms to stop her from falling against him.

"I wanted to get out of this suit."

Dan looked over her shoulder and saw Tom talking to her father, who was back at poolside. "I see." His mouth was fleetingly grim, then he smiled. "Well, I'm glad we ran into each other. I wanted to speak with you anyway. I met one of my neighbors in town and he reminded me that there's a Valentine's Day dance at the country club tonight. I just wouldn't feel right keeping you away. Will you do me the honor?"

Karin thought for a moment. The last thing she wanted to do was go dancing. But Dan had been so considerate that she couldn't refuse his invitation. "I'd be delighted." She smiled with a brightness she didn't feel.

Her knee-length, slate-blue jersey dress wasn't what she would have worn if she had been free to choose from her entire wardrobe. But it was the dressiest outfit she had brought to Palm Springs—suitable for dinner at Dan's, but hardly elegant enough for the country-club dance.

She tugged nervously at her long, fitted sleeves as she sat between Dan and her father, watching the expensively gowned women enter the ballroom. There were two other couples at their table, contemporaries of Dan, and the older women did their best to include Karin in the conversation.

After a while she began to feel quite at ease, and by the time they were enjoying their baked Alaska she felt perfectly comfortable in her casual clothing. Spooning up some ice cream, she watched the dancers sway to the languid beat of a slow foxtrot and her contentment dissolved more rapidly than the dessert on her plate.

Danielle, looking absolutely gorgeous in a strapless red sequined sheath, was circling the floor in Lucas' arms. Her hands were clasped behind his neck and Karin doubted if a paper clip could fit between their bodies. Danielle freed one hand and stroked it along the firm line of Lucas' jaw. He smiled down at her; he looked superbly masculine in an expensively tailored white dinner jacket that highlighted his dark tan. And Karin swallowed hard, the flavor of her dessert buried beneath her pain.

Dan and her father, talking with other other, hadn't noticed Lucas, and Karin didn't want them to see how upset she was. Smiling brightly, she excused herself and walked quickly to the ladies' room. How could she have been so stupid? Why had she come? She should have realized that Lucas would be here, flaunting his love for Danielle. Didn't she remember hearing about Tahoe? Hadn't she seen them together at the Depot? Weren't they sharing a house? Blindly she reached for a tissue and dabbed at her eyes.

"Something bothering you?"

198

Karin turned and saw Danielle leaning against the open door, staring down at her.

"Or perhaps it's some*one?*" Danielle settled herself on the bench next to Karin.

"I have something in my eye," Karin said.

"I don't doubt that," Danielle sneered. "Probably a first-row view of Lucas and me."

"Oh, is Lucas here?" Karin asked, taking a deep breath and trying to regain her composure.

Danielle threw her head back and laughed. "Don't ever try for an acting career—you'll never make it." Sliding her red-tipped fingers behind her neck, she flipped her hair over her bare shoulders. "I saw you watching us. You turned practically green with envy."

"I assure you, that's not what happened."

"And I guarantee that it's *exactly* what happened." Danielle grinned confidently.

Karin turned to Danielle haughtily. The actress's disdainful attitude had dissipated her misery and replaced it with anger. "I really don't care what you think."

"Well, that's just too bad, because I'm only trying to stop you from making a complete fool of yourself."

"How thoughtful of you, but please don't trouble yourself. I'm a big girl—I don't need your help."

"Oh, but you do. That's what I've been trying to tell you. Lucas doesn't love you—he never will." A small wicked smile curled her crimson lips. "I explained the situation to you earlier, but you wouldn't listen. Lucas is mine, and despite any temporary interest he may have in you, he'll never be satisfied with a candy-coated debutante. He needs a real woman. He needs me."

"Then it's wonderful that you've found each other."

"Don't play games with me. I know all about your financial situation. You need money, and Lucas has it. His good looks aren't a turnoff, either." She lit a cigarette and blew the smoke in Karin's face. "Well, keep your hands off him—he's mine. In fact, he's flying back to New York with me. I'm considering a new play."

"I have no interest in Lucas." Karin shrugged scornfully. "You saw me return his ring."

"Yes, I saw that little showstopper. But I've also been paying attention to the follow-up scenes. I saw you making a play for him at the Depot. And don't think I don't know why you're here. You realized your mistake, didn't you? Pride doesn't pay the rent or warm your bed. Now you want Lucas back. He's told me all about it, and we've been having a good laugh at your expense. I could let it continue, but I feel sorry for you. After all, we're both women."

Karin stood and glared at Danielle. "You know, I've never been ashamed of my sex before, but the thought of having even that much in common with you nauseates me." She slammed out of the room.

Lucas was leaning on the back of her empty chair, chatting with her father, when she returned to the ballroom. She stopped walking and looked behind her, searching for a retreat. But the sight of Danielle's advancing figure made her continue on to the table.

"Hello, Karin." Lucas' eyes met hers and she couldn't still her wildly beating heart.

"Lucas." She nodded without smiling, breaking eye contact.

Her father shifted in his seat, turning his attention to Dan, and Lucas reached for Karin's hand.

"I have to talk to you." His eyes flickered to the open French doors.

"About what? Is friendship on the agenda? Or is that topic still taboo?" She glanced over his shoulder just as Danielle came up behind him.

A small muscle twitched at the side of his jaw as he stiffened away from her. "My friends are my own business. I refuse to have them screened, either by you or by your butler." He turned and put his arm around Danielle's waist.

"Hello, darling." Danielle stood on tiptoe and kissed the corner of his mouth. "Did you miss me?"

Lucas smiled enigmatically. "How could I not?" His eyes moved slowly over Danielle, then switched to Karin. He was considering, evaluating, judging, and Karin knew that she would never win the blue ribbon in this contest. She couldn't match Danielle's sophisticated beauty even if she were wearing the most elegant gown in her wardrobe, but in her simple dress she felt like a grubby little teenager. She half-expected Lucas to reach into his pocket and offer her ice-cream money. But he didn't. Instead, he grinned confidently and said a general good-bye to everyone at the table; Karin's own farewell was limited to an impersonal nod. She returned it, sat down and somehow managed to get through the rest of the evening.

Her meeting with Lucas had ruined the entire weekend. It was futile to pretend that his relationship with Danielle didn't bother her. Relationship . . . "friendship," he called it, and had once again made it clear that the subject was not one which he cared to discuss.

His attitude was just further proof that his interest in Karin was based on who she was and not on any great love he felt for her. Well, if she had ever needed a reminder of her status in life, something to restore her sagging self-esteem, the time was now. Never before had her morale reached the depths it was wallowing in today. She loved Lucas and needed him, but her pride wouldn't let her accept him on his terms. Not now—not ever. She closed her eyes as she remembered what Danielle had said, that Lucas had talked about her, laughed about her. The thought was so painful that she bit her lower lip, hoping that the physical sting would ease her mental anguish, but nothing helped. The heartache of her one-sided love for Lucas was an affliction she would have to bear for the rest of her life.

Anxious to avoid her father's questions, she departed Palm Springs early Sunday morning without ever discussing the details of his new job. As she left the desert and drove toward the coast, heavy sheets of rain flooded her windshield, making the outer atmosphere as dismal as the state of her heart.

Chapter Ten

Lucas kept his distance, and two weeks later, with the advent of March, the skies cleared. The rain stopped and the sun warmed away the cold dampness that had seemed to pervade the entire atmosphere. The weather might have improved, but Karin's spirits had not, and she accepted eagerly when Jim called to invite her on a whale-watching cruise to Catalina Island.

Whale watching was a popular pastime along the Southern California coast all through the winter and spring months. At the start of winter the gray whales left their Bering Sea homes in Alaska and traveled five thousand miles to the warm lagoons of Baja California, where they had their breeding grounds.

In the past, Karin had always watched the southern migration from Dana Point Harbor, but because of her personal problems she had missed it this year. Now she would be able to see the forty-foot mammals returning to Alaska with their newborn calves.

They left early Saturday morning on a boat Jim and several friends had chartered for the occasion. The mood was festive, and Karin enjoyed the company of the other women as they puttered around the ship's galley, preparing coffee and sandwiches. Jim called her and she ran up on deck in time to see a pod of whales spouting and propelling their massive bodies out of the water. For a short time the sight of all that new life made her forget her troubles with Lucas.

Although it was too early in the year for most people to visit Catalina, the sudden break in the weather and the chance to see the whales had brought out so many boating enthusiasts that it looked as if an armada was invading the small island. Karin thought that the local residents must view this influx of tourists with the same apprehension that had assailed the natives when the first Spanish galleons approached Avalon in 1542. Although she was sure they welcomed the tourist dollar, she knew they were deeply committed to preserving their privacy and the rural flavor of the island. She understood their desire to retain the relaxed environment of their island home and supported their efforts to maintain its beauty for generations yet unborn.

They docked at Cabrillo Harbor, rented bicycles and followed the narrow, bumpy route down to Pebbly Beach, then stopped and admired the shadowy beauty of the undersea gardens before having a picnic lunch in the sandy cove.

Karen crumpled up her sandwich wrapper and looked up at the cloudless blue sky. "It's so beautiful here; I could stay forever. I hate the thought of going back."

Jim put his hands over her shoulders and let his fingers drift beneath her hair. "Do you really mean that? About staying over?"

His fingers felt clammy against her skin and she stood up, brushing them away. "Of course I mean it. I love Catalina, and one day, when the weather's warmer and Dad's really feeling better, I intend to take him here for a nice leisurely vacation."

"Well, it's only Saturday. My partner's covering for me for the weekend. We *could* stay over till tomorrow."

"Don't be silly. We came with the others; we'll have to go back with them." Karin was enjoying the day with

Jim, but she had no plans for stretching it into an all-night affair.

"So you'll go along with whatever the others want?"

"Jim, I don't know why you're doing this. It seems like a pointless discussion."

"It's not pointless at all, Karen. I like you a lot. I think we should get to know each other better—spend some more time together."

"Fine; I'm not busy tomorrow night. Maybe you'd like to come for dinner."

"Breakfast sounds better." He put his hands on her waist and turned her toward him.

"No way," Karin said, moving back from him. "After all this invigorating fresh air I intend to sleep deliciously late. I probably won't even get out of bed until noon."

"That's exactly how I feel. Maybe we could relax together." His eyes moved suggestively down her body. "Then we'd get to know each other much better than we could across any dinner table."

Karin felt a chill marching slowly up her spine. "Stop talking like that, Jim. I know you're only fooling, but you're making me nervous." Tossing her sandwich wrapper into the trash bin, she headed toward her bike.

After lunch, they pedaled to Avalon and walked through the town, wandering in and out of the small shops which dotted the waterfront area. The stores stocked a variety of items, catering mostly to the tourist trade. Karin and Jim walked through the different shops, and in one of the boutiques Jim found a sheer black nightgown and held it up to Karin. "What do you think?"

Karin glanced at it quickly and looked away. It reminded her of something from a men's fantasy magazine. "There's not very much to it," she said wryly. "Were you thinking of it as a gift for your mother?"

"No." Jim pulled the gown off the hanger and held it

up against her. "I'd much rather see it on you." He pressed the gown closer to her body and lowered his eyes appreciatively.

Karin pushed the gown away from her. "I can take a joke as well as anybody, Jim, but I think you're carrying things a bit too far. If you'd really like to buy me a present, here's something I'd much rather have." She picked up a pink and white seashell, handed it to him and left the store.

Jim's behavior was really beginning to bother her. She thought of him as a friend, nothing more, but he was starting to make overtures that had definite sexual implications and went beyond mere joking. She sighed deeply and hoped she was mistaken. The thought of being stranded on Catalina with this new Jim was beginning to take all the joy out of an otherwise pleasant day.

Jim came strolling out of the store and found her leaning against the railing. He handed her a small paper bag. "Hold on to it. You never know when it might come in handy."

From the feeling of the package, Karin was sure that it contained more than the curlicued conch, but she wasn't about to get involved in any detailed discussions. Once she got home she could quietly dispose of the gown. There was no sense in creating a scene now.

"Come on," Jim said, motioning toward the others. "No tour is complete without exploring the casino. It must really have been something during the big-band era." He took her hand and they walked down the street.

Karin held the bag in her free hand and had to resist a strong desire to deposit it in each trash bin they passed. By the time they had finished touring the casino, where some of the nation's biggest bands still entertained on special occasions, it was late in the afternoon.

"Hadn't we better be starting back?" Karin asked Jim.

Jim cleared his throat and hesitated.

"Is something wrong?"

"A bit of a problem." His face turned red and he looked away. "Remember you said you'd do whatever the others wanted?" He shrugged innocently. "Well, they want to stay over."

The small hairs at the back of her neck quivered to attention, but she tried to remain calm. How stupid could she be? After all, hadn't Jim been hinting about this all day? Why should his announcement come as some great surprise? A disappointment, perhaps, but not a surprise. She should have been prepared. She searched her mind for a solution. "We can take a plane back."

He shook his head. "Afraid not. They're all booked up."

"We'd be staying on the boat? Is there enough room?" Her mind began flashing danger signals. There was no point in hiding her anger.

"We'll have all the privacy we need."

"I'm not worried about privacy—and we're both too old to be going through this out-of-gas routine." Why you, Jim? she thought sadly. Why you? Why did you have to ruin a beautiful day? "I thought you were my friend." She felt miserable enough to cry.

Jim shrugged. "Some things never go out of style, and I've told you that I want to be more than just a friend. I like you too much to let our relationship continue on this platonic level. Besides, we have no choice. I've been trying to tell you about staying over all day, but you can't seem to get the message. Quiet dinners and daylight picnics aren't enough for me anymore. I have much more exciting plans for the evening. I'm sorry if you don't feel the same way, and I'd like to try to change your mind. You can sit up all night if you want, but there's no way you can leave until morning."

"I'd rather check that out for myself. After today, I don't trust anything you say." She turned away from him and began walking down the main street of Avalon. This was just what she needed. Jim, whom she had thought of as her friend, a man she could trust, was turning into a lech. So much for her father's theories about breeding. She wondered what he'd say about his friend's son now.

"Look, it's getting dark. You can't go wandering through town alone." Jim was following her closely. His voice was solicitous, almost pleading.

Karin stopped in the middle of the street and glared at him. "Why? Because it might be dangerous?" She was too tired to play games with him, any kind of games. "Don't tell me you're concerned about my welfare—my reputation?"

"He might not be, but I am." Lucas' deep, authoritative voice came from a small round table just beyond the white picket fence of a sidewalk café.

Karin stared at him in disbelief. "What are you doing here?" She was sure she was seeing things; she had thought about Lucas so much that her fantasies must be mingling with reality.

"That doesn't really matter, does it? Just be grateful that I am." He stood up and reached over to open the little gate that separated the tables from the sidewalk.

He's real, Karin thought. Even my fantasies can't dominate a scene like Lucas can. A small part of her heart felt more secure and began to smile.

"Karin's with me. We don't need your help," Jim said.

"That's not your decision to make. It seems to me that she's looking for a way to get home. My yacht is moored in Avalon Harbor, and I'll be leaving for Newport in a short while."

"I'll take care of Karin," Jim said, draping his arm around Karin's shoulder.

"I'm not staying with you," Karin said, dipping her shoulder and moving away from him. She looked at Lucas. He was so ruggedly handsome in his blue and white jersey and white duck trousers that for a minute her mind went blank and all she could think of was how much she loved him. Then she glanced at Jim and forced herself back to the ugly reality of her predicament. Jim had made his intentions for the evening perfectly clear, and just thinking about them had a nauseating effect. She couldn't stay with him; she just couldn't. She looked back at Lucas, remembering how vehemently she had lied to him, declaring her undying hatred for him. It was only last week that she had decided not to have anything further to do with him; yet, despite everything that had happened between them, she felt she could trust him, and right now she had no such faith in Jim's behavior. Without saying anything, she walked through the gate Lucas was holding open.

"Are you sure you know what you're doing?" Jim's voice was petulantly angry, almost like a small boy who had lost some childish contest.

Karin nodded and sat down, placing her package on the table. She didn't even want to look at Jim, let alone speak to him. She hated him even more for making her dependent on Lucas once again, but under the circumstances, she felt she had no choice. She heard him muttering angrily as he strode off.

"Thank you," she said to Lucas.

"Don't mention it. But I do think you should stop going out with Jim. . . . He doesn't appreciate you as much as I do." He signaled the waitress and she brought Karin some coffee and refilled Lucas' cup. He reached for the paper sack and began opening it. After placing the conch on the table between them, he drew out the sheer black negligee and draped it between his fingers. "Hmm, I can see why Simpson was so disappointed. He had the evening well planned—costumes and all."

Karin blushed and looked away. "I can't believe it; it's so childish. Did he really think I would spend the night with him? I would have slept on the beach."

"It's illegal—unless you have a camping permit. But you don't have that problem. I'm going to take you home—and you know my motives are strictly honorable."

Karin lifted her eyebrows and looked at him.

"Will you settle for respectable? I still want to marry you."

"For all the wrong reasons."

"You can't be sure of that. You never suspected my reasons until you listened to Tom."

Karin didn't answer. There was no point in telling him that Tom's statement had only supported her own conclusions. She didn't want to get involved in a long discussion about Danielle. Right now, all she wanted was to get home. "I appreciate your help, Lucas, but that doesn't change our relationship."

"Which is?" Gentle amusement played around his lips as he waited for her answer.

"Most unusual." Karin couldn't help but smile back at him. "We can't seem to get along, but I always need your help."

"If you marry me, I'll be around all the time."

"Will you?" Karin continued the question silently. Or will you spend most of your free time with Danielle while I stay at Casa del Mar playing the role you cast me in seven years ago?

"Why shouldn't I?" Lucas watched her quizzically.

"You have other commitments," Karin said, thinking of Danielle. "You're much too busy to devote all your time to me."

"Marry me and see," Lucas answered.

Karin shook her head. The whole discussion was pointless. Lucas would never admit the truth: that his friendship with Danielle would always be more important than his marriage to her. She pushed her chair back and stood up. "I'd really like to go."

"Your wish is my command." He glanced at the check and tossed some bills on the table. Then he took Karin's arm and led her into the street, where he tossed the negligee into a trash bin. "You don't mind, do you? I'd never want you hiding your beauty beneath anything so tawdry."

"I hate it," Karin said. "Throw it away, cut it up, burn it; I don't care what you do with it so long as I never have to see it again." She shuddered at the remembrance of how cheap Jim had made her feel and she was even more embarrassed that Lucas had found out about the entire episode.

"Okay," he said. "Don't get so excited. Calm down and forget about it. Let's pretend it never happened. Talk to me about something harmless, like the weather."

Karin was as eager as he to change the subject, but the weather wasn't on her mind. "What are you doing on Catalina?" she asked.

"I just had my boat repaired and I wanted to take her out for a trial run."

"And you just happened to run into me? A mere coincidence, it hardly seems plausible."

"Maybe I knew you'd be here? Maybe I was looking for you?"

"Who told you where I was?"

Lucas shrugged. "Does it matter?"

"It might."

"Why don't you think of it as kismet—that we were always meant to be together?"

"Always?" Karin sneered. "Where's Danielle?"

"Why are you so interested in Danielle? I told you, she's only a friend."

Friend meaning lover, Karin thought. "I don't know," she said. "I guess your *friend* fascinates me."

"Well, you're going to have to be fascinated from afar. Danielle's in New York. She never stays here very long; her work is centered around Broadway."

And her lover is out here, Karin thought. How nice for you both that air travel makes things so convenient. But she didn't tell Lucas about the conversations she had had with his mistress at both the antique shop and the country club.

"You didn't spend much time in Palm Springs; you left right after the dance."

"I only wanted to see my father." She wondered if Lucas had tried to see her, then dismissed the thought. He'd have had no time for her, not with Danielle snuggling in his arms. His voice interrupted her conjecture.

"He looks well, doesn't he?"

"I think so, but I hardly see where it's any concern of yours."

Lucas grinned. "Didn't he tell you? He's working on a project for me." He bent down and whispered into her ear in a conspiratorial manner. "I spoke to him yesterday and he mentioned you were going to be here today—something about whale watching. That gave me a definite destination for my trial run. I hoped I might run into you. Just think of it as Karin watching, a most rewarding activity and something that definitely needs doing. I plan on making it a full-time job."

Karin ignored his teasing and concentrated on his statement about her father. "I don't believe it; you can't be serious. My father would never have anything more to do with you."

"Why not? Your father and I are both intelligent men. He needs a job and I can use his talent. Why shouldn't we get together?" She felt his warm breath turn into the lightest nibble of a kiss. "He and I in business, you and I in . . ." He didn't bother finishing his sentence; instead, his lips began exploring the nape of her neck.

She tried to remain calm, but her heart began racing and her knees felt weak. "You know why." She tilted her head away from him. "I don't want anything from you." Not anything less than your love, her mind whispered. Your love and an explanation about your friendship with Danielle.

"But you can't seem to manage without me, can you? It's only a matter of time before you realize how much we need each other. Just don't take too long. We're wasting valuable time." He flashed a smug smile, tightened his grip on her arm and led her up the gangplank of a large yacht that was moored between two smaller ones.

Karin glimpsed the name as he led her on board. "The *Buccaneer*. How appropriate."

"I'm glad you approve."

"I didn't say I approved—I merely said it was appropriate."

"Same difference." He nodded to the captain and led Karin along the deck to a door that opened into a large lounge area.

The motor started up; the captain gave the crew some orders and the yacht began moving slowly out of its moorage. A steward came in with a silver ice bucket containing a bottle of French champagne. He poured some into a crystal goblet and handed it to Lucas. Lucas nodded, and he filled another glass, which he gave to Karin, then he filled the remainder of Lucas' glass.

"A bit much for the short ride to Newport," Karin said, but she knew nothing was too much for Lucas. He believed in an excess of everything—land . . . and women. Well, she wasn't going to be the latest addition to his expanding conglomerate.

"There's no need to rush back." Lucas smiled. "I pay the crew to be available at all times. This yacht is far too valuable ever to be left unmanned. So, we can go practically anywhere you want. Just name your destination." He thought for a minute. "If it's a really long trip, we'll have to stop somewhere to take on provisions, though."

Karin turned and looked out the window. The yacht was circling the island; it was definitely not heading back to Newport.

"You're not serious?" she said, staring at Lucas in disbelief.

"Of course I am. Why else would I be devoting so much time to you? Now, will you let me put the ring back on your finger so we can set the wedding date?" His narrowed eyes challenged her over the rim of his champagne glass.

"I'm not talking about that. I meant are you serious about not returning to Newport?

"That depends."

His voice brought her back to reality and she tried to speak sensibly. "On what?"

"On how long it takes to convince you to marry me."

"You're insane." And you're making me lose my mind, she added silently. Why can't you just love me and forget about Danielle?

"Not really. . . . After all, you did say I was a bit of a buccaneer. Now, just what do you think a buccaneer would do if the girl of his dreams was being uncooperative?"

Karin stood up and looked at the lights shining from the harbor. The yacht was moving away from the developed tourist areas, but it seemed to be staying close to the island, circling the dark terrain of rugged mountains and rolling pastures. A nearby boat flashed a spotlight, illuminating the shore, and briefly revealing a flock of wild mountain goats before they fled the glare.

Putting down her glass, Karin walked out on deck and leaned against the rail. The spotlight shifted, exposing a seal rookery nestled among the rocks jutting into the water. Lucas came up behind her. His arms went around her and rested on the rail; his warm breath caressed the top of her head.

"I'd like to go back to Avalon." She had to get away from him before she gave in to the intensity of her emotions. She clutched the rail, trying to resist the temptation to turn and press herself against the strength of his body.

"Why? Are you lonely for Jim? Have you changed your mind about spending the night with him?" His hands moved over the rail, covering hers.

"No. And I don't intend to spend it with you, either. I'll find some other way to get home." Her voice was low and ragged as she struggled for the breath to speak.

"There's no need. I said I'll take you home and I will—when I'm ready. Now, come inside; our dinner's getting cold." He seemed so calm, so totally unaffected by the tension she was feeling.

Karin didn't move, but continued looking toward the shoreline. She despised her weakness for Lucas more than ever. Why did she have to love him? Why couldn't she be as ruthless as he was?

"Forget it!" Lucas' voice was harsh and commanding. "There's absolutely no way you'd make it to shore."

"Don't be ridiculous. I'm not about to jump overboard. You're carrying this buccaneer bit too far. I'm not afraid of you; I'm sure you have to be back in Newport before long. After all, so many people depend on you. Everyone I know seems to be working for you." Her voice was almost a whine as she tried to hide her feelings of betrayal.

"Even your father. . . . I wonder what he'd say if he found you had spent a few nights with me on board ship? He's still old-fashioned enough to insist that I marry you." Lucas' voice was low and thoughtful. He turned and walked back to the cabin.

Karin followed him. "You wouldn't."

"It's a definite possibility. After all, we buccaneers have never been known for fair play." He walked to a small, round, cloth-covered table in the corner of the lounge, glanced toward Karin and held out a chair. "But right now the only thing on my mind is dinner. After that, we'll think about satisfying our other appetites." His hand moved from the back of the chair to her shoulder. She felt his fingers playing along the slender column of her neck, drifting upward until they caressed the curving line of her jaw.

The movement was so unexpected that she couldn't control the shiver that tore up her spine. His hand lingered for a moment, then he moved away and settled himself in the seat opposite her. When she looked up, she saw an enigmatic smile sparkling in his eyes and lips. He didn't say anything—he didn't have to—he had felt the tremulous strength of her reaction.

Karin was so eager to avoid any further eye contact that she paid more attention than was necessary to the cream-of-asparagus soup that the steward placed before her. She began eating almost immediately, hoping that the presence of the food would prevent any drawn-out conversations.

"You're starving," Lucas said. "Didn't Jim feed you?"

"There was so much to see. We didn't want to waste time eating, so we had a quick lunch on the beach."

"Then you haven't had a really good meal yet. Well,

don't worry; I'll soon remedy that. I'd never let you go hungry." Even without looking at him, she could sense his cynical smile. "But I have more interest in your welfare than he does—I mean to marry you. And I certainly want a healthy wife, a healthy mother for my children."

The steward removed the empty soup plates and placed sautéed veal and small buttered potatoes before them. Lucas kept refilling her champagne glass, and she was so tense that she sipped it almost constantly without realizing what she was doing. His mention of children and all that they implied had sparked a strange warmth in her and she kept drinking the champagne, hoping it would quench the fire Lucas' statement had ignited. But all her efforts were in vain; Lucas had started the blaze and only he could satisfy its hunger. During most of the meal she kept her eyes lowered, concentrating on her plate, but every so often she glanced surreptitiously at him through the feathery fringe of her lashes.

"That's very provocative, you know." His voice was a soft caress; her eyes lifted and his gaze met hers.

"What?"

"When you flutter your eyelashes and look at me like that, as if you were flirting with me."

"I'm not flirting with you!"

"No? Then what were you doing?"

"I was just looking at you."

"Why?"

"Maybe I'm trying to understand you." She stopped, unable to confess that his erratic behavior, shifting between arrogant indifference and genuine concern for her welfare, had her thoroughly confused. "Why must you make such an issue of it? What's so terrible about me looking at you?" Pushing her chair back, she walked quickly to the deck, where she stood by the rail, trying to calm herself. She was so upset that she didn't even have the strength to protest when he came up behind her and draped his arm across her shoulder, drawing her to his side.

"There's nothing to understand. I like you looking at me, and I like looking at you." He turned her toward him and ran his hands over her arms. "I also like touching you; I'd like to have you touch me." His voice was husky as he clasped her hand and held it to his cheek, pressing it against his skin so she could feel its rough, masculine texture. He guided her hand across his lips and nibbled at her palm, his tongue flicking lightly, tasting her skin, making it tingle until her entire body was one sensuous quiver.

His lips traveled from her palm to her shoulder and he nuzzled the delicate hollow below her neck, lingering to savor the pulse that quickened beneath his caress. Then he lifted his head and caught the corner of her lips with his, slowly moving them across until they covered hers fully.

Karin was helpless against this tender assault and she found herself kissing him back with a hungry yearning that she could no longer deny. As he sensed her response, his kiss deepened and his gentle entreaty became a possessive demand. He released her hand and his arm went around her body, molding her soft curves to the hard length of his. Her hand rested on his shoulders, and as a surging warmth exploded within the depths of her soul, she pressed her fingers into his neck, letting them comb through the bluntly cut hair that grew just above his collar.

When he lifted his head, she gasped for the air that his impassioned kiss had denied her, then she began searching, tenderly exploring the carved line of his jaw and reaching once again for the exciting warmth of his lips. She felt his breath whispering against her ear.

"I want you so much. We could go to Mexico and be married immediately."

Marriage! His words surrounded Karin like an icy shroud. She knew why he wanted her, and love had nothing to do with it. His love was reserved for another woman—Danielle—and Karin's pride wouldn't let her accept his offer of marriage when she knew he didn't love her and had no intention of giving up the woman he did love.

The memory of Danielle's smug smile as she had wandered through the antique shop searching for those personal items that would make her a permanent part of Lucas' home and life, combined with her warning at the country club, gave Karin the strength to push away from him.

He stepped back, reached down and caught her hands in his, preventing any further flight. "What's wrong?"

"Nothing's wrong. I just don't like what you're doing." She twisted her hands free.

"Liar!" He gripped her arm, forcing her back against his chest. "You're enjoying this as much as I am." His hand moved under her sweater, seeking the curve of her breast and cupping it possessively.

His touch sparked a blaze deep within her throbbing heart. Although her mind and her pride urged her to resist him, she knew that her treacherous flesh would soon betray her. His power over her responses made her feel helplessly weak and she hated the way she continued to crave his masterful explorations. Her inability to force herself to do what she knew was right brought tears to her eyes and she tasted the salt as they fell between her lips.

A sudden rigidity moved through Lucas' body and he stepped back, holding her at arm's length. "You're worse than your father ever was—you won't even try to change. You're still the same spoiled brat you were as a child. I was good enough for you when you thought I was Lucas McKay, wealthy builder, but you can't bear the thought of marrying Lucas McKay, the farmer's kid who lived at the bottom of your hill." The dark anger in his eyes moved over her. "Well, don't worry. There are plenty of women who don't cry when I touch them."

Looking down at his hands, he tightened his grip on her arm and she could see him fighting for control. Karin whimpered at the cutting pain of his fingers and he released her so quickly that she staggered momentarily. He glanced at her disdainfully. "But, of course, *you're* too genteel to be caressed by hands that have worked in the field." All desire had fled from his eyes and they were a study in pure undisguised hatred. "Get inside. I'll take you home—I'll never bother you again." He turned from her and looked across the undulating sea.

Karin stared at his back. He was hunched over the rail, both hands grasping it as he looked down into the water. His stance was that of a man stripped of his confidence, bearing no resemblance to his usual haughty carriage. She couldn't remember seeing Lucas like this before. For the first time he seemed to have lost control of his emotions. His unusual behavior made him seem more human, more vulnerable, almost as vulnerable as she was.

For a moment she was tempted to go to him and explain that he was wrong: that she couldn't care less about his background, that she loved him as he was now—and would forever—but that she could never accept his relationship with Danielle. Nor could she accept that he was marrying her to achieve some childish goal he had set for himself, not because he loved the woman she had become.

The entire situation was a tangled, hopeless mess, and Karin felt too unsure of her own emotions to risk another confrontation with Lucas, who seemed to have withdrawn into a world of his own. With one last glance at him, she opened the door and returned to the lounge.

She was huddled on a small padded bench, her feet tucked under her and her eyes focusing blankly on the water, when the yacht began turning away from Catalina Island. Their speed increased, and instead of drifting aimlessly, they were now headed for a definite destination. Karin waded through her muddled thoughts and tried to understand what was happening to her. Lucas wanted to marry her, yet he had never said he loved her. That in itself was bad enough, but it was something she might have persuaded herself to live with, if not for Danielle. Danielle and Lucas—the picture tore at her heart. Yet Lucas refused to even discuss the relationship that existed between them.

He couldn't really believe that his background meant anything to her. She shook her head and smiled inwardly. Actually she would have preferred it if he were still a farmer. Then she wouldn't have to deal with her dual feelings for Lucas McKay, the man, and Lucas McKay, the land baron. That would probably also eliminate Danielle as a problem. The beautiful brunette's sequined gowns would never share a farmer's closet.

But Lucas was what he was, and all her wishful thinking wouldn't change the situation. He loved Danielle, yet he wanted to marry Karin. She loved him, but she couldn't accept his conditions. Could anything be more painfully hopeless? If only there was something she could say to Lucas, some way to reach him. Her morbid thoughts tortured her as the yacht raced toward the shore.

She didn't see Lucas for the rest of the trip, and when they reached the Balboa Bay Club, the steward told her that he had been instructed to drive her home. Once more Karin thought about talking to Lucas and explaining that he had been wrong about her, but the steward told her that he was no longer on board; he had left for home as soon as they had docked, a home which brought irrepressible images of Danielle's personal touches to Karin's mind. She told herself that she could never accept sharing Lucas with the beautiful actress and that perhaps everything had happened for the best. There was no point in speaking to Lucas. His opinion of her was unimportant; he didn't love her, and knowing that, nothing else really mattered to her.

Chapter Eleven

$\mathcal{T}$he next week dragged by. Lucas made no attempt to contact her, and although Karin told herself that he was only doing what she had asked, she couldn't convince herself that it was what she really wanted. She felt as if she had lost her best friend, her only friend, and was delighted when Stephanie invited her to lunch. They went to a small seafood restaurant which was known for its fresh, well-prepared food and inexpensive prices.

"Have you seen what they've done to the store?" Stephanie asked.

"I'd rather not. I prefer to remember it as it was." Karin picked at her shrimp salad. "I've purposely been avoiding the area." She didn't bother to mention that she was also purposely avoiding Lucas.

"But you're wrong. It's just beautiful; you'd love it."

Karin looked at Stephanie quizzically. "I'll grant that it must be a lot cleaner, with everything new and all, but you know how I feel—new isn't necessarily better."

"I feel the same way. How could I manage an antique shop if I didn't? But in this case, new really *is* better. Why don't you come and see for yourself?"

"You've been made manager?" Karin fought back a little twinge of jealousy. She liked Stephanie far too much to covet her success.

"Yes. Didn't I tell you? All the former owners who want to stay on have been given a chance to lease the new shops at very low rates, and the sales help have been encouraged to remain. American International thinks things will run smoother with experienced employees. Since you'd taken another job, they made me manager. I guess it was a lucky break for me. Anyway, we're going to be needing additional help. The shop is expanding; we're going to feature furnishings from Spain, Mexico and the old West. Everything is being done to preserve the flavor of the area."

"Everything except the building itself."

"That's just it. The building isn't what you think it is. You'll have to come and see for yourself. I really wish you would. Besides, as I started to tell you, we're going to be hiring some new people and I'd love to have you back. We work so well together. I'm sure, with all your experience, American International would be willing to pay you much more than you're getting now."

"It's out of the question," Karin said. "I can't possibly go back."

"Why not?"

"I'm happy where I am, and much as I'd like to be working with you again, there are other factors which would make the job unpleasant." Lucas' image flashed in her mind.

"But I told you, the building isn't what you think it is. All the old shops are moving back. You'll know everybody."

Karin shook her head. She would know everybody, all right. Even Lucas McKay. He was bound to come around. No doubt Danielle would accompany him, probably buying more accessories to make his home reflect her personal touch. No, Karin could not go back. She had to build a new life for herself, one without Lucas McKay. But the subject was too painful to discuss with anyone, even Stephanie, so she didn't elaborate on her reasons for not wanting to return to the store. Fortunately Stephanie was astute enough not to pursue the topic.

"At least promise me that you'll come to see the new shop. We'll be opening in two weeks."

Karin paid the cashier and walked out the door. "I'll try, but it may be difficult." Karin knew that she would never go back. She couldn't risk meeting Lucas, yet, she still wanted to continue her friendship with Stephanie. "Perhaps we can meet for dinner some evening." She checked her watch. "I'd better be getting back. My lunch hour is almost over." She left Stephanie at her car and ran down the street.

The week ended as uneventfully as it had began. Her entire life seemed to be one long series of non-events now that Lucas was avoiding her. The disturbing realization that she very much wanted him to ignore her stated wishes and come after her again wove through her thoughts as she drove to Palm Springs the following weekend. It was nearly the middle of March and Karin thought that the weather should soon be turning mild enough for her father to come home. Even the swallows would be returning soon.

Her father looked completely recovered. He was deeply tanned, showing none of the sickly pallor that had dulled his complexion during the past year, and he seemed to have regained his old vitality and zest for life. Dan was letting him use the study, and he was so engrossed in his work that although Karin knew he was glad to see her, he seemed almost to resent the interruption.

"Why don't you go out to the pool? After all, you're only here for the weekend. I'll join you as soon as I've finished this layout."

Karin could tell he was eager for her to leave so he could continue working, but she had a question that demanded an answer. She just couldn't wait any longer. "Why didn't you tell me you were working for Lucas McKay?"

Her father shrugged. "I didn't want to upset you after what happened between you two. Besides, I'm working for American International."

"Lucas McKay *is* American International." She looked at him angrily. "I can't believe you'd do this. It's sacrificing all your principles." She didn't want to tell him how hurt and betrayed she felt at the thought of her own father defecting to the enemy. And Lucas was the enemy, wasn't he? Somehow, she wasn't quite as sure as she had always been.

Paul Andrews put down his pencil and leaned back in his chair. His eyes narrowed thoughtfully as he studied his daughter's face. "I've done you a grave injustice, Karin, and left you with a false impression about the type of man I am. I may be hardheaded and set in my ways, but I'm neither a snobbish tyrant nor a helpless invalid. It takes a lot of convincing to make me change my mind, but once I see I'm wrong, I'm not too proud to admit it. And Lucas is the same way. I never even knew about you inviting Tom to your birthday party. If the butler refused to let him in, that was a decision he made on his own. I've explained that to Lucas. I think he believes me, so we've been able to establish a new relationship based on our mutual respect for each other."

Karin thought she was hearing things. Her father couldn't be saying this, he just couldn't. "Mutual respect? You called Lucas an upstart—someone with no breeding—new money."

Sighing, Paul Andrews rubbed the back of his neck. "I'm an old man, Karin, and I've done many foolish things in my lifetime. But as you've said, times have changed, and I know some of my beliefs are hopelessly outdated; perhaps they were always inappropriate. In any case, I'm convinced that Lucas McKay is an extraordinarily talented gentleman."

Karin looked startled. "Coming from you, that's quite a compliment."

"He deserves it. Do you realize that he was one of the youngest real-estate brokers in California? He earned his tuition by buying older houses, repairing them and selling the remodeled structures at a substantial profit. By the time he received his architectural degree he was a fairly wealthy man."

"American International is a major home developer; it doesn't even deal in resales."

Paul Andrews laughed. "Remodeling was just the start of Lucas' career. After he had graduated, he began building houses on his family's farmland. With his profits, he bought as much adjacent property as he could afford." He shook his head in approval. "He's a millionaire several times over, and he's achieved that status through his own labor and ingenuity. How can I help but admire such a man?"

"But he's ruthless," Karin protested. "He's a heartless businessman. He has no use for anything except American International." And Danielle, she added silently.

"Hardly," her father answered. "Lucas is actually very concerned about people and their needs." He used his pencil to tap the blueprint. "This retirement community, for example, it's going to be an ideal place for senior citizens. Someone like me." He smiled. "Once you get married."

"I'm not getting married."

"There's no reason why you can't. I've told you how I feel about Lucas. I'd be proud to have him for a son-in-law."

"I see," Karin said, feeling as if she had lost her last ally and not having the heart to tell her father that Lucas no longer wanted her as his wife.

"I hope you do. Because whatever happens between you and Lucas from now on, it has nothing to do with something that happened seven years ago."

"There's nothing happening between Lucas and me," Karin said. "I haven't seen him in weeks." She didn't tell her father about all the hateful things Lucas had said to her on his yacht: his vow to never bother her again, a vow he was now keeping.

"He's been in New York. But he should be back next week to reopen the Mission Shopping Plaza. I understand it's going to be quite an occasion. All the county officials will be there as well as several celebrities."

Karin made a wry face. She knew one celebrity who was sure to be there, Miss Danielle Matthews. She wouldn't miss this for anything. It would probably be her victory celebration. Now that her father had convinced Lucas that he had no basis for his vendetta, there was no need for him to marry Karin and Danielle could have him all to herself. She remembered how Danielle had crowed about Lucas going to New York with her. Well, why not? Wouldn't she be crowing if Lucas loved her? But he didn't, so what was the point in contemplating what-ifs?

"Well, *I* won't be there," Karin said. "I haven't changed my opinion about destroying charming old shops and replacing them with a concrete monolith. I hate what Lucas is doing." Silently she acknowledged that what she really couldn't bear to see was Lucas with his gloating companion, Danielle, but she wouldn't admit this to her father.

"You have to be there," Paul Andrews said. "Dan can't make it and I'm counting on you to drive me."

"I can't."

"Why not? Because of Lucas? Don't you think now is the time to tell him how you really feel about him?"

Karin looked at her father in surprise.

He smiled. "Didn't you think I knew? Women don't get upset about a man they don't care about. I think you should let him know that you love him . . . now that all that other nonsense is out of the way."

Karin shook her head. "There's no point." Now that all that other nonsense was out of the way, Lucas had no reason to marry her. Besides which, her father hadn't witnessed his tirade on the yacht when he had told her how he really thought of her—as the same snobbish brat she had always been. She could just imagine his triumphant response to her confession of love and the image left a queasy weakness in the pit of her stomach.

"Well, you're too old for me to tell you how to manage your personal affairs, but I work for American International and they expect all their employees to be at the opening. I can't afford to miss it. In fact, I'll come home with you this weekend to save you the trouble of picking me up next week."

There was no arguing with her father when he spoke in that tone of voice, and Karin resigned herself to the fact that she would have to accompany him to the opening of the remodeled shops. She soothed the nervous tension that arose when she thought about seeing Lucas again by telling herself that he would be so busy entertaining visiting dignitaries, especially the one from New York, that he wouldn't have any time for her. Indeed, he no longer had any reason to pursue her since his peace with her father had probably put to rest the vengeful demon that had been behind his offers of marriage.

Her father made no disparaging comments about the condominium into which Karin had moved. Instead of complaining that it was unimaginative and boxlike, he said that it was a wise choice since the rooms would be easy to maintain and the grounds were cared for by a homeowners' group. She couldn't believe her ears when she heard him suggest certain minor architectural and landscaping changes which he thought might improve the aesthetic appeal of the development. If nothing else had come from this entire miserable experience, at least her father had made a good adjustment to their new life-style and she no longer had to live with the tension of keeping the truth from him.

When she left for work on Monday morning, he was already making plans to approach the homeowners' organization with his suggestions. Karin was delighted, and when she checked with his physician later that day, he told her that her father was almost fully recovered, although he did suggest that it might be wise for him to refrain from strenuous exercise or driving a car for the next few weeks.

The doctor's report and her father's good spirits were so encouraging that Karin decided to celebrate by preparing a special dinner. On the way home from work she stopped off at a small gourmet shop and bought the expensive white veal that her father enjoyed so much. Then she selected some wild rice, baby asparagus and a good bottle of Chenin Blanc. The bill came to more than she had spent for a week's supply of the meatloaf and baked macaroni she had been eating while her father was in Palm Springs, but she felt she could afford to be extravagant just this once. All their debts had been paid off, both she and her father were working, and she certainly needed some cheering up after all the moping she had been doing over Lucas.

When she reached the door to the house, she was so loaded with packages that she couldn't free a hand to search for her key. The lights were on in the living room, so she rang the bell and waited for her father to answer the door. When he did, she saw that he was wearing a dark blue business suit, white shirt and tie.

"How did you know I was planning a celebration dinner?" she asked, smiling at his dignified appearance.

He reached for the packages, but she held them firmly. "Thanks for opening the door. I needed a third hand to find my key. I'm fine now—I'll just put these sacks in the kitchen. I can see I'm going to have to change while the food is cooking. I wouldn't want to be underdressed for the occasion, not when you look so nice." She began walking through the living room but stopped when she saw the man leaning against the fireplace mantel, an ice-filled glass in his hand.

"Lucas invited me out to dinner. We have business matters to discuss." Her father's voice was hesitant, as if he was uncertain of the reception his statement and his guest would receive.

For a moment Karin was too stunned to move. She remained in the center of the room, the packages still in her arms, and just looked at Lucas. She could see his shoulder muscles flexing beneath the smooth wool fabric of his well-tailored dark gray jacket. His lips were taut and unsmiling, and the drawn lines of his jaw seemed to accentuate the small pulse that was throbbing below his cheek.

"Hello, Karin." His voice was coldly subdued.

"Hello, Lucas." Suddenly she realized that she was standing there staring at him. She only hoped the hungry love she felt for him was not so openly obvious that he had noticed it. His own attitude toward her was one of such apparent dislike that she couldn't bear to stand there and have him look at her. "I have to put these things away." She ran into the kitchen.

After putting down the packages, she walked to the sink and looked out the window into the night. Her hands clutched the tile edge of the counter. There hadn't been a sound in the room, but she sensed Lucas' presence even before he spoke.

"You're welcome to join us." There was a tentative

quality in his voice that she had never noticed before; his self-assured arrogance was strangely absent.

She remembered the night on his yacht when he had lost control over his emotions. Then, as now, she had been confused by his unexpected behavior. She wanted to accept his invitation, to be with him again, but what if he was only being courteous because of her father? She couldn't take the chance of being hurt again.

"No, I don't think so. Dad said it was a business meeting. Besides, I have all this food." She turned to indicate the sacks on the table and her gaze met his. For one brief instant, before either of them realized what was happening, they remained that way. It was as if everything else in the universe had ceased to exist and there were just the two of them exchanging confidences, searching deeply for the meaning in each other's eyes.

"The food will keep, and so will the business." Lucas' words were more a plea than a statement, and his eyes maintained a steady contact with hers.

Karin's inclinations wavered between running as far away from him as she could to escape the savage attraction he held for her and dashing into his arms, seeking the love and approval she so desperately wanted—needed. If only he would say something that indicated he really wanted to be with her and wasn't inviting her merely to be polite.

They stood apart and he made no attempt to approach her, took no steps to shorten the distance that still existed between them and kept them from understanding each other. If only he would touch her and say that he cared about her, then she could chance telling him how much she loved him. But so long as he remained silent and separate, she could not take the first step toward him. She was too unsure of herself— too unsure of his feelings for her. Pride and fear kept her frozen where she was.

Lucas continued to watch her, his eyes narrowing as

if he were deep in thought. "Tom told me he saw you in Palm Springs."

"He came to see Dan. I was in the pool."

"But he did speak to you." He hesitated for a moment and tightened the jut of his jaw. "Before the Valentine Dance."

"Yes."

"He apologized for what he said at the party, told you he was wrong, asked you to reconsider."

Karin felt the blood leave her face. She remembered saying that she loved Lucas and hoped Tom hadn't repeated that part of the conversation. She couldn't bear having him know how much she loved him—not when he didn't care for her, when he was so obviously in love with another woman. She closed her eyes as she visualized Lucas and Danielle laughing about the way she had succumbed to Lucas' charms. She wouldn't—couldn't—give them that satisfaction. Her pride would not allow it. This was one time when her mind would have to control her emotions. She shrugged casually. "Tom was trying to be polite, but I told him he had nothing to apologize for."

A small muscle began throbbing at the side of Lucas' jaw. "He also said that you weren't completely indifferent to the way I felt about you." She saw his fists tighten at his sides. "Yet when I saw you at the dance, you said nothing. You refused to even speak to me. Then when I tried again—saw you on Catalina—you cried when I touched you, as if I repulsed you. I thought I had you all figured out, but Tom says I'm wrong, that you don't despise me." His teeth clenched at the end of his sentence and one fist struck the counter.

Karin turned away. That's the problem, she thought. I don't know how you feel about me, not really. And if I despise anyone, it's myself for wanting you so much when Danielle insists I can never mean anything to you.

I'm so confused I don't know who to believe: you, Tom, Danielle, my father, my mind, my heart. She turned back to him, facing him silently.

Her heart pounded rapidly, vibrating through the silent room, asserting its dominance over all other considerations, and she knew what she had to do. I'm going to find out, right now. I'm going to make you admit how you feel about me—and also how you feel about Danielle. I won't be put off anymore. Whatever I feel for you is far too important to be smothered by something you refuse to talk about. If you love Danielle, then say so. Stop torturing me with your vague explanations of friendship.

She opened her mouth to speak, but the words never came out because the spell between them was broken by her father's voice. "Someone to see you, Karin." His gaze shifted from his daughter to Lucas. "Shall I tell him you're busy?"

"No, I'll be right there." Despite her determination to demand an explanation from Lucas, her father's entrance had restored a sense of reality to the situation. She lost her nerve and clutched at the excuse to delay the confrontation. She was too uncertain about Lucas' response to take the risk. But she was sure about one thing: hearing him admit that he loved Danielle and no longer had any interest in her, even as an unloved wife, would send her already battered confidence into a depression from which she might never recover. She shook her head and turned away from Lucas. He made no attempt to stop her as she fled into the living room.

Jim was standing just inside the door, a huge bouquet of dark red roses in his hands. He smiled at her, a petulant, little boy's smile. "A peace offering." He held out the roses and started walking toward her. "Will you forgive a foolish mistake?" He placed the roses in her hands and covered them with his. "I should have known better."

"We'll be leaving now," her father said, nodding to Karin and Jim as he walked past them.

Lucas followed. "Hello, Simpson." His greeting was for Jim, but his accusing eyes never left Karin's face.

She struggled to free her hands, but got all caught up in a tangle with Jim and the roses. "I . . ." This wasn't what she intended at all. Lucas couldn't possibly think she was interested in Jim. He couldn't, but she was sure he did. She had to find a way to tell him. She tried to think of something to say, something that would explain Jim's presence, but the words just wouldn't come. They froze beneath the icy stare that Lucas was directing toward her. The cold arrogance that had disappeared for a short while had returned, and she cringed beneath the harsh judgment of his gaze. She realized that there was nothing she could say to melt the icy shield Lucas had erected between them. His open contempt for her shrouded the room in silence and she could hardly blame her father when he suggested to Lucas that they had best be going. The already harsh lines of Lucas' mouth twisted in a sneer as he followed her father out the door. He hadn't even bothered to say good-bye to either Karin or Jim.

"Problems between you two?" Jim asked.

"It's nothing," Karin said, so completely distracted that she walked away, leaving him holding the roses. She was barely conscious of his presence and wished he would have the decency to just disappear, but he seemed intent on gaining her attention.

"This is great. I mean, if your father has gone out with McKay, then you're free to join me for dinner."

"I don't want to go to dinner with you."

"Why not? Because of Catalina? I told you I was sorry . . . haven't you ever done anything you've regretted?"

"Oh, yes." Karin laughed wryly. "That I have." Her thoughts flew to Lucas. Her entire relationship with him was one long series of regrets. If only she had been friendlier in the Sacred Garden. If only she hadn't given him back his ring. If only she had accepted his offer to join him for dinner. Her gaze shifted to Jim. If only Jim hadn't shown up with his apologetic bouquet. She could write a book about the things she regretted. But what good would it do? Once Lucas learned that she was the author, he would never even bother reading it.

"Then why can't you forget . . . pretend it never happened . . . give me another chance?"

"There's no point in it, Jim. I wouldn't be good company."

Jim studied her for a moment. He placed the roses in her hand and looked down at her. "It's McKay, isn't it? I should have known. He's out of my league; I can't compete with him."

"There's nothing for you to know, no one for you to compete with. But I'm too tired for explanations. Good night, Jim."

He hesitated for only a moment. "Good night, Karin." He turned and walked out the door.

The house was deserted and she was alone with her thoughts. She went into the kitchen and began unpacking the groceries she had bought with such eager expectations. Suddenly all the gourmet food seemed tasteless and unappealing. After putting everything away, she made herself a cup of hot cocoa and prepared for bed.

She was just beginning to doze when the front door opened and she heard the sound of voices—Lucas' and her father's.

"Let me help you to your bedroom," Lucas said.

"Nonsense! I tell you I'm fine. I swear, you're getting as edgy as Karin."

"There's no point in being a hero. I'll feel better once you're in bed."

Karin slipped on her robe and went into the living room. Her father's collar was open and he looked pale. "What's wrong?" she asked, running up to him. She felt cold fear racing through her veins. She never should have told her father, never should have made him move. All this excitement had been too much for him. How could she have been so selfish, so thoughtless? "Sit down and rest. I'll call Dr. Stevens."

He shrugged her off. "You'll do nothing of the sort. There's absolutely nothing wrong with me. A piece of chicken lodged in my throat—I started coughing, and Lucas got nervous. But I'm fine now, and I'm going to bid you both good night. Thanks for the dinner, Lucas. I'll see you on Sunday."

"Let me help you upstairs." Karin reached for his arm.

He threw her hand off him. "Will you stop treating me like an infant?" His voice was laced with anger. "I told you I'm fine and you'd better start believing me." His eyes narrowed as he looked from her to Lucas. "Maybe it's time for you to get married and start raising a family of your own. Then you'd be too busy to cluck over me like a worried mother hen." He scowled and marched up the stairs.

Karin put her hand on the banister. One foot lifted to the first step.

"Don't," Lucas warned. "He meant what he said. Leave him alone."

Karin sighed and turned away. "What happened?" she asked Lucas when her father had slammed the door of his room.

"Just what your father said. Maybe he's right. Maybe I was more upset than I should have been, but I like your father and I don't want anything to happen to him." The disturbed shadows in his eyes told Karin that his concern was genuine.

She walked over to Lucas, the soft folds of her blue

silk robe clinging to the lines of her body. "I'm grateful
for all you've done, Lucas." She put her hand on his
arm. "Please stay for a while?" She led him to the white
sofa, sat down, smiled and patted the seat beside her.

His eyes contemplated the length of her body and he
hesitated for a moment as if he were undecided about
what to do. Then he sat down and leaned back against
the cushions, lifting his arm so that it rested just above
her shoulder. "Maybe I should stay awhile just to make
sure that your father's really okay." Crossing his legs,
he shifted into a more comfortable position.

"I can make some coffee," Karin offered, twisting
her hands together nervously, wondering if she would
ever learn to relax when Lucas was so close to her.

"That's not necessary," Lucas said curtly. He looked
around the room. "Jim left early, I see. A pressing
business engagement, I suppose. But then, we both
know how devoted he is to his business—in a gentle-
manly way, of course, not at all crass, like some other
men I could name."

"Please, Lucas, don't be like that. I don't want to
talk about Jim."

"Why not? Do you think discussing him with me will
sully his good name?"

"No, of course not. It's just that I want to tell you
how happy you've made my father. He feels useful
again. If there's anything I can do to repay you . . ."
She leaned forward and his gaze flickered to the deep
cleavage that was now revealed by the open collar of
her robe.

"Are you making me an offer?" he jeered. "With
your father sleeping in the room right above us? Did
you make the same offer to Jim?"

Her hand slapped his face in the precise instant that
she rose to her feet. "How dare you?" Then, mortified
by what she had done, she buried her face in her hands.
"I'm sorry, Lucas, but you shouldn't have said that. I

was only trying to thank you for helping my father." Once again she placed her hand on his arm.

He looked down at her hand as if her touch was distasteful to him and shrugged it off. "I don't want your gratitude—I don't need it. Maybe you ought to take your father's advice—talk to Jim, start raising a family."

Karin backed away and put her hand to her throat. "I don't understand." Whatever else she had expected from Lucas, it wasn't this.

"Of course you don't. I'm not from your social set, remember? You made that quite apparent when you chose to stay home with Jim. How could you be expected to understand the feelings and reactions of a man whose background is so far beneath yours?"

"You're wrong! Lucas, I don't feel like that—and as for Jim . . ."

"Don't lie to me, Karin; I don't want your gratitude or your lies. I don't want anything from you—not anymore." Without another word he slammed out the door.

Karin felt as if she had been completely destroyed. Lucas didn't even care enough to listen to her. Whatever his previous intentions had been, it was quite clear that she now wanted nothing more to do with her.

Chapter Twelve

*W*hen Karin awakened on Sunday morning she was seized by an overwhelming desire to stay in bed. It seemed the least painful way to get through the day. All during the week she had avoided any discussion of her relationship with Lucas by changing the subject each time her father brought it up, but today she would be attending the grand opening of the new stores in San Juan Capistrano, and even if she tried to be as inconspicuous as possible, there was no way to avoid seeing Lucas. She kept searching for a way out, but all thoughts of escape came to a swift end when her father rapped lightly on the door.

"Are you up, Karin? We're leaving in an hour."

"I'll be ready." Sighing, she sat up and swung her feet to the floor.

Despite her intention to remain completely in the background, she was sure to meet at least a few people she knew, so she chose her outfit carefully. A chilling March wind was drifting in from the ocean and she decided on a brown tweed ensemble. The skirt was straight, with three small pleats at the side just below the knee, the darker brown knit top had a mock turtleneck and a short boxy jacket matched the skirt, while several gold chains of varying lengths brightened the somber effect. She slipped into dark brown high-heeled pumps and brushed her hair so it curled softly under her chin. After applying a light touch of lip gloss and eye makeup, she quickly checked her appearance in the mirror, then walked into the living room and told her father she was ready.

The road into town was one huge traffic jam and Karin tried to find the lane which moved the fastest. But at last she gave up. "It's like a game of checkers," she told her father. "First one lane moves, then the other. I might as well stay put. I didn't expect so many people. They're really getting a good turnout for the opening."

"Not everyone is going to the opening, but they're sure to notice it. Lucas planned it that way."

Karin turned her gaze from the road for a moment and looked at her father quizzically.

"It's St. Joseph's Day, La Fiesta de las Golondrinas. Didn't you know? Most of these people are probably going to the mission, but they're sure to see the new stores, and that's what Lucas wants."

"Hmmph," Karin muttered, half to herself. "He's even trying to put the swallows to work for him."

"What was that you said?" her father asked.

"Nothing . . . nothing at all."

American International had purchased the empty land between the stores and the railroad tracks and had turned it into a freshly paved parking lot. Well, Karin thought as she got out of her car and locked the door, he's eliminated the parking problem; that should definitely increase his volume of business. She began walking toward the stores with her father. From the back, it seemed that very little had been changed. Except for a fresh coat of white stucco and the new edging on the red tile roof, everything looked basically the same. So he hadn't put up a huge skyscraper, Karin thought. At least that was one thing in his favor.

She caught her breath and stopped walking when she rounded the corner and saw the front of the building. The haphazard structure which used to resemble a beachfront arcade had been remodeled to give the appearance of a small Mexican *mercado*. The same shops were there, but the white stucco fronts, with their red tile roofs and dark oak trim, were all uniform. Terra-cotta Mexican paving stones covered the old broken concrete horseshoe-shaped walkway. Instead of commercializing the area, Lucas had brought back the spirit of the old Californios. Karin bit her lip as she remembered accusing him of having no respect for the past. Now, more than ever, she felt ashamed of the undeserved criticism she had directed toward him.

A small podium had been set up at the head of the horseshoe and the sides were lined with three-tiered wooden grandstands. Karin's father seated himself near the front, but she shook her head when he patted the place next to him and moved to the back, standing half-hidden in one of the doorways.

Danielle was nowhere in sight. Karin thought that she must be busy with her play in New York—either that, or she was home in Newport making things cozy for Lucas' return; so at least she would be spared the sight of Danielle's possessive hovering over Lucas. She would have to learn to be thankful for small favors, she thought wryly.

A member of one of the town's earliest families made a speech about the history of the area, then the president of the local historical society began complimenting American International, and its president, Lucas McKay. She was truly delighted with the appearance of the remodeled shopping center, she declared, but the really marvelous news, which Mr. McKay had asked her to delay announcing until this occasion, was that he had purchased Casa del Mar and was donating it to the historical society to be used as their headquarters as well as a public museum. In addition, he would assume all restoration costs. She went on to mention that Casa del Mar had been built by an ancestor of his, since his mother could trace her lineage back to the Spanish grandee who had originally been granted the land but had been forced to sell it so many years ago. She made reference to the fact that the family had been able to retain a nearby farm which had since been turned into a housing tract.

The announcement was such a shock to Karin that she gasped audibly. Imagine her telling Lucas that he had no feel for the land—no understanding of the area! How could she have been so wrapped up in herself? So conceited? And to think she had accused him of being callous and arrogant! And he had taken all her insults, never stopping to correct her, never trying to defend himself, never making her feel as awful as she felt now. She couldn't control her tears, couldn't choke back her sobs. When people started to look at her, she was so embarrassed that she turned and ran, with no definite destination in mind. She simply had to escape. She couldn't stay here—she was too ashamed. Leaving the *mercado*, she stepped out into the street and looked quickly around her. The mission beckoned. It had always been her refuge, the one place where she could think clearly. Darting between cars, she ran across the street.

Tourists were gathered outside, eyes scanning the sky, watching for the return of the first swallow. Karin waded through them, paid her admission and walked quickly down the main walk, past the fountain and pool, through the old columns and arches of the front corridor and into the Sacred Garden. Ivy and blooming vines draped the ancient walls, but the solid bank of poinsettias that grew alone the front of the Campanario had lost its vibrant red winter foliage.

Two white pigeons glided to her feet as she passed the old stone fountain and seated herself on the bench just below the Campanario, but Karin held out her empty hands and they flew away, searching for a visitor with more to offer. Once again Karin was left alone with her thoughts. She wished she could relive the past few months and return to that day last October when she had first met Lucas—that day in the Sacred Garden, in this very spot. How differently she would respond . . . if only she had another chance. If only . . . if only. How many women had moaned these hopeless words after they had lost the man they loved?

She had been so wrong about Lucas. He was not the heartless businessman she had accused him of being. Not only had he remodeled the ramshackle little stores so that they were now a beautiful adjunct to the mission, he had also donated Casa del Mar to the historical society. Those were hardly the acts of a man who cared only about money and material achievements. And as for heritage—well, hadn't the president of the historical society said it all? After what Tom had said, she naturally assumed that Lucas had always wanted to own the big house on the hill—and her as well—merely for his own gratification. She had been wrong about the house. Was it possible that she was also mistaken about his feelings for her?

She shook her head and looked down at the pigeons that had just landed by her feet once again. They were so tame and trusting. Trust . . . perhaps that was what had always been missing in her relationship with Lucas? Even before Tom's ill-fated remarks, she had never believed that Lucas really loved her. He had never told her so. She knew that she aroused a physical desire in him, but then, so had many other women. The newspapers had found plentiful grist for their gossip mills in the amorous escapades of Lucas McKay. And there was Danielle, always hanging on to Lucas, making it quite apparent that she would never willingly relinquish her hold on him.

But Karin hadn't even made Danielle fight for Lucas. She had just given him up, never believing any of the explanations he had tried to make until she had convinced him that she was a spoiled snob who thought she was too good for him. Now it was too late to do anything—or was it? Danielle had shown that she was willing to fight for Lucas. Why couldn't Karin make the same effort? What did she have to lose—her pride? It seemed like a meaningless possession when she thought of how happy she had once been in the warmth of Lucas' arms.

She decided to go to Lucas and apologize. She would tell him that she was sorry for all the horrible things she had said, that she did not despise his touch and that she would prove it, if he would only give her another chance. But would he? There was only one way to find out. He was probably still in the arcade. She stood up to leave the gardens and return to the remodeled shopping center—and Lucas.

"You forgot your sweater." Lucas stood there, holding a hand out to her. His hand was empty, but his words were full of meaning.

Tears welled in Karin's eyes as her insides turned to water. Love and gratitude merged to form a lump in her throat and she was choked by emotion, unable to speak.

"I thought I'd find you here. It's also my favorite place in the mission."

"Lucas!" Happiness glistened through her tears and she couldn't control the breathless quality of her voice. She was so delighted to see him that she couldn't stop staring at him. His deeply tanned skin and dark hair reminded her of the ancient Spanish conquistadores who had guarded the mission against harm. A conquering air of virile masculinity came from every inch of him and his dark gray business suit could not conceal the aura of powerful domination which surrounded him. Her legs grew weak beneath her and she sank back on the bench.

"I saw you leave the ceremonies. Didn't you feel well?"

She shook her head. "I'm fine. I just needed to get away." Now that he was here, she only wanted to look at him; the words she had planned just wouldn't come.

"You didn't see Jim's new office?" His remark was more a question than a statement.

"No, but I'm sure it's beautiful . . . the entire shopping center is. I owe you an apology. You've done a lot to improve the appearance of the town." She kept looking at him, letting her eyes feast on the sight of a fantasy come true. I love you, she thought. Why are we wasting time on all this nonsense when the only thing I want to do is tell you how much I love you?

Lucas looked at her as if she hadn't spoken. "Is it all over between you two?"

Karin looked at him in confusion, then she understood. He was referring to Jim. Lucas was jealous of Jim, and there was no reason to be, no reason at all. She hastened to reassure him. "There wasn't anything to get over. We were never more than friendly business associates."

"Business associates?" Now Lucas was confused.

"He's a realtor, and I've had a lot of real-estate transactions lately." She smiled up at Lucas. He still hadn't moved any closer. Several pigeons walked between them, eavesdropping on their conversation with total disinterest.

"Dinner, cruises and red roses for a client?" Lucas lifted his brow doubtfully. "I thought your fathers were old school buddies?"

"That's true, but I never had much contact with Jim until I became his client, a very good client. He earned quite a commission on the sale of Casa del Mar."

"The buyer has no regrets."

"Nor does the seller, and I'm glad to see that it's going to be made into a museum. It has too much historical importance to be kept from the public. It's an irreplaceable part of our American heritage. You've done a wonderful, selfless thing."

"Not really. In fact, it was quite selfish of me. I had no choice." His voice was soft and husky, swollen by emotion. "It was the only thing I could think of doing." He walked toward her and sat beside her.

She looked at him quizzically. "I don't understand. How can an act of charity be selfish?"

"It was the one way I could prove to the woman I want to marry that I loved *her* and not the house she lived in. That some stupid remark I made—and forgot about—seven years ago meant nothing." He reached out and took her hands in his. There was the same tentative plea in his eyes that had been there when they had spoken in her kitchen just a few nights ago, nights that seemed like a black eternity which was finally drawing to an end.

This time she wasn't going to let anything stop her from doing what she had been wanting to do for so long. She had been granted a second chance, a chance she didn't deserve, and now she was determined to let her heart guide her body to the place where they both belonged. Sliding across the old stone bench, she closed the distance between them and rested her head against his chest. "I love you, Lucas. I think I always have."

His arms encircled her, but she could still feel a certain rigidity in his body, as if he didn't quite trust her confession. "Then, why? Why did you fight me so much? I really thought you couldn't bear to have me touch you; your mind seemed to deny the response your body was so eager to give."

"I was afraid and unsure—of both of us. You can be very arrogant and intimidating." She hesitated for a moment, then drew herself out of his arms. He seemed surprised, but made no attempt to stop her. She didn't want to risk destroying the beauty of this moment, but if there was to be trust, then there must also be truth. She had reassured him about Jim, but what about her own apprehensions? She needed an answer. "What about Danielle?" Her voice was little more than a whisper; she could hardly bear to say the actress's name.

"What about Danielle?"

"I love you very much, Lucas, but I could never share you with another woman. It would destroy me."

"Why should you ever have to share me with any other woman? I haven't felt any desire for another woman since the day I found your sweater here and you accused me of being a masher."

Karin smiled. "Well, you have to admit, it was a rather old line. 'Don't I know you?' Really!"

"But it *was* true, wasn't it? I did know you, and I wanted to know you better. I still do. I want to marry you and father your children and know what it is to sit beside you when our hair turns gray." He reached for her again. "I never realized I could love any woman as much as I do you. I thought you hated me . . . I tried to forget you, to stay away from you. But nothing worked. You're a part of me and I can't live without you."

Karin wanted to go to him more than anything; she felt totally deserted without his arms around her, but she knew that once he touched her, she would never care about anything else again, and there was still Danielle between them, a chilling haze that was clouding their happiness. She lifted her palms against his chest. "Danielle came to see me in the antique shop. She said she wanted to get some personal items for your home on Linda Isle. She said she was living with you. When we met at the country club, she said you were in love with her and always would be. She said I could never satisfy you."

Lucas' eyes turned cold as they narrowed into hers. "And you believed her?"

Karin shrugged. "She was so sure of herself, and you never said that you loved me."

"I loved you from the moment I saw you. I thought my actions made that obvious." He shook his head in disbelief. "You've heard that old cliché about love at first sight. I've always thought it was a bag of nonsense —at least until I met you." He raked his fingers through his hair. "Maybe it's this garden, this mission. Maybe there's a magical quality here that makes people fall in love. I don't know. I only know that I've loved you from the first moment I saw you here." He paused and lowered his voice. "And I'll never stop loving you, not ever. I thought my behavior made that apparent to everyone in sight."

"Not to me. Everything happened so fast . . . and Danielle was very convincing."

Lucas made a sound that was more a snort than anything else. "She's an excellent actress. Didn't that thought ever cross your mind? How could you have believed anything she told you? Couldn't you see that she was just trying to come between us?" He reached out and gripped her upper arms, drawing her to him. Once more the angry arrogance had returned to his gaze. "Why didn't you ask me about it?"

"I did, and you always told me not to question your friendships." Karin didn't know where she found the breath to voice her words. "I hated having to ask you about your mistress, especially when she kept telling me that it was her you really loved."

Lucas sighed and released her. "I deserved that. I was too blinded by my love for you to see that you needed reassurance. I never realized that Danielle was telling you such vicious lies. She may have thought that there was more depth to our relationship than there was, and if she did, I'm sorry for any pain it caused her. It was unintentional, I assure you. As far as I was concerned, we were just good friends. You were the only woman I ever loved and I thought you were questioning my friendship with Danielle because she was an actress, beneath your social class, not good enough for you or the man you intended to marry."

"Well, she's certainly not good enough for my future husband." She smiled coyly. "I'm the only one who's perfectly suited for him." She snuggled against him and ran her hand over the rugged texture of his cheek.

Lucas squeezed her hand. "I've been telling you that for months now. I'm grateful for whatever it took to convince you."

"Three little words, Lucas—I love you." Her lips tantalized the throbbing pulse in his neck.

"Then I'll have to keep repeating them, won't I?" He drew her tightly to him, his warm breath feathering her hair.

"Constantly." She pressed even closer, unable to satisfy her mounting desire. Then one last disturbing question invaded the ecstasy of her thoughts. "Were you in Tahoe with Danielle in February?"

His thumb caressed her fingers. "I want to put your mind at ease about Danielle and me." He paused for a moment and looked deeply into her eyes. "Despite the stories she's told you, and I'm beginning to realize that they were quite imaginative, I haven't even thought about her since I first saw you sitting here six months ago. I've been as faithful as the swallows. I was in Tahoe on business—only business. If Danielle was there, I never saw her. Maybe she was looking for me, but I wasn't looking for her. I just wanted to get my business finished so I could get back home to you, so I could convince you to marry me. I was totally miserable every minute I was apart from you."

He brought her hand to his lips and kissed each fingertip. "And as for living with Danielle, she was staying at the house in Newport but I was at the cottage in Capistrano. Despite whatever mistaken impression

Danielle may have had, after I asked you to marry me I never wanted to share my bed with any woman but you. I tried to make that clear to her in Palm Springs during Christmas, but I guess she's so used to having her own way that she couldn't take no for an answer. But once you had moved out of Casa del Mar, I was able to bring in the restoration crew, and I lived in the cottage to oversee things myself. The next time I saw Danielle was when she asked me to meet her for a farewell dinner at the Depot. Since there was no longer anything sexual between us, I saw no reason to refuse. She was leaving for New York the following day." He smiled wryly. "You do remember that night?"

"How could I forget? You seemed so happy to see her."

He smiled again. "You noticed. I'm glad. But did you also notice that my heart did somersaults when I saw you sitting there at the table by yourself? I was so bewitched by you that I forgot all about Danielle. It was all I could do to keep myself from destroying Simpson when he returned and casually thanked me for entertaining his girl. And you did nothing to dispel that impression. I was determined to get even by making you jealous, and Danielle was the perfect vehicle. I'm glad it worked. But I'm sorry for all the misery I've caused you. That was never my intention, and I'm sorry if Danielle used my stupidity to hurt you even more. It's a good thing she returned to New York."

"But she didn't stay in New York. She came to Palm Springs, and you went back to New York with her right after the Valentine's Day dance."

He quirked an eyebrow. "So you really were checking up on me. Well, you never had anything to worry about. The relationship between Danielle and me is pure business. That's why I went to New York. She needed some money for her new play."

"And you gave it to her?"

"It was the least I could do. My money is something I don't mind parting with, but my love is another matter. I can't share that with anyone but you. I think Danielle understands that at last, and I don't think she'll bother us anymore. She's very busy now, cementing a liaison with her new producer. I don't think she's going to be coming to California for a very long time."

"And if she does?"

"I'll take my beautiful wife to see her at the theater."

"I'm not sure I'll want to go."

"Of course you will. Danielle was right about one thing. You'll never be able to satisfy me. My need for you is insatiable; I'll never have enough. I intend to love you so thoroughly that you'll be convinced that I have neither the time nor the energy for Danielle or any other woman." He took her in his arms. She snuggled against his chest and he murmured into her ear, "Of course, I'll have to expect a reasonable amount of affection in return."

She raised her lips to his and whispered just before they met, "Would you settle for an unreasonable amount? There's nothing at all reasonable about my feelings for you. I'm totally irrational where you're concerned."

The touch of her lips seemed to release the fiery response which he had been holding under control and Karin returned his kisses with a hungry yearning that had been building since she first saw him enter the garden. Her lips parted in rapturous delight and she clung to him with the passion of a woman who had finally found the source of a truly contented love.

When at last they drew apart, she was breathless and he pulled her head back down onto his chest. "I love you so much, Karin. I've never been so happy."

"Nor I." She made an effort to lift her head. "But I don't think the good padre will appreciate such carryings-on in the mission."

"He won't mind when I explain the situation to him. They still perform weddings in the Serra chapel, don't they? Somehow, it seems appropriate; we always come together at the mission. How would you like to marry me before the three-hundred-year-old golden altar that the good father brought all the way from Barcelona, Spain?"

"I'll marry you wherever and whenever you say. I'll never doubt you again, and our love will have an eternal beauty, just like that of this mission."

Lucas moved away and reached into his pocket. "Then you should be wearing this. I never stopped carrying it. I kept hoping that one day you'd put it on again."

"And I'll never take it off."

"Not even to put your wedding band on?"

"Umm . . ." She smiled and settled herself against his chest.

A fluttering noise from above made them lift their eyes toward the sky. "The swallows," Karin said. "They've come back."

"Of course," Lucas affirmed. "They always do." Once again his lips sought hers and all thoughts of swallows vanished from her mind.

If you enjoyed
this book...

...you will enjoy a Special Edition Book Club membership even more.

It will bring you each new title, as soon as it is published every month, delivered right to your door.

15-Day Free Trial Offer

We will send you 6 new Silhouette Special Editions to keep for 15 days absolutely free! If you decide not to keep them, send them back to us, you pay nothing. But if you enjoy them as much as we think you will, keep them and pay the invoice enclosed with your trial shipment. You will then automatically become a member of the Special Edition Book Club and receive 6 more romances every month. There is no minimum number of books to buy and you can cancel at any time.

MORE ROMANCE FOR
A SPECIAL WAY TO RELAX

$1.95 each

1 ☐ TERMS OF SURRENDER
Dailey

2 ☐ INTIMATE STRANGERS
Hastings

3 ☐ MEXICAN RHAPSODY
Dixon

4 ☐ VALAQUEZ BRIDE
Vitek

5 ☐ PARADISE POSTPONED
Converse

6 ☐ SEARCH FOR A NEW DAWN
Douglass

7 ☐ SILVER MIST
Stanford

8 ☐ KEYS TO DANIEL'S HOUSE
Halston

9 ☐ ALL OUR TOMORROWS
Baxter

10 ☐ TEXAS ROSE
Thiels

11 ☐ LOVE IS SURRENDER
Thornton

12 ☐ NEVER GIVE YOUR HEART
Sinclair

13 ☐ BITTER VICTORY
Beckman

14 ☐ EYE OF THE HURRICANE
Keene

15 ☐ DANGEROUS MAGIC
James

16 ☐ MAYAN MOON
Carr

17 ☐ SO MANY TOMORROWS
John

18 ☐ A WOMAN'S PLACE
Hamilton

19 ☐ DECEMBER'S WINE
Shaw

20 ☐ NORTHERN LIGHTS
Musgrave

21 ☐ ROUGH DIAMOND
Hastings

22 ☐ ALL THAT GLITTERS
Howard

23 ☐ LOVE'S GOLDEN SHADOW
Charles

24 ☐ GAMBLE OF DESIRE
Dixon

25 ☐ TEARS AND RED ROSES
Hardy

26 ☐ A FLIGHT OF SWALLOWS
Scott

27 ☐ A MAN WITH DOUBTS
Wisdom

28 ☐ THE FLAMING TREE
Ripy

29 ☐ YEARNING OF ANGELS
Bergen

30 ☐ BRIDE IN BARBADOS
Stephens

SILHOUETTE SPECIAL EDITION, Department SE/2
1230 Avenue of the Americas
New York, NY 10020

Please send me the books I have checked above. I am enclosing $_____
(please add 50¢ to cover postage and handling. NYS and NYC residents
please add appropriate sales tax). Send check or money order—no cash or
C.O.D.'s please. Allow six weeks for delivery.

NAME _____

ADDRESS _____

CITY _____ STATE/ZIP _____

Silhouette Desire
15-Day Trial Offer
A new romance series
that explores
contemporary relationships
in exciting detail

Four Silhouette Desire romances, free for 15 days!
We'll send you four new Silhouette Desire romances
to look over for 15 days, absolutely free! If you decide
not to keep the books, return them and owe nothing.

Four books a month, free home delivery. If you like
Silhouette Desire romances as much as we think you
will, keep them and return your payment with the
invoice. Then we will send you four new books every
month to preview, just as soon as they are published.
You pay only for the books you decide to keep, and
you never pay postage and handling.